SHAME

a ruin novel

#1 *New York Times* Bestselling Author
RACHEL VAN DYKEN

Shame
A Ruin Novel
by Rachel Van Dyken

Copyright © 2014 RACHEL VAN DYKEN

SHAME
Copyright © 2014 RACHEL VAN DYKEN
ISBN: 978-1-946061-72-0
Cover Design by Jill Sava, Love Affair With Fiction
Formatting by Jill Sava, Love Affair With Fiction

SHAME

PROLOGUE

Hope is itself a species of happiness, and, perhaps, the chief happiness which this world affords: but, like all other pleasures immoderately enjoyed, the excesses of hope must be expiated by pain. —Samuel Johnson

Lisa

"Tell me you love me!" he screamed, fists clenched. He was high on pills; then again, he was always high on pills.

"Tay…" I licked my lips and tried to maintain a sense of calm. "…get down."

He threw his head back and laughed. "No, no, no, I don't think so, not until you tell me!" He moved to the ledge of the bridge and leaned over, laughing, swaying, and dipping his feet below the edge, making a giant joke out of nearly killing himself. He turned quickly, almost falling. I gasped, and he righted himself and stared me down, his face twisting with rage. "Say it."

"Tay—"

"Say it, damn it! Say you love me! Say it, say it, say it, say

1

it!" His voice went hoarse from screaming as he pounded his chest.

Things hadn't always been like this.

I used to think we were in love.

I used to think our relationship was… just passionate.

"I'm going to jump if you don't say it, Mel." His smile was cruel. "Do you really want that on your conscience for the rest of your pretty life? Do you even realize who I am? What my death would do to you?" He laughed again as tears streamed down his face. "I may as well be a god to you. That's how much I own you. I'll always own you."

"Tay…" I stepped forward, my heels clicking against the cement. "…I love you, I love you so much, now please…" my voice shook, "please just get down."

"I always knew this moment would come." He went completely still; the wind blew his dark, wavy hair across his forehead. "When I wouldn't be able to control it anymore, when you'd finally try to run away," he sneered. "When you'd lie to my face!"

I shook my head, panic rising in my chest. He'd always been dramatic, controlling, bat-shit crazy, but recently he'd been threatening to kill himself more and more. He'd almost succeeded the month before. "Taylor, please baby, I love you. I can't live without you!" I held out my hands in front of me. "Just come off the ledge."

He threw his head back and laughed, almost losing his footing. "It's hilarious how much I control you. I'm going to ruin your life, you know that?"

"Taylor!" I yelled. "This isn't funny! This isn't a game. Just get down!"

He did a little jig on the ledge and laughed harder. "I took care of everything, you know… everyone will find out. I took notes. It was too easy… too easy to take you, but you made me feel, and I don't want to feel, Mel. Not anymore. It hurts too bad. But you know what? In a bit, it won't hurt anymore, and I'll be happy knowing that I'll haunt you for the rest of your life. You see, even in my death, your soul is mine. Your body is mine."

His smile was cruel. I fought the urge to throw up as each word pounded into my brain — as absolute truth.

"I own you," he whispered. "One more chance, Mel. Do you love me?"

His head tilted so far to the right I thought he would lose his balance.

In that moment, the hate won over the fear. I was so tired of being afraid, so tired of being controlled, just so, so tired.

"No," I whispered. "I hate you."

He closed his eyes and whispered, "Finally," before falling backward off the bridge.

Pieces of my life were falling slowly, painfully. Falling like snow falls onto the ground. Frozen pieces dissolving into nothingness as the ground sucks in the water, and the process repeats.

More snow falls.

More water soaks in.

And after the snow has fallen.

After the ground has drunk its fill.

All you're left with is a beautiful landscape of white, the

type of white that, as a little kid, you can't wait to run out and play in.

I used to have that type of excitement. I used to imagine my life was like that, a fresh blanket of snow. I'd always been close to my mom, and whenever it snowed, she was always a fan of making me wait. She said that I needed to be patient; I needed to allow the rest of the world to see the beauty of the snow. So I'd wait, tap my foot, wait some more, complain, and finally, laughing, she'd let me run out into the white perfection.

One day, Mom stopped me. She pointed to the snow and said, "Honey, this is your life, a blank canvas. Follow your destiny and know that each step you take will be another footprint made in the snow, but make the footprints strong. You want them to lead somewhere. You want the footsteps to have meaning."

I never thought much about her words — I was a kid. All I cared about were snow angels.

And as I grew, I lost interest in the snow. My interest was darkness, not white.

They let me go.

They let me run in the opposite direction.

Funny, because that's how I found *him*. He promised to walk along with me in the dark, promised to entertain, promised to be by my side. And I trusted him. So when he told me to do things I knew I shouldn't…

I did them.

When I wanted to run back to the snow, when I felt like reverting back to that same excitement of childhood, he'd show me one more thing that pulled me to the other side.

He pulled me.

He pushed.

Until I had nothing left.

And in the end, I ran away. I ran away from the dark and promised myself to start over.

Gabe helped with that — my best friend. I did everything in my power to help save him because in the end, by saving him, I was saving me.

Unfortunately, the thing about running, the thing about trying to start over — eventually, that hope is dashed by your past coming up to greet you like the fires of hell.

My past came knocking sooner than I could have imagined.

In the form of a ghost.

A person I had no idea existed.

A person who knew my shame.

A person I fell in love with.

My college professor.

Don't roll your eyes. You don't know my pain. You don't know my story. You don't know the hope I've held in my heart for years. Hope that one day I would be different. Hope that one day the person I chose to give my heart to would see me as beautiful, pure, like the snow. And wouldn't look at the darkness and walk in the other direction.

"Tristan?" I sniffled. "Say something!"

"You want me to say something?" he sneered. His blue eyes might as well have been steel as they pierced through every inch of my body. "Fine."

I braced for impact.

"I hate you." He said it slowly as if he wanted me to hear each word and commit it to my memory. "I love you."

"What?" Tears fell across my lips. "What did you say?"

"Both." He put his hands on his hips. "I feel both."

I took a tentative step toward him. "Which wins?"

"The one you give power to," he said seriously. "The one I choose to give power to."

"Love?" I begged, pleaded, my voice hoarse.

Tristan's smile was sad as he took a step back and gave his head a solid shake. "No, sweetheart. I'm sorry, but no."

He left.

Hope died in my chest.

I stared down at the ground, closing my eyes, wishing for snow, wishing for a do-over. Wishing I could go back and make the footprints straight in the snow, wishing I wouldn't have chosen death.

But that's the thing about choices; you don't regret them until after they've been made. It may be a second later, or a year.

Shame always comes.

And you're about to know mine...

ONE

Simple fact about me: I get bored easy, and she was an easy target. Young, beautiful, with the fiery eyes of a temptress. "Impress me," I'd say, and she'd laugh and go about doing exactly that. My body liked it; my mind craved it. She forced the demons down better than any drug, and I freaking worshipped her for it. —The Journal of Taylor B.

Lisa

I ran back to my dorm and nearly collided with the door before I was able to grab it. I hated having to dig through my purse to find my stupid key card; it seemed like it always hid for at least ten minutes while I pulled out my keys, my wallet, my gum, my cell, that little tiki key fob I still hadn't added to my main ring of keys yet. I mean, the list went on and on and on. Finally, of course, I'd realize I kept my key card in my back pocket only to have stood in front of the damn door while it rained!

Ugh. College.

I took the stairs two at a time and unlocked my dorm room.

"Loser pants," Gabe said from the couch without looking up. "You left your door open again."

"I gave you a key." I rolled my eyes.

"You gave Saylor a key," Gabe grumbled. "I had to freaking steal that thing, make like seven copies, and return it."

"Seven?" I put my bag on the counter and walked around to the mini-kitchen to grab a bottle of water from the fridge. "Why seven?"

"Fun story about marriage." Gabe thrust his finger into the air as if letting me know he was about to make a speech. Though by now, I knew his speeches bordered on inappropriate most of the time, hence the dread pooling in my stomach. "Saylor loses everything. It's like sex…" He paused. "Sex with me, mind you, not any other dude because let's be honest, when it's from me, it's just—"

"Gabe," I sighed. "Get there faster."

"Right." He turned off the TV and turned around to face me.

God, it was still weird seeing him with blond hair. A few months ago, his whole *secret* identity had come out. Ashton Parker Hyde, the pop star and actor who was the object of every teenage dream five years ago, had gone into hiding, and since I'd been his closest friend, I'd followed him. My reasons were different from his, obviously. He was escaping a painful past. I was trying to forget mine

We'd both been famous, but I was a child model, easily forgettable. He had been a god. No seriously, ask social media. They stalked him like crazy. You'd think he'd dye his hair back to black just to get a break once in a while, but nope, as far as he was concerned, Ashton was here to stay, though he went by Gabe. He rationalized that just made everything easier for his professors and new wife, Saylor, who, because of his hidden identity, had nearly castrated him.

But that's another story. I shook my head, clearing the

cobwebs, and threw him one of my waters. "You were saying?"

He grinned. I had to look away. He was too pretty, and I kind of hated how both he and Wes, another Lifetime-Channel-story-come-to-life, were both the happiest people on the planet, while I was living by myself and receiving stalker hate mail.

"She's forgetful." He shrugged. "So I keep seven of everything."

"Again, why seven?"

"It's the number of completion." He rolled his eyes. "Duh."

"Is there a reason you're here and not home? With Saylor?"

He looked guilty down at the couch. "I, uh, cable was out?"

"Try again."

He looked behind me and pointed. "The, um, fridge light needed to be changed."

I grinned. "It's fine."

"And—" He shot up from the couch and ran to the door, opened and closed it. "You need grease in the, er..." He scratched his head. "...hinges."

"Wow!" I clapped twice. "You know what a hinge is."

He flipped me off.

I stuck my tongue out.

In two steps, I was in his arms, my cheek resting against his muscled chest. Two tattooed biceps squeezed tight around me as he rested his chin on my head. It was comforting just being in his arms.

I'd missed him.

I hadn't been without him for years. It had always been us against the world. Then he'd gone and gotten married, and I'd felt truly lonely for the first time since leaving LA.

"I'm worried about you," Gabe whispered, pulling back and

cupping my face with his hands. "You need… a… bodyguard or something."

I closed my eyes and shook my head. "No, I'm fine."

"You're too pretty."

"I'm fine!" I laughed again and stepped out of his embrace. I didn't want him to know how freaked out I'd been the last week. The hate mail — aka fan mail — had gotten worse. I kept changing my PO box, and people kept discovering it. I mean, it was the usual stuff, the *you're so pretty and I watch you* stuff, which I could deal with — mostly. But a few of the letters had had pictures of Taylor.

And that didn't sit well with me.

If Gabe even knew, he'd flip his lid.

"I'm not above embedding a GPS unit in every article of clothing you own, including your favorite Donald Pliner sandals." He crossed his muscled arms and leaned against the back of the couch.

Sighing, I held up my hand, walked over to the table, and dug through my purse, pulling out my Taser and my Mace. "Happy?"

"Badass." He nodded in approval. "Your Taser's pink."

"I'm a girl." I shrugged my shoulders. "It seemed… happier."

He snorted, rolling his eyes. "So the person you Taser laughs instead of pisses his pants? Killer. Good thinking."

"Gabe." I shoved everything back into my purse and chewed my lower lip. "I swear, I'm totally and completely fine. Just stressed about starting sophomore year and all."

His blue eyes narrowed. "When did you cut your hair?"

My hands flew to my cropped black hair; I'd just recently cut it to my chin, hoping it made me look different than the most recent pictures of me. I'd added a few streaks of blue to the front too. Holy crap! I was turning into a freak from witness protection.

"Needed a change," I lied. "What's with the fifth degree, Gabe? You used to dye your hair all the time."

"I was hiding." He threaded a few pieces of hair through his fingers. "It looks good on you."

"Thanks." I felt my face heat. "Now, is there anything else I can do for you, *Dad*, or am I free to take a shower and run to the student center to grab my textbooks?"

"Classes started last week." Gabe frowned. "Why the hell are you still not getting your textbooks? If you flunk your classes, I'm going to be pissed." He started pacing in front of me. "I mean, this is your future and—"

I couldn't fight the smile as I crossed my arms.

"Shit, I do sound like your dad."

"Pretty soon, you're going to be waiting on my couch with a shotgun when I go out on dates." It was out before I could stop it.

"WHAT? You're dating someone!"

"Whoa!" I held up my hands. "Easy! I'm not dating anyone, and do you really think I'd introduce them to you first? They'd probably pass out!"

"Please, I'm not that intimidating."

My eyes took in his golden-blond hair, fully tatted-up body, and piercing blue eyes. "Right, not at all. What was I thinking?"

"Bitch." He winked. "And if you do start dating, make sure you tell Wes so we can get a full background check on him."

I shook my head. "Letting both of you at the guy would cause him to run in the opposite direction, and I'm pretty sure the point is to have him stick around. That is if I can find one at this godforsaken school." The lie fell easy from my lips. I hadn't had any guy stick around; I wasn't able to stomach it, not anymore.

"Flash 'em." Gabe nodded encouragingly. "It's the only way."

"Um, weren't you just threatening to kill a guy for even dating me?"

"Solid point." He cursed. "I'm stuck between being your friend and your dad. Not working, not working well, Lisa." His eyes twinkled. "Now, if there's anything I can fix, or do, or buy, or—"

"Go home to your wife." I pushed him toward the door. "Tell Saylor hi, and remember we have dinner this Sunday night, alright?"

He groaned aloud. "Stupid Wes and his benefit dinners."

"Stupid Wes and his benefit dinners that bring in money for the Pacific Northwest Group Home you own?"

Gabe paused. "Fine, see ya then. Love you." He turned quickly and kissed my cheek.

I shut the door behind him and leaned against it. Trembling, I walked over to my backpack and dug out my mail. With shaking hands, I ripped open the letter.

> *Come out, come out, wherever you are! I know your*
> *secret, wanna know mine? —Anonymous.*

"Stupid bastards."

I ripped the letter in half and grabbed a granola bar before heading back down to the student center. A shower could wait. I needed my books.

The last time I'd been at the center, I'd seen a guy I could have sworn looked like someone from my past.

I hadn't seen him in a week, so I knew it was my imagination... after all... Taylor? The Taylor I knew was dead.

I would know... after all.

I'd killed him.

TWO

One night I asked her to trip one of the other models then throw food in her face. Mel hesitated, but only for a minute, before not only doing just that but laughing and posting a picture to Facebook and The Site. When she came back, she asked, "How'd I do?"

I gave her a smug smile and said, "Better, you can do much better." And then I kissed her. It was a hungry kiss, a possessive one. The demons laughed in my head as she embraced my neck, and I took everything she'd been willing to give. Every. Last. Drop. —The Journal of Taylor B.

Tristan

My fingers drummed along the dashboard of my truck as I waited by the student center for her to walk by. Students milled about, most of them laughing, talking on their cell phones, looking excited about the school year. Campus was extremely busy since classes were about to start. It was probably useless, waiting for her like this. Every time someone walked by, I leaned over my steering wheel to get a better look, only to be left disappointed. Irritated, I shook my head at myself. She had to get books at some point. After I scared her off earlier that week, I'd been monitoring her, asking around about her. The good news? I was university staff, so it didn't look too creepy. It just sounded that way.

I groaned.

The university had given me a week to get adjusted from the sudden move, meaning I hadn't even taught my first class yet. Meaning, I should probably be preparing for class, but I couldn't, not until I saw her again, not until I knew it was her. Should I be in my truck acting like an insane person? Negative. What I should have been doing was finishing off the syllabus for first semester.

But I'd always been a procrastinator, not that I'd ever tell my students that, especially since they always assumed someone as young as I, who had a doctorate, was crazy-smart and totally by-the-lines.

If they only knew.

I checked my cell. Maybe she wasn't coming. I'd probably missed her. I rubbed my face with my hands and cursed myself for the fiftieth time that week.

I really should have kept my mouth shut, but instead, I'd said her name, scared the ever-loving crap out of her, caused her to nearly fall over, and then run in the other direction.

Honest moment. That was the first time I'd ever had a girl run away from me, and I wasn't so sure how I felt about it. The least I could do was apologize.

I snorted. Right, how would that go? *"Um, I'm sorry I look just like him?"* Or how about, *"I'm here because of you"*?

Right.

That sounded totally sane. She'd laugh, I'd laugh, I'd ask her out to coffee, she'd say yes, I'd hand over all his stuff, tell her what I thought of her — what I really thought of her — and be on my merry way.

Stick to the plan, Tristan.

The plan only included a semester at UW.

A semester to find out the truth.

Even if it hurt her.

After all, she'd been a bigger player in the mess that was his life than I'd ever realized — until it was too late.

Without even knowing it, she had pushed him until he'd finally snapped and lost his mind. I still felt the overwhelming sense of guilt when I thought of him. He'd been nothing but a kid — both of them had been kids.

I wasn't heartless; I understood that he was a monster in the making; if his notes were anything to go by, she should have run away rather than encouraged it. What type of girl stays in an abusive relationship like that? In my mind, she should have seen the writing on the wall. All I had to go off was the journal... the journal of a lunatic, and I was only halfway through that specific piece of evidence.

"Whatever. She's not coming," I said to myself, then started my truck, just in time to see a flash of dark hair. Pausing, I watched, praying she would turn around.

And when she did, I swear I almost choked on my tongue.

Lovely.

She was absolutely lovely.

When she'd run off the other day, she'd looked a bit stressed, and her hair was longer then. Now it was short, elongating her neck, showing off her sharp chin, full lips, and gorgeous cheekbones.

My heart started hammering against my chest; my hand hesitated on the ignition. Did I approach her now? Soften her up? Would that even lessen the blow? The plan had been to befriend her at least. I fought between being angry at her and wanting to pull her into my arms and kiss her.

Whoa! Where had that errant thought come from? My

internal response wasn't expected; it had come out of nowhere, a protective need to jump out of my truck and touch her face.

She turned around and adjusted her sandal, bending over right in front of my parking spot.

I groaned aloud.

She wasn't just lovely — she was freaking gorgeous, beautiful, a supermodel walking amongst a sea of boring faces.

In that moment, I wanted her to look at me. Desperately.

But she didn't.

Instead, she fixed her shoe and continued on her way.

I watched her for five seconds, but the seconds felt like minutes ticking by. She licked her lips, tucked her hair, and looked behind her several times as if someone was following her. Then she looked in my direction, but not long enough to make eye contact.

It was enough, but I had a strange feeling I'd need to repeat the process, not because I needed to know the girl responsible for everything — but because I felt such loss when my vision cleared and she wasn't in it.

Which was honestly the most messed up thing I could have ever thought. It was betrayal, pure, and simple. She hadn't ever been mine.

She'd been his.

The last thing I needed was to join the same downfall.

THREE

The demons clawed from the inside out, dying to be free. She entertained them for a while. Hell, she entertained me for a while, but in the end, it was never enough. The first time I told her I needed more, she panicked. I explained a man of my tastes couldn't hold on to just one girl. When fear entered her eyes, I was so turned on, I almost hated myself, so I told her to strip in front of me and walk around the hotel naked in her heels. She did it, and when she finished, I told her to take pictures of herself and send them to three of the girls who had crushes on me, telling them that clearly, I wasn't interested if I had that. She did it. She did it all. And in the end, I rewarded her for it. But the emptiness remained. Even with my body sated, my mind wasn't free. I was never free. —The Journal of Taylor B.

Lisa

I was already late for class, thanks to another crazy note in my mailbox, and when I'd gone to the student center to change my PO again, the student assistant had rolled her eyes and told me that maybe I should just stop having a mailbox.

Right.

Stop having a mailbox.

Like a hermit who lived in the woods and shot rabbits, I'd given her the best smile I could manage and then resorted to pleading when she didn't budge. My heart had been in my throat the whole time, my hands shaking. She'd seen me as an ungrateful nuisance; if she only knew how scared I was.

How scared I always was.

By the time we'd straightened everything out, I was already late for my Psychology of Emotion class. It was a sophomore-level class that I needed for my teaching major. In theory, it made sense that elementary ed majors had to take a lot of psychology, but that didn't mean I had to like it.

Psychology just reminded me how messed up I was — how messed up *he'd* been.

I pulled a granola bar from my pocket and sprinted with it in hand all the way to the Social Sciences building. By the time I made it, I was six minutes late, sweating, and pretty confident I'd inhaled at least two bugs. The granola bar had softened with my tight grip. I tore open the wrapper, scarfed it down in a few bites, and anxiously looked around the building.

Room 202. I glanced at each door and finally stopped in front of the right classroom. With a huff, I pushed the door open and froze.

Every eye turned to me. With a gulp, I self-consciously tucked a piece of short hair behind my right ear, allowing the rest of my hair to curtain across my hot face.

"You're late," a smooth voice said.

I chewed my lip and walked straight toward an empty desk. "Sorry," I mumbled, scooting past two students and finally stopping to turn around. "It won't happen ag—"

The professor tilted his head.

Words caught in my throat. I couldn't speak, was finding it hard to breathe, and even though I told my body I needed to sit down and stop making a fool out of myself, all I could do was stare.

The professor cleared his throat, his Adam's apple bobbing up and down as he examined me with cold gray eyes. "You were saying?" His hair was a dark brown with pieces of copper sewn through. His skin, tan. He was... too young to be a professor, too pretty. And totally the same guy I'd run into the week before and freaked out over. Could my day get any worse? Clearly, I'd overreacted when I'd first seen him; he looked nothing like Taylor. Taylor's hair had been darker, his face harsher.

"It won't happen again," I squeaked, my voice high-pitched with nerves.

"Glad to hear it," he snapped, turning away from me and grabbing a textbook. "Now, where were we before the interruption?"

The smart ass next to me raised her hand while simultaneously giving me a haughty stare.

Like I cared.

Puffing out my cheeks, I pursed my lips and blew out slowly, seeking calm that was proving elusive, as I pulled out my textbook and placed it gently on the desk.

"Dr. Blake..." She leaned forward, her boobs popping out of her tight black tank top. "...I think you were talking about the passion section of the syllabus."

"Ah." He snapped his fingers. "I believe you're correct." He looked down and examined a piece of paper, and then his lips curled into a smile as he glanced up. "Sophie, is it?"

Swear, the girl sighed out loud as she nodded her head eagerly. I glanced around in disgust and noticed most of the girls having similar screw me now reactions. What's the big deal? So he was young and attractive? Who cared? How about passing class and making an impact on the world?

"Passion…" He spoke in that same low, fluid voice that had me slightly hypnotized before shaking my head. "…will be discussed after the emotions segment. This class is the simple study of emotions and the brain. Why do we do what we do? Do emotions drive our decisions? Or are they unnecessary in how they affect every single one of the choices we make? This class will help you decipher between logic and emotion, and hopefully, once the semester is over, you'll know your own emotions and your own brain better." His voice cracked. "At least that's my desire."

The way he'd said *desire* had my head popping up involuntarily. His eyes were on me. I squirmed in my seat and jerked my gaze toward the board behind him.

"I'm not going to keep you the full time this morning…" He cleared his throat. "…because I have an assignment for you."

"Of course he does," a guy to my left said under his breath.

I offered him a quick smile.

Dr. Blake handed some papers to a student in the front row. "Pass these back."

Once the paper hit my desk, I almost groaned.

"Wow, torture on the first day. How'd we get so lucky?" that same guy whispered.

It was like he was reading my mind. I couldn't make out his face because I didn't want to stare at him long enough to make him think I was interested. So I kept my eyes trained on my paper.

"A study of the face," Professor Blake read aloud. "I want you to study your peers. On the paper you'll see each emotion written out. I want a definition of the nonverbal cues you see. If you have permission from the person you're studying, take a picture and upload it with your assignment when you're finished. Gentlemen, this is not an excuse to stalk."

The guy snickered. "Bummer," he said under his breath, while my entire body froze.

It wasn't a joking matter, and I hated that I was the only one in the room who couldn't laugh at what was supposed to be a joke. My breathing picked up as I gripped the sides of my desk.

"The assignment's due tonight by midnight. Class dismissed."

Students shuffled by me, but my butt was firmly planted in my seat.

"Hey…" The guy next to me stood and hovered over my desk. "…you okay?"

Slowly I looked up. He seemed harmless enough. A dark black hoodie hung around his muscled chest. Bright blue eyes peeked out beneath really thick lashes and glossy brown hair.

My eyebrows furrowed. "Yeah, yeah, forgot to eat breakfast."

He smiled. "Been there. By the way, I'm Jack." He held out his hand.

Not knowing what else to do, I took it and whispered, "Lisa."

"Cool." He nodded. "Well, I guess I'll see you later. Apparently, we have homework!" He said the homework part loud enough for Professor Blake to lift up his head and glare.

The minute Jack walked out of the room, the tension picked up, sucking out any sort of comfort I'd felt at his encouragement. Scattering out of my seat, I quickly grabbed my things and headed for the door. I was almost free when I heard a throat clear.

"Lisa, a moment of your time."

Funny how some sentences can sound so innocent, right? A moment? Is a moment — some time with your professor after being late — totally normal? But that one sentence wasn't normal. Had I known how abnormal it was, I would have never turned around.

That was my first mistake.

Turning around and meeting his steely gaze.

Taking that first step in his direction, not knowing that in a few short months, I'd be helpless against his pull. Defenseless.

I stopped in front of the table in the front of the class and sighed. "Yes?"

Up close, he was prettier than he'd been from far away. I almost lost my nerve but met his gaze straightforward as if I didn't realize he was beautiful, as if I wasn't terrified of that same beauty and the intensity behind it.

"Sit," he ordered.

I would have plopped on the floor had a chair not been right beside me. He demanded obedience, and, for some reason, I felt like I owed it to him.

I had no idea how true it was.

How I owed him more than obedience. My very soul.

"I expect students to be on time." He folded his hands in front of his chest and leaned against the desk, his head cocked to the side, his grin friendly yet… distant. "Is that going to be a problem in the future?" His smile dropped briefly as his eyes darted away, almost in disgust. "For someone like you?" His gaze returned, heated, then went completely cold.

Stunned, I could only stare in response. Was he serious? Someone like me? What did that even mean? Finding my voice, I answered, "You mean a sophomore like me?"

"No…" His jaw clenched. "…I meant it exactly how it sounded."

"Well." I cleared my throat and found a shred of confidence, probably the last bit I had for the day before I broke down and cried. "It sounded like you were implying that I was different than any other student here, and, I can assure you, I'm as normal as they come."

"I'm sorry to be the only person willing to tell you the truth," he said slowly. His full lips bared another smile, but it wasn't kind. It was mocking. You know that feeling you get when someone stares at you, and it's almost like you have no clothes on at all? But instead of it being out of lust, it's total disgust? That was the look he was giving me like I had no business being in school like I had no business breathing the same air.

I'd never felt more cheap than I did in that moment, and I was fully clothed, a rarity for someone of my old profession. Designers had made me feel beautiful, my friends had made me feel flawless, and this man had stripped every bit of confidence with one mocking grin.

"You're a bit of a celebrity around here, Lisa."

I looked down.

"So…" His right foot tapped against the ground. "…I know it must be difficult to fit in, but the later you are, the more attention you command. Do you understand what I'm saying? If you truly desired to blend in…" His voice trailed off.

"I'd be on time." My voice wavered as I blinked back tears. "I swear it won't happen again." I lifted my head. "I had an issue with my mailbox again, and then the girl wasn't being very helpful, and I forgot breakfast and—"

He held up his hand. "I don't need your excuses or

justifications. I just need your attendance and focus for the next semester. Think you can handle that?"

I took a step back and nodded.

"Good." He stood, towering over me. His shoulders relaxed but only slightly. A piece of copper hair fell across his eyebrow, giving him a boyish look, though he exuded nothing but anger and sensuality. I was loath to admit that last part because he was such a jackass. "You may leave now."

Had Gabe been there, he probably would have been up in the professor's face. Even Wes wouldn't have stood for it, and Wes didn't even like killing spiders. Respect was huge for them, and this guy was using his authority in all the wrong ways, throwing his weight around like I was nothing more than an annoyance.

"Lisa?" Professor Blake's eyebrows shot up. "Don't you have a class to go to?"

"Right." I clamped my mouth shut even though I wanted to talk back. The last thing I needed was to get in trouble or not pass my classes; they were all I had. If I didn't focus on school, I'd focus on the stalker or even my past. Both of those were out. I couldn't go there, refused to even dwell on it. "Thanks, Professor, for your... um, advice."

He seemed surprised; his face scrunched up a bit before he coughed into his hand and turned away.

Somehow my response had made him uncomfortable. I just didn't know why.

I checked my watch and groaned as I stepped into the hall. If I didn't run, I was going to be late. Again.

FOUR

I never had a pet growing up. What I had was Mel. Damn, she was spirited. I enjoyed breaking that spirit; I relished in the evil I'd made her do and laughed when she started falling with me when I no longer had to pressure her to pick on the weak. My greatest accomplishment was the day she'd come up with the idea to end all ideas. A death dare for all the new recruits in our group of friends. That was the night I told her I loved her — but I didn't really love her. I loved what she made me feel. I loved that, instead of being afraid of me, she fed the beast. She fed me more than my heroin addiction, more than the coke, more than the girls, the fast cars. She filled me temporarily, but I knew it would come to an end someday. She had a conscience, whereas I did not, so it would end, and I'd have to change tactics with her. —The Journal of Taylor B.

Tristan

I hadn't expected her to be so docile. It was a direct contradiction to what Taylor had written about in his journal. For a minute, possibly a second, a seed of doubt started to grow, but I squashed it down. I was doing this for me, for my family. I had no proof that she was the same girl Taylor wrote about, only a sneaking suspicion; the names matched, the description matched, and I'd found a few pictures of her in that same journal.

What had happened? How had she pushed him over the

edge? Why hadn't she told someone? She was so young; so was he. Granted, I knew an apology was probably in order, but I didn't even know what the hell I was apologizing for or how to do it. I was torn between feeling guilty about how he'd supposedly treated her and furious that she'd been responsible for him jumping off that bridge.

My body gave an involuntary shudder, pissing me off all the more. I wasn't this guy, the one hell-bent on revenge. I didn't even recognize the foreign feeling anymore. On the outside, I was the same; but inside, it was like a storm was brewing, just waiting to implode from the inside out. I gripped the edge of the desk and took a few soothing breaths, closing my eyes, returning my focus to the words on those pages, the words that sealed my fate, the ones that sealed hers.

She'd helped destroy him.

So by rights — I should destroy her. That's how life worked, the yin and the yang.

If my parents could see me now. Yeah, it wouldn't be pride; then again, they'd done nothing to help. If anything, they'd been the first catalyst, followed by *her*.

Her bright blue eyes flashed in my line of vision.

They matched that blue streak in her hair.

The one I couldn't stop staring at, the one that kept distracting me from my lecture. I hadn't actually planned on ending class so early, but the woman was too distracting. One look and I was just as lost as he'd been. She was like a poison, one I needed to suck out, to destroy.

Falling for her would be easy.

Getting her to fall for me would be the hard part. Relationships were built on trust, and I was going to gain hers. But first? A healthy dose of fear and respect. After all, I knew exactly how her mind worked. She responded to challenges. Fear gave her courage. So I was going to be a damn fearsome professor — and she'd love me more for it.

Guilt nagged again as the harsh words about Mel came flooding into my line of vision. If what he'd written was true, she'd been in hell with him.

I pushed it away.

I wasn't the good guy anymore — the one who never swore, drank, or did drugs. I was going to become him, if only for a semester. I would use his journal as a guide, and, in the end, God willing, I'd find peace.

I patted the journal in my coat pocket. "It's okay. You'll finally be at rest." I was going to discover what had really happened if it killed me. I owed him that much.

Guilt nagged again… I swallowed it down, unwilling to admit that everything I did was driven by fear. The pill bottle in my pocket rattled. I slapped my hand over it and swore aloud.

He'd found the only way to be free.

I didn't want that same destiny.

FIVE

"Do you still love me?" she asked one night while we were lying together in bed. I always stayed at hotels with her, never at the house. I didn't want to mix business with pleasure.

"Of course I do, baby." The lie was smooth, effortless. "Why?"

"You seem distant."

Because I was; because she was nothing to me, a body, a means to an end, an entertainment, a pet, a project, a distraction. Didn't she realize by now? I didn't feel things; it was impossible with all the drugs I'd taken for my sickness, or whatever the hell my parents called it. Please, if I was a sociopath, I would have been bombing things. Instead, I bullied kids, I entertained myself, and I did drugs. There were worse things in the world. Right? —The Journal of Taylor B.

Lisa

"**J**ust hold still!" I yelled, holding up my phone while Gabe gave me the finger. I grimaced and dropped the camera away from my face. "Nice, thanks for that."

"I'm a giver." He smirked.

Saylor, his wife, smacked him on the arm and rolled her eyes.

"Ouch."

I scrunched up my face when he leaned in and took Saylor's mouth with his, kissing her senseless in the local Starbucks like they were doing a romance scene in a movie. I coughed.

They didn't pull apart.

So I took a picture.

I earned another finger, but Gabe still didn't dislodge from his wife.

"Whoa!" Wes's voice sounded from behind me. "They been at it long?"

"Are all newlyweds disgusting?" I voiced aloud.

Wes moved around the table with his wife, Kiersten, and gave me a goofy shrug. I wanted to roll my eyes, but Wes was too nice and hot. Let's not forget the hot part. Both he and Gabe were like walking poster boys for GQ. Both blond, now that Gabe had decided to dye his hair back to his original color. It was like staring at two really bright superstars.

Hating them was like hating the Easter bunny. Try all you want, but you'll eat every piece of chocolate in the basket, just you wait.

"So, classes?" Kiersten leaned forward. "I heard you got stuck with that hot new psych prof."

Wes growled low in his throat.

"Down, boy." I braced my hands on the table and laughed. "Besides, he's not that hot."

"A girl passed out." Kiersten's eyebrows shot up. "Like in class."

"Dehydration?" I shrugged, taking a sip of coffee.

"Or…" She leaned forward. "…the rumors are true."

"Rumors…" Gabe backed away from Saylor, his lips swollen. "…are always based on truth."

"So you really did do a naked dance in your underwear last week after getting drunk downtown at Pike Place Market?" I tilted my head and waited while Gabe rolled his eyes and popped his knuckles. "Exactly."

He opened his mouth.

I took a picture.

With a grimace, he snatched my phone away from me. "Never thought I'd have to tell you to lay off the pictures, Miss Paparazzi."

I slumped in my seat. "It's for an assignment with that hot professor."

"Aha!" Kiersten jabbed her finger at me. "I knew it."

I pinned her with a look. "Sarcasm, friend, sarcasm."

"Boys get girls pregnant," Gabe offered, while Wes choked on the coffee he'd just stolen out of my hand.

Serves him right!

"Don't date them."

"You're going to be a great dad." I smiled sweetly. "What? You're just going to lock your girls in their rooms and go—" I mimicked his voice. "—uh, you see boy parts are bad, they make girls have lots of babies, like rabbits, and you know how rabbits make dad nervous and—"

"Hilarious," Gabe's eyes narrowed. "And please don't talk about kids yet…"

Saylor laughed quietly next to him, then squeezed his arm.

My heart dropped.

A very long time ago, I'd wanted to be that for Gabe, then Taylor happened, and well… I shuddered, blocking out the painful memories, the things I'd done, the things he'd done, the things we'd done.

"You okay?" Wes asked, his voice soft. He was way too

perceptive for my taste. If I'd wanted to share, he'd be the guy I'd talk to, but I was a vault. Sharing meant admitting my guilt, and admitting meant I'd probably go insane just like he had.

"Yeah…" I straightened in my seat. "…I just don't want to fail my class, and I need to write down nonverbal cues and take at least one picture. And pretty sure I need to ace this first assignment on account that I was late to my prof's class, and I got in trouble."

"He spank you?" Gabe's eyes mocked across his coffee.

"Yes, Gabe," I said calmly. "Because that's how they punish bad students here at UW — with a yardstick and a smile."

"I wish." He whistled. "What I wouldn't give to have Saylor—"

I plugged my ears.

He threw his head back and laughed while Saylor turned bright red and put her hand over his mouth to shush him.

"So…" Wes ignored Gabe as was his usual and leaned across the table. "…why don't you take pictures of people here in the coffee shop? I mean, ask permission, but most people here are super interesting, right? Studying? Stressed out? Tired?" He pointed to a guy in the corner. "He looks like he's running on five cups of coffee and one hour of sleep. Go ask, take the picture, make some notes, project done."

"You make it sound so easy," I grumbled.

He grinned. "I'm Wes Michels."

I hung my head lower and grimaced.

"Phone." He held out his hand and stood.

Within minutes, not only had he snapped two pictures for me but had taken notes on two pre-med students who had stayed up all night cramming for what they'd assumed would be a pop quiz, only to find out that they'd been in the wrong class on the wrong day.

"And that's why I'm not pre-med." Gabe shuddered.

"Really?" Kiersten asked. "I thought it was because big words scared you?"

"Supercalifragilisticexpialidocious. What now?" He nodded. "Keep talking, Kiersten, or keep walking."

"Spell it." She smirked.

"So this professor…" Gabe changed the subject. "If he tries anything, use the Mace or the rape whistle."

"Right." I nodded. "I'll be sure to do that. In class. With a hundred other students. When he looks at me cross-eyed."

"Good," he huffed.

"I was kidding."

Saylor patted Gabe's shoulder. "Gotta let the baby birds out of the nest someday, Gabe."

"No, that's actually not true, and this is why—"

I leaned forward and banged my head against the coffee table a few times. "Okay, guys, as much as I love all this fun banter and exhausting dialogue, I really need to go finish this assignment, so you two—" I pointed at Gabe and Saylor. "—kiss away. And you guys—" I pointed at Wes and Kiersten. "—go solve world hunger or something."

Wes tapped his chin. "Done."

"Wiseass." I grinned. "Now, you guys go be all mushy and hot elsewhere. I'm going to finish this assignment if it kills me, and then I'm going to go take a nice long walk."

"And think about your hot professor?" Kiersten asked.

"Bye, guys. See you at the benefit."

"Dress nice!" Gabe called as I walked off.

"Wear pants!" I called back as I pushed open the door to

Starbucks and rammed smack-dab into heat.

My bag fell onto the ground with a thump. "I'm so sorry." I bent to pick it up and noticed the shoes.

Brown shoes.

Ones that belonged to feet. Feet that I recognized from before. My gaze slid up the dark jeans and settled on a trim waist, finally landing on the same scowl I'd seen a few hours back.

"Maybe if you weren't so late all the time, you wouldn't be in such a hurry?" Professor Blake's eyebrows shot up as he offered me his hand.

Left with no choice but to take it, I grasped his fingers, gasping as the contact singed me from head to toe. *Hot* professor was a serious, serious understatement. Swear, his gray eyes saw through my clothes.

His breathing changed just briefly before the mask went back on. He nodded to the papers clenched tightly in my hand. "Working on your assignment?"

"Yup." I rocked back on my heels. "Caffeine's my drug of choice and all that."

He smiled.

Not a mocking smile, but a real smile, one that I felt all over my body like someone had just attached me to a freaking tanning bed and turned it on high. I took a step back, nearly colliding with another body leaving Starbucks.

"Whoa! Class meeting!" The male voice said from behind me. "Hey, do I get an A if I spot the professor out of class? You know, like seeing a bear in the wild?"

Professor Blake's eyes darkened as he turned slightly away from me. "No, Mr. McHale."

"Damn." He crossed his arms and laughed.

"Assignment's due at midnight," Professor Blake said in clipped tones, then sidestepped both of us and walked into the coffee shop.

I exhaled in relief and started walking toward my dorm.

"Hey, wait up!" Jack called from behind me. "You finished yet?"

"No." I wanted to kick every pinecone I saw but refrained, just barely. "I have a few more to write down."

"Me too." He smiled warmly. "Let's do it together." He blushed and then shook his head. "I mean the assignment."

"I knew what you meant." I laughed. "I'm a girl. We don't think on that same… level."

Jack eyed me up and down. "More's the pity."

"You gonna try to flirt or work?"

"Can I do both?"

"No."

"Fine." He slugged his backpack over his left shoulder. "Let's go watch people."

I fell into step beside him, and when the coast was clear, when he was jabbering on about homework, I looked over my shoulder to see Professor Blake watching me from the window at Starbucks.

"Hey, you coming or not?" Jack asked. His smile was easy, nonthreatening.

I couldn't figure him out; then again, I didn't have to overanalyze everything.

"Yeah." I quickly turned back around. "Yeah, I'm coming."

SIX

It was almost too easy, bending her to my will, allowing her to think she was important. I wanted to see how far I could push her, so I broke up with her. I've never seen a girl cry so much in my entire life. Hell, she had to have medically dehydrated herself. When she was done wailing, I nodded toward the door and crossed my arms. She stomped out and slammed the door behind her.

Minutes later, she came flying back in and wrapped her body around mine, kissing me forcefully across the mouth. "I can't live without you," she whispered.

And I laughed because I had a dirty little secret. She was going to have to, and I'd laugh — from hell. I'd get the final laugh. "I know, baby, I'm so sorry." I kissed her back, satisfied that the game was still on, that she was still clueless to who I really was, what I really was, and what she meant to me. Absolutely nothing. —The Journal of Taylor B.

Tristan

Warmth from the coffee mug seeped into my palm. I stared down at the steaming dark sludge. Bitter. The coffee was bitter. Or maybe it was just my life? Possibly me? Nothing gave me any sense of satisfaction — coffee, food, sex. Ha, now that was a good one. Sex. Did I even know how to perform anymore? Not likely. After all, I'd been the good guy, the golden boy, the one who didn't do things like get girls pregnant or steal their virginity on prom night. *My* name wasn't Taylor.

It was easy to see why she'd become a sort of addiction to him; she'd be that way to any guy with working eyes. Getting her legs out of my head had taken a lot more thought than I'd originally intended.

I gripped the cup in one hand and pulled out my iPad with the other. I still had some work to finish but hated the feeling of being alone in the classroom. I needed noise, a distraction. Odd, how a constant hum of voices soothed me. Funny, it hadn't really soothed him — it had led to his destruction.

Class, not voices.

"Tristan?" A voice interrupted my dark thoughts.

I lifted my head, and damn-near ran for the door. "Wes." My voice croaked. "It's been… a while." Try years. Lots and lots of years. I tried to look busy shuffling papers, but Wes was one of the guys — way too nice, way too available. He plopped down across from me and leaned forward, his eyebrows arching in interest.

"Let me guess. You're the new hot professor."

I almost spit out my coffee then tossed my pen onto the stack of papers I'd just shuffled, which hadn't needed shuffling. "I'm sorry, what?"

"Got the girls going crazy." He sighed loudly. "Man, some things never change."

Or they do. Like, a lot.

"Right." I laughed, making direct eye contact with the guy. "I didn't know that word had spread…"

"It's college." Wes leaned back, finally giving me the space I needed. "What did you expect?" His mouth dropped open at my shrug. "What last name you go by these days?"

Wes knew way too much about me, but then again, he would. He would know everything about me, about my family. Everything except Taylor. No, that had been our dirty little secret, covered up very nicely by our ridiculous resources and total lack of morals.

"Tristan Blake." I licked my lips and offered a half-shrug. "My usual."

"Ah… decided to leave out…" Wes grinned knowingly. "Good call. Don't want any assassination attempts or kidnappings. That would probably ruin your credentials at the job. By the way, why are you working? Thought you were in DC?"

What was this? Twenty questions?

I shifted the coffee in my hand and tried to appear nonchalant. "I needed a change. You know how things are up there, all work and no play."

"Right." Wes nodded, his eyes turning a bit skeptical. "Which is your MO, so why UW?"

"Actually, I have a lot of work I still need to do." I pointed down at my iPad and shrugged. "Can we catch up later this weekend?"

"The benefit this weekend." Wes didn't even blink. "Your dad said he'd send a rep. I'm guessing that rep is you?"

Damn it. I really needed to learn to check my other calendar. "Yeah, most likely."

"Great." Wes stood and held out his hand.

I shook it firmly.

"See you Sunday!"

He motioned for a redhead to follow him; his wife, I guessed. She was tall, lithe, gorgeous, pretty much exactly the type of girl that I'd imagined Wes would settle down with. I'd seen her enough on the news to know they were an ideal couple, and I shuddered to think about how crappy of a friend I'd been when Wes had gone through his cancer. Yeah, I'd sent him cards and called a few times, but nothing compared to actually being in Seattle while he struggled. No, the only thing that could have brought me to Seattle was my own selfishness.

Gabe and Saylor, another couple who had been on the news non-stop since it was discovered that the pop star was actually alive and not dead, followed them out, both offering me tentative looks as if they weren't quite sure if I was a friend or someone they needed to steer clear of. It's possible it was because I wasn't smiling and probably looked about ready to break my pen in half — not their fault. Mine. All my fault. Like everything else.

Gabe stopped at the door and turned, giving me a curious stare. And the funny thing? I imagined in that moment that I was normal again: I was working on the hill, doing what I loved, doing what I believed in. I would have been friends with them. After all, I'd had loads of friends, family, coworkers. That's the thing about life. You don't realize what you have until it's completely ripped away from you.

Or until you find out the brother you never knew...

Was murdered.

And your father tried to cover it up.

I'd always wanted a brother. And now I had nothing. Nothing. Before I'd even started, before I'd even got my hopes up, all hope had been stolen from me by a girl with black hair and shimmery blue eyes.

I gripped the coffee cup tighter, my jaw popping in irritation.

Time was going to run out faster than I'd anticipated. I could only keep a low profile for so long. Dad thought I was taking a much-needed hiatus.

And it was true. To a point.

I'd take my *vacation*, then things would return to normal. Life would return to normal. Food would taste good again, and I'd stop feeling guilty for the life I should have saved. For the life I'd never known existed.

SEVEN

I was so drunk that night anything with two legs looked good. But I picked her over and over again. Only this time, it wasn't consensual. We were in the elevator. She'd said she always hated elevators, making my pleasure that much more heightened. I fed off her fear when I stripped her of her dignity. Then again, she'd stripped me of mine. Made me feel when the last thing I wanted to do was feel — I hadn't felt any type of emotion for a long time. It scared me. It made me want to hate her, hate her for being all the right things at the wrong time. So I raped her. I raped her twice. And I told her to say thank you when I was done. I was a beast, but damn, she really was my beauty. —The Journal of Taylor B.

Lisa

"I look like I belong in a romance novel," I huffed, staring at myself in Kiersten's full-length mirror. We were getting ready at Wes's mansion. And when I say mansion, I mean straight up, HGTV, hold-your-breath, Jay-Z-ain't-got-nothing-on-him mansion. I'd been around wealth all my life.

It was nothing compared to Wes Michels'.

Kiersten laughed and pushed me in the shoulder. "I remember a time not so long ago when you dressed me up for a party. Consider it payback."

I raised my hand. "Didn't I also help with the wedding dress? So, technically, those two times should cancel out by default — meaning I shouldn't have to wear this."

"What's so bad about it?" She crossed her arms. Her dress was white, puffy, like something out of a fairytale.

"It's black," I said, lamely lifting the lacy overlay with my fingers. The sweetheart bodice was so tight I could barely breathe. If she was Cinderella, then I was the evil queen. Granted, it was a black and white ball. I just hated black. Black reminded me of him, of his soul, of the things he'd done to me, of things he'd made me wear when he was in one of his moods, when he wasn't happy — which was on a daily basis. I'd been too in love, too young, too naive to understand. Until it was too late.

"Where'd you go?" Kiersten braced my shoulders. Her green eyes were wide with concern. "Are you sure you've been feeling okay?"

Peachy, I wanted to say. Nothing like getting totally awesome stalker mail in my mailbox and dealing with a hot professor who looked like he wanted to kick my ass for breathing. Then there was Jack, who hadn't left me alone since I'd helped him with his homework last week.

If I was honey, he was a bumblebee. I mean, he was funny and cute, but I had no interest in guys.

Another secret I'd kept.

One that I'd lied about to make Kiersten think I was one of those normal roommates. Yeah, guys were hot; I found them attractive, but I couldn't do it anymore. Last year, I'd actually almost puked on a guy I was making out with. I'd tried to have the meaningless sex, the crazy make-outs, and every single time I ended up so sick, I'd had to leave.

Probably why most guys thought I was a tease.

If they only knew that their mouths reminded me of death. Their hands? Of rape.

"Lisa!" Kiersten scolded. "This is a masquerade ball. Fun is kind of part of it. Think you can wipe that grimace off your face and pretend to have a good time? Leave all the homework stress here, and let's go."

I looked down at the mask in my shaking hands. He'd made me wear a mask once.

"You're right." I forced a silly smile. "Sorry. It's just my classes are super hard this semester."

Her right eyebrow shot up. "Change majors."

I scrunched up my nose.

"Okay, then your only choice is to have fun and be awesome."

"Fine," I huffed, still clenching the mask in my hands as we made our way out of the room. Kiersten linked arms with me.

"Whoa!" Gabe was waiting at the bottom of the stairs. "Lovely, ladies, just lovely."

Saylor rushed up to us, wearing an awesome black-and-white-checkered dress that Alice would have worn in Wonderland. The overhead light flashed on the mask she held. Red. Why couldn't I have a red mask? Stupid black.

"Damn." Wes pulled Kiersten away from me and kissed her across the mouth. "If I wasn't already married to you, I'd ask again."

"Yeah." I coughed. "So it's not awkward at all being the third wheel. Totally fine with it, guys. Totally fine."

Gabe snickered while Wes gave me a shy look and shrugged. "Who says I don't have a date waiting for you at the ball?"

"Oh my gosh, Wes Michels! I knew you could do it!" I

lunged into his arms and kissed his cheek. "You and your loads of money created an exact replica of Prince Charming?"

He burst out laughing. "Nope."

"Channing Tatum?"

The girls sighed behind me while Gabe huffed.

"Sorry."

"Ryan Gosling?"

"Naw." He winked, clearly enjoying our little game. "But I think you'll like him. After all, I've been told he's really hot. Besides, I kind of grew up with him — well, at least went to prep school with him until his family moved away."

"Ah, childhood friend." My eyes narrowed. "Admit it. You're setting me up with the friend in high school that got no play."

"Actually…" Wes's cheeks went a bit pink. "…pretty sure he got the most play in the entire school."

The room fell silent.

Gabe walked up to Wes and patted him on the shoulder. "It's okay, man. Let it out."

"How is that possible?" Saylor asked what everyone was thinking.

"Hey!" Gabe crossed his arms and glared.

"Trust me. You'll see," was all Wes said as we filed out of the house and into the waiting limo.

I wasn't sure I wanted to see, especially considering I was defective. The type of girl who couldn't even kiss a guy without getting traumatic flashbacks. I was both a tease and a prude. How the heck had that happened?

"To the masquerade, Govna!" Gabe shouted in a fake British accent once we were all seated inside the limo.

I gave an exaggerated cringe. "And that's why you never

took any of those UK roles. Your accent sucks, Gabe."

He rolled his eyes, and everyone fell into easy conversation about the masquerade, about the money it was raising for Gabe's foundation, about the new technology Wes's family's company was adding to all the local hospitals. They were like one big happy world-saving family. All doing something to benefit others, while I couldn't stop thinking about myself, about my failure, about my sadness.

Everyone was excited for the future.

Everyone but me.

EIGHT

"Tell me a secret," I whispered in her ear. I was a collector of secrets. I used them as currency and knew if I had all of hers, I could own her like she owned me.

"I don't like being mean," she finally said. "But I love you."

She was eighteen. She didn't know what love was. If I was love, then she was seriously deranged, maybe even more so than I. Then again, I was a great actor. I was charismatic, good-looking, rich — and the best part? She had no freaking clue who I really was. Didn't even know my last name. How great is that? I'd like to think that in the end, when this is all over, when I'm gone, I'd done one thing right. I'd at least protected my family from the demons. —The Journal of Taylor B.

Tristan

The black mask covered up my entire face, leaving only spots to breathe and two holes for my eyes. My hair fell in waves over my forehead as I hurried through the doors into the main ballroom. Usually, at functions like this, I had my hair slicked back, professional-looking, but I'd run out of time to do anything but leave it as was, which meant I probably looked like an untamed hellion.

Everything was transformed. The Hilton hotel downtown

may as well have been the setting to some regency-inspired movie.

I was nervous. Not that I had any reason to be. It wasn't like Lisa was going to be there or that I'd have to fight that ever-growing attraction to her that pissed me off on a daily basis. Grinding my teeth together, I pulled on my white gloves then adjusted my black tie. My suit was head-to-toe black, custom-made, only something a Westinghouse would wear.

After all, tonight I wasn't the undercover professor. Damn, just saying it in my head sounded so wrong.

Tonight, I was son to a very important, very wealthy man. And I had to play the part I'd been born to play my whole life. The part of perfection. Perfect straight smile, smooth talker. I wasn't vain enough to think I was actually all of those things, but I knew damn well how to pull it off so that every single person within my vicinity was eating out of the palm of my hand.

The orchestra played softly in the background as people swayed in rhythm in the middle of the parquet dance floor. The chandelier's golden glow mixed with the silver moonlight dripping through the windows and gave the room a fairytale ambiance. Tall, white-tapered candles stood at intervals across each buffet table, casting flickering reflections off silver chafing dishes.

And the masks. Good God, the masks. They were everywhere, hiding the guests' faces… and their secrets. The rich liked that — the masks. They made them feel mysterious.

The place looked… nice. Then again, for five hundred a head, the place had better look nice. It was hard not to think about the money being spent, considering that was part of my job, though a small part. Make sure to throw enough money to make the family look good. Make sure that my father looked good.

I made my way across the room, gliding between the bodies of people, and sidestepped an elderly woman, only to run directly into someone in the process.

Black lace brushed against my gloves as I lightly laid my hands on her petite shoulders to steady her. I cleared my throat and mumbled, "Apologies."

Bright blue eyes peered up at me through a black mask. It covered half of her face, making her red lips look so inviting I almost leaned forward to have a taste.

"Oh." Her voice was husky. "…it was me anyway. I can't see out of the mask."

I smirked, still not removing my hands from her shoulders. "I'd keep it on."

"Why's that?"

"Rules." I nodded sternly, then offered a smile. "You don't want to be known as a rule-breaker, do you?"

"Hmm…" She tapped her chin. "…that depends."

"On?" I leaned forward, breathless with anticipation.

"What I get for breaking them," she whispered.

Her dark hair was pulled back into a low tight bun; pieces fell across her face, tempting me to tuck them behind her ear then kiss her until she begged me for more. My reaction to her was borderline-violent. I'd never felt such a strong attraction to a complete stranger — unless you counted Lisa, and counting her just pissed me off. She'd been his, not mine. And, if my suspicions were true, she'd driven him to complete madness. No thank you.

"Dance?" I slid my hands down her arm then tucked her into my body, making it impossible for her to escape.

"Is that within the rules?" she teased.

"Only if we keep our identities hidden."

"Really?" She laughed. "Are you joking or serious?"

"I never joke." I shook my head and leaned forward, whispering across her ear. "But tonight, for you, I'll do anything."

"Wow!" She pulled back and placed her hands on my shoulders as we fell into step with the other dancers. "You're really putting on the moves, Mr. Rule Breaker!"

"Ah, and here I thought I was being so subtle about my feelings toward you."

A splash of rose bloomed in her cheeks then faded. She broke eye contact, worrying her lower lip before her gaze flashed back to me as though she couldn't resist herself. Maybe it was male pride speaking, but that was my desire — for her to be so caught up in the moment, in this moment, that she forgot herself, forgot everything but my hands on her. A buzz of awareness burst through my veins.

"You're beautiful," I stated honestly, smoothly.

"Um, th-thank you."

"I don't believe in flirting or being coy." I twirled her around twice then pulled her against my chest. "I believe in honesty and truth. When a woman smiles, and it takes your breath away, she damn-well better know it that instant. Otherwise, what's the point in thinking it? The point in staring? I'd rather she be aware of her effect on me. It makes things fairer that way."

"Fairer?" she croaked.

"For when I kiss her." I twirled her small body again, and her dress swished against my legs. "It won't be a surprise when my lips touch hers. It won't come as a shock when my fingers graze her neck, now will it?"

Her chest heaved. "I'm trying to figure out if I like your honesty or if it's a bit terrifying."

"Fear…" My lips grazed her ear. "…is a tool, not a weakness."

She jerked away from me so fast I thought she was going to tumble on her rear.

"Wh-what did you say?"

"It's a common phrase." Her face, or what I could see of it, had gone completely pale. I narrowed my eyes and leaned in for a closer look. "Are you alright?"

"Yeah, just…" She removed her hands, and self-consciously rubbed her arms. "Sorry. I've had a rough week."

I reached for her hand and tugged her back to my body. "What happened?"

"Sorry," she repeated and laughed weakly. "I don't make habits of confiding in complete strangers."

"I graduated with honors from Harvard, double-majored in psychology and law, and have had background checks on at least ten individuals at this very party. Security is waiting in every corner of the room for someone to yell bomb or pull out a gun, and I own every single one of them. I'm safe. Now… let's talk about that week."

NINE

I asked her what she thought about death.

She shivered in my arms and said she didn't like talking about it. Why discuss something so horrible when we were so young?

I laughed along with her and kissed her forehead, my heart twisting in my chest as the demons told me to hurt her when all I really wanted to do? Lie next to her, touch her, make her feel safe, even if it was from me. Even if it would always be from me. Something was happening between us, and I was powerless to stop it. How do you stop the wind? How do you quit the rain? You take shelter, but what if the shelter is the reason for your downfall in the first place? —The Journal of Taylor B.

Lisa

"**S**ecurity?" I was probably gawking. Who the heck was this guy? I mean, I knew Wes and Gabe took security at their events really seriously. But who else was hosting? I tried to think back to the invitation. Had a third name been engraved on it?

"You seem to be focusing awfully hard. Your week *must* have been hell." His smooth voice drew my attention back to his face.

I wasn't one of the girls, the ones who fawned over male beauty. I mean, I'd been in the modeling industry since I was twelve. I saw pretty on a daily basis, but he wasn't pretty. He was so far beyond good-looking that I had to keep averting my eyes like a total middle-schooler.

Tall, muscular with beautiful thick hair that had twists of gold and copper, though it was messily arranged around his mask like he'd just gotten off a motorcycle and decided it was good enough. His hands were huge; they cupped my hips like they were made to fit my body. And his smile? Bright. Beautiful. Trusting. And, admittedly, I was a little frightened that my first instinct, my gut reaction, was to trust him, to follow him down the rabbit hole and ask for more and more until I was sated. I didn't react to guys like that. His touch didn't make me recoil, his smile didn't leer, and he was honest about what he thought, saying exactly what he was thinking without hesitation. That type of confidence was sexy, and he wore it well.

In fact, he reminded me of the professor, though the professor was such a stiff I doubt he even knew what a masquerade was, let alone owned a suit as nice as the one this guy was wearing.

"So," he prompted, his full lips curling into another devastating smile as his light eyes twinkled with amusement. "Tell me a secret."

I froze.

I had nothing against secrets. But that had been a game Taylor and I had played… something intimate, something he'd used against me repeatedly in order to get me to do his bidding when he was angry or jealous.

I shivered in response.

"Or…" His smooth voice matched his captivating smile, and the mystery man changed tactics. "…just tell me a truth."

"This last week…" I swallowed, ignoring the painful reminder in my chest. "…I had to switch mailboxes seven times."

"Seven?" His eyes widened. "Not happy with your PO location? Hmm, I highly doubt that. The only reason a woman would go to all that trouble would be to hide from something or someone… tax evasion? No, too young." His eyes scanned me. "Crazy ex-boyfriend, then? Or stalker?"

I opened my mouth to speak, but he gave a slight shake of his head. His eyes examined me from head to toe. "Too polite to report a crazy stalker or ex-boyfriend. My guess is you've been trying to hide from the individual and hope it will go away with a simple address change."

"It will," I defended. "Besides, ever since information was released into the public—"

His eyes narrowed. "The public?"

"Never mind." I shook my head. The last thing I needed was to let him know who I really was. That *always* gave me unwanted attention. "So I'm in college." Not the smoothest subject change I'd ever tried, but it worked. He seemed amused. His lips curved into a grin. Something was so familiar and ridiculously hot about that grin.

"Twenty?"

I gawked as his mouth nearly brushed mine with the ending of his answer. "Huh?"

"Your age."

"Yeah."

"Sophomore?"

"Can you stop psychoanalyzing me now?" I said, breathless.

He laughed heartily. His head fell back just slightly, giving me a view of his strong neck.

Something was seriously wrong with me if I was lusting after the man's neck.

"Alright, so tell me about your week; let me guess your new professor is an absolute prick."

I joined in his laughter, recalling all the times that week that Professor Blake had picked on me in class. "Yeah, something like that. I think he hates me."

"Who could hate you?"

"Ah, there's that flattery again."

He dipped me, the motion stealing any control I'd deluded I'd had in his arms. He brought me back against his chest and said in a husky voice. "I prefer truth."

I fought to not roll my eyes. "Fine, and apparently, it's really easy. Apparently, I offend him by breathing."

"The only reason a man would be offended by your breathing is because of the distraction it causes."

"Me living is a distraction?"

"To me?" His eyes narrowed as he twirled me then pulled me back into his arms. "To the male species?" He lowered me into a dip, his face inches from mine as he whispered, "I imagine your presence is a distraction everywhere you go."

I swallowed convulsively as the music ended, and he brought me back to an upright position.

A man tapped him on the shoulder and whispered in his ear. Feeling a bit uncomfortable, I wrapped my arms around myself while he engaged in conversation. I read no expression on his face. It was like he'd gone blank.

When he turned back around, that dead-sexy smile was back, and I could have sworn my knees knocked together a bit.

"Walk with me."

I nodded and grasped his gloved hand with mine.

He smoothly led me through the crowds. We came to a stop once we reached the stage; he released my hand and jogged up.

Uh, did Wes and Gabe know that this guy was going to make a speech?

I looked behind me for the guys. The music stopped.

When I glanced back up at the stage, Wes and Gabe were joining mystery man. They slapped him on the back and then pumped each other's hands. Okay, who was this guy? Seriously?

"Thank you all for coming," Wes said into the microphone. "With your help tonight and the generous donations of W. Enterprises, we were able to raise over one million toward our goal of two million by the end of the year! Thank you so much!"

Gabe clapped along with Wes. They stepped out of the way while my mystery man stood tall amongst the two guys, not dwarfing them but easily holding his own. He coughed into his fist then shoved both hands into his pockets; it looked practiced as if he wanted to show an heir of vulnerability. His eyes flashed toward mine, giving me a dark possessive look, before addressing the crowd.

"As CEO of W. Enterprises, I'm more than happy to thank all the donors, and on behalf of my father, we truly appreciate everyone's continuing support toward bettering the healthcare in the greater Seattle area."

More applause.

But the pieces weren't falling into place. So he was a CEO of a company? That fit, I guess. He was dressed well, and he'd mentioned security, but what CEO had that type of security?

The guys filed off the stage. Gabe purposely bumped into me and winked before wandering off, probably to find Saylor, and Wes stopped right in front of me.

"So…" His grin was shameless. "Having fun with Charming, Miss Cinderella?"

I narrowed my eyes at him and crossed my arms. "You mean that's the guy—"

"I think I deserve an *I'm sorry, Wes, for doubting your ability.*"

I held up my hand. "Not happening."

"Of course, the great Wes Michels knows the prettiest girl in the room." Mystery man walked up to us. He wrapped an arm around me, tugging me closer to his body. I liked it. I shouldn't, but I did.

"Funny, I don't see my wife." Wes winked. "And yes, Tristan, this is—"

"No last names!" I blurted, sounding like a complete idiot.

"We don't want to break the rules." Mystery man leaned down, his breath hot on my neck. "Do we?"

Oh we do, we really, really do. "Nope." My voice came out like a squeak. "Sorry, Wes, but no names until the unmasking at midnight!"

Wes held up his hands and grinned. "That should be very, very interesting." He covered his face with his hand and looked away. "Yeah, I'm going to go find my wife… and dance. You two…" He licked his lips. "You have fun until midnight, then."

"Until midnight." I nodded, leaning further into the warmth of the solid body next to me. He smelled like expensive cologne — not overpowering, just inviting. So inviting, I fought the urge to turn my head a bit and breathe him in.

"So…" His low voice vibrated. "…shall we dance under the stars?"

Laughing, I pulled away and stole a glance at his face. "Who are you?"

"Nobody important."

I sighed.

"And you? The most beautiful girl in the room… who are you?" His eyes took on another dark hue, captivating me, making me want to lean in, discover his secrets.

"For tonight?" My body shook with desire. I wanted more. For the first time in a really long time, I wanted more, and I wanted it to be him. "Your dance partner."

He brought my hand to his lips. His light eyes brimmed with hunger as he placed a gentle kiss across my wrist. "And tomorrow? What am I tomorrow?"

Was I shaking? "I guess we'll see."

"So strategic in her answers. I love a woman who knows her mind." He dropped my hand and led me toward the double doors. When he pushed them open, we were suddenly on a balcony looking at the Seattle skyline.

"Beautiful." I breathed. "And look, no rain!"

"Please don't tell me you're one of those." He laughed, leaning against the railing as he tucked his hands into his pockets.

"What do you mean?" I turned toward him, my breathing labored at the sight. He looked so predatory. Even relaxed, he seemed ready to pounce.

"One of those horrible people who spread rumors about Seattle having nothing but rain when the exact opposite is true." His head tilted in amusement. His full lips pressed together as he glanced briefly at the skyline, then back at me, revealing a sensual smile that took my breath away. It was scary the way a complete stranger could make me feel, the desire he evoked in me with one look.

"It does rain a lot here." I found my voice and took a

tentative step toward him.

The tip of his tongue slid through his mouth, grazing his top lip, almost like he was thinking about licking my lips, not his. "I'd like to call it mist."

"Fine, it mists a lot in Seattle." My eyes couldn't look away from his; like a trance, I kept watching his face, entertained by each movement he made.

"Magical," he whispered reverently. "The mist. No way would I be coming out and saying that about you after only knowing you for a mere hour… don't you think? After all, I'm honest, but I don't want to come on too strong by telling you that under the stars, you look like an angel… a dark angel."

I tried to shrug, to appear unaffected by his words. "Hmm, isn't darkness bad? Wouldn't that mean I'm fallen?"

He laughed, pulling his hands out of his pockets and gently tugging me the rest of the way toward him. His legs braced either side of mine as my dress puffed around him. Strong fingers grazed my jaw as he kissed me softly on the cheek and whispered, "I'm pretty sure those are the best kind."

TEN

"Prove you love me," I demanded one night when we were at a party.

She gave me that stare, the one that said she was afraid but didn't know how to fix it. "Tay…" She shook her head. "…you know I love you. What more do you want me to do?" She was on the verge of tears.

I felt equal parts bad and good. Her reaction sated me. Her tears destroyed me. I needed to be numb again. It was the only way to keep the demons out, the only way to keep everyone out. The pain was too much. So I reached into my pocket and pulled out a handful of pills, then tossed them into my mouth and whispered, "Fine, you just killed me then." —The Journal of Taylor B.

Tristan

She was like a drug. With each glance she gave me, I wanted to take more; with each word she shared, I leaned in. Something about her was dark. I wasn't one to normally be attracted to that sort of thing. I was the golden child, after all. But it was fun — in that single stolen moment — being myself and wondering what if I didn't have to worry about the journals, or Taylor, or Lisa? What if it was just me in this moment with this stunning woman?

What would I do?

I closed my eyes and leaned my forehead against hers. A

shaky breath escaped her lips. "I'm going to kiss you now."

"Are you trying to prepare me or ask permission?" she whispered, her voice beckoning me like a siren's call.

"Both." My lips hovered near hers. "I figure it's only fair."

"Fair?" She pulled back slightly. "How so?"

"Ten thousand." I angled my head and watched the pulse jump on her neck. "That's how many nerve endings, on average, are in your lips. Consequently, when your body anticipates pleasure, the build-up is the best part. Imagine, those ten thousand nerves are swelling, allowing blood to surge through them in anticipation of... what?" I swept my tongue across her lower lip and whispered, "Of being touched. I ask permission, not because I'm being a gentleman. It's actually the complete opposite. I ask permission, so your brain anticipates the pleasure before I've ever even touched you."

I tasted her lower lip again and abruptly dipped my tongue into her mouth. Then just as quickly retreated. "The human body is an instrument. Know how to master it... and well..." I let my voice drop as I moved my hands slowly to her shoulders and tugged her body flush against mine. Our mouths met softly at first. I deepened the kiss, memorizing her taste, knowing I wouldn't experience a kiss like this again in my lifetime. The way her scent, her soft moans destroyed my body, wrecked me from the deepest part of me, was nothing short of life-altering.

And I'd like to think I'd kissed a lot of women.

I'd studied the psychology of sexuality.

I was an expert in pleasure.

But she was schooling me, absolutely wreaking havoc on every logical thought as her soft whimper cascaded over me.

Blood surged through my body as it tightened with awareness at her proximity.

She pulled back, her lips swollen. "That was... not a good enough warning."

Laughing softly, I cupped the back of her head and gently drew it toward mine and kissed her again, angling my lips differently, searching her, consuming her, drawing pleasure from her lips as if it was my life goal to discover every single secret she owned.

Her arms wrapped around my neck. She was shy; she didn't push against me, didn't wrap her legs around me, or moan into my mouth like I was having sex with her rather than kissing her.

My hands moved down her corset to her hips, and I lifted her into the air and walked her backward toward the brick wall. The whole time, our masks collided. In frustration, I ripped hers off, then mine. The shadows of moonlight hid our faces as I kissed her harder, losing myself in her.

Her nails dug at the back of my neck as she jerked my head harder. Groaning, I let her fall to the ground as I placed my hands on the brick wall to keep myself from ripping the dress from her body.

Shouting started from the ballroom.

"Ten, nine...!"

"Eight," I whispered against her mouth. "Seven."

"Six." She sighed, her breathing labored as her tongue found mine again. "Five."

"Four, three." I pulled back and trailed kisses down her neck. "Two."

We broke apart, both breathing heavy. "One."

People burst out onto the balcony as the fireworks started, lighting up the sky. And our faces.

And the only thing I could say as she gasped in horror was, "Oh, shit."

ELEVEN

The pain completely stopped that night. I remember falling to the ground. I was smiling like a damn fool, and she was sobbing. I kept whispering, "Your fault, your fault..." when really I knew I was the one who'd taken the pills. But I also knew if she ever left me? I was as good as dead anyway. I needed to keep her with me at all costs. Even if it meant hurting her. See? I really did have to protect her from me, but in the end, I didn't really want that. I was too selfish to want that. —The Journal of Taylor B.

Lisa

I covered my mouth with my hands and almost passed out on the spot. Mystery man was my professor; professor was my mystery man.

The very same person.

Mr. Blake.

Or Mr. Freaking Blake.

Holy crap. I needed professional help. The one guy I was able to kiss in over two years without wanting to puke, and it's my *professor*? *REALLY?*

The one who hates me. Oh no, I even told him my professor was a prick.

Tristan's eyes turned murderous as he whispered, "Oh shit," then looked down at the ground, then back up at me.

My mouth was still hanging open, and lucky me, my lips were still swollen and tingling from our kisses.

Could I get kicked out of school? Could he lose his job?

"I should…" He shook his head. "…go. I should go."

He looked like he wanted to stay like he wanted to say something, but when he opened his mouth again, all that came out were more curses. Funny, the mask had protected me, given me one night as the innocent princess who could have a kiss with a prince.

The minute the mask was pulled off…

He saw me for what I was.

Lisa, the notorious model, Melanie, who'd fallen off the face of the planet, changed her name, and couldn't be on time to save her life.

I felt dirty, shameful, almost like he knew all my secrets, knew my past, even though I knew it was impossible.

With tears clouding my vision, I rushed past him and into the ballroom. The more I thought about the rejection, his horror-stricken face, the faster I walked until I was full-on running. Wes and Gabe were on the far side of the room, glancing around, probably for me. I ducked through the nearest door I could find and caught my breath in the hallway.

"Well, well," a deep voice said from behind me. "Has the slut finally discovered her prince?"

I turned around so fast my heel broke.

A leather-gloved hand covered my mouth. The man's face was concealed with a full black mask, only there was no place for his lips, and where eyes should be, he had them covered in black material. His suit was black as well.

I tried to scream, but the leather glove muffled things.

"I've been watching you," he said, his voice grainy as if the mask was keeping it from coming fully through. "And I'm going to make you pay for what you did. You're a real bitch, you know that?"

I fought against him and screamed again. My legs kicked, but he just laughed. My entire body seized with fear. The laugh was mocking, psychotic. I scrambled against him, at the same time fighting for air as the leather bit into my mouth and pushed against my nose.

The door to the ballroom burst open. "Lisa?" Professor Blake caught sight of me, then started running in our direction.

"This isn't over." The man pushed me onto the ground. Air rushed out of my lungs at the impact. I coughed, my lungs burning from the combination of terror and not being able to breathe very well. The guy was already down the stairs and out of sight by the time I looked along the hall.

Professor Blake reached me and pulled me into his arms. I started sobbing hysterically against his chest, unable to control myself. In all the time I'd received those letters, I never thought that would happen. Who would do that? Who even KNEW?

"Shh," he whispered into my hair. "It's alright." With his arms still around me, he pulled a cell phone out of his pocket and barked orders into it. "He just left the ballroom floor, took the west stairs. Find the bastard."

I closed my eyes and breathed in his scent. I knew it wouldn't last long. After all, I was crying in the arms of a guy who didn't really like me that much. To top that all off with the fact that he was my professor? Yeah, talk about pointless. But still, his smell was comforting, his embrace familiar, strong.

"Do you think you can stand?" he asked after a few minutes.

"Yeah," my voice rasped. "I broke my heel, though."

With a nod, he helped me to my feet, then lifted me off the floor and into his arms like I weighed a feather, which, with my height, I knew wasn't exactly true. He leaned against the door and pulled it open, then returned his hand to my legs as he carried me into the ballroom.

"Tristan?" Gabe yelled over the music. "What happened?" Gabe charged toward us. A look of pure rage crossed his features as he took in my face and then Professor Blake's — Tristan's. The name was nice, better than Professor Blake, less forbidden.

"She was attacked," Tristan answered.

At the same time, I started to say, "Professor Blake—"

"You son of a bitch!" Gabe lunged for him, but Wes intervened just in time, his arms wrapping around Gabe as he pushed him to the side and approached.

"Stop!" I half-sobbed. "I was attacked by someone else, not Professor Blake."

"Tristan." His eyes flashed, daring me to argue. "It's Tristan."

I gave a weak nod and shivered, too upset to fight.

"What happened?" Wes asked gently, looking at me then at Tristan.

"A guy…" My voice shook as I hugged myself.

Tristan pulled me closer to him.

"He, um, he had a mask on, but it covered his mouth so I couldn't make out his voice very well, or his eyes. He said he was going to take care of me, just threatened me."

Pallor crept into Gabe's face. He narrowed his eyes and pressed his lips into a thin line as he pushed past Wes. His expression softened, and he cradled my face against his palms. "Lisa, is it—?"

"Fine," I lied. "It's totally fine. Nothing I haven't handled before, Gabe. You know that."

He didn't buy it. His hands gripped tighter. "You know it's never been like this," he ground out. "No crazy fan has ever made actual physical contact."

"Security," Tristan said from beside me.

"Damn." Gabe released my face. "I didn't even think of that."

"If she's in his class…" Wes shook his head, looking more irritated by the minute. "We'll need security for both of them."

"What?" I drew in a quick breath. "Not that I'm uncaring, but can't Tristan hold his own? In a fight? He towered over the guy."

Wes shared a look with Gabe, one I couldn't interpret. "Right, but Tristan's father—"

"Will be notified," Tristan said smoothly. "I'll talk to the security detail tonight and make sure the house has an extra guard. Besides, nobody's aware that I'm here, remember, Wes?"

"But you just made a speech—" I shook my head; something wasn't making sense.

Gabe cleared his throat. "But, Lisa, they think he's here just to make the speech then go back to—"

"My job, which, coincidently, is not a full-time college professor." Tristan shrugged. "I took a few months away from the company to clear my head…"

"Can you do that?" My eyes narrowed. The confusing distraction of Tristan's background was a welcome change from the terror still pumping through my veins.

"He can probably do whatever the hell he wants, all things considering." Wes shrugged and gave Tristan a brief nod. "We should probably get you back to the dorms, Lisa."

"I'll take her," Tristan offered.

Wes's hand froze on my arm, while Gabe's nostrils flared with irritation.

Tristan wrapped his arm around me. "We should talk. I'll deliver her safely and make sure she's in her dorm."

Gabe didn't seem to be on board with the idea, but Wes slapped him twice on the shoulder and tilted his head toward the door. "We'll leave you to it then. Have a good night, and, Lisa, call one of us if you get scared. And for the love of God, please use the pink Taser Gabe keeps teasing you about before I buy you a gun and hide it in your nightstand."

I nodded and watched them walk away, knowing each step they took meant I was even more alone with Tristan. Was I crazy? Allowing him to watch over me? I was half-tempted to run after Gabe; then again, that wouldn't make things less awkward when I sat in class Monday morning and had to face Tristan or, I guess, Professor Blake again.

Without turning around, I whispered, "Are we going to talk or make out, Professor?"

That got a chuckle out of him before he sobered and tucked me into his side. "Well, technically, I have a house in Hawaii."

"What?"

"It's not midnight in Hawaii… not yet."

"Oh." I swallowed and looked away shyly.

"Come on." He kissed my head and walked me toward the door. "I think I know how to end this night on a good note."

TWELVE

"You almost died." She wept against my body as I tried to lift my hand to tuck her hair behind her ear. "Please don't ever do that again, Tay. Never again!"

"You care." My throat felt like it was on fire. I talked anyway. "You really love me?"

"I do."

"Then I want you to do something for me..." My voice trailed off, and I freaking had a heyday as her face went completely white. —
The Journal of Taylor B.

Lisa

We walked hand in hand to the front of the hotel. Tristan presented his valet ticket. I was shivering, but not because I was cold. I still felt that creepy guy's hands on me. And it sucked because he'd ruined what would have been a good memory of Tristan's hands.

I was pretty sure I was the last thing Tristan wanted to touch now. I wanted to pretend that our masks remained in place, that the kissing was still making me forget, rather than remember the type of girl I really was. Insecurity was a hard-enough battle when you're female. Add that with the industry I grew up in, and then Taylor himself? And I struggled on a daily basis, fighting the looks people gave me and battling a strong sense of chronic self-loathing I carried with me night and day.

Just the thought of my demons, of Taylor, caused my body to give an involuntary shudder.

"Are you cold?" Tristan shrugged out of his jacket and placed it on my shoulders. It smelled like him — and I felt safe again.

I glanced over, and my mouth went completely dry. His black button-up shirt fit every muscle and crevice of his body like a glove. Clearing my throat, I forced myself to look away, even though I wanted to do a few double-takes.

A black Tesla pulled up to the curb.

"That's us." Tristan caught the keys as the valet threw them in his direction and opened my door for me.

I was almost afraid to get in. One didn't hang out with Gabe and Wes and not know cars. I'd always thought cars told you a lot about a person. And the fact that he drove something both expensive and environmentally friendly? Well honestly, it just screamed CEO and tree-hugger.

Soft leather seats cushioned every curve of my body as I leaned back against the headrest. The navigation turned on, and an old Jay Z song started playing in the background. I seriously wanted to laugh, but I was afraid I'd forgotten how, especially after tonight.

Gabe didn't know about the rape when I was younger.

I wasn't even sure if it was rape. I mean, is it rape when you're in a sexual relationship with someone, and they still force you? Bile rose in my throat at Taylor's words. I'd blocked it out, just like I tried to block him out, from the way his smile made me do anything to his smooth commands. I swore I'd never allow a guy to control me again. Not that way.

Unable to stop shivering, I clutched Tristan's coat closer around my body as he silently drove through the city.

"Lisa," he said, turning down the music. "Are you sure you're okay?"

"Oh, yeah." I tried to appear nonchalant. "I get attacked all the time. I've got the damsel-in-distress bit down pat."

"Don't." He hissed. "Don't make a joke out of something so serious. I'm asking you if you're okay. I want a straight answer. No eye-rolling, no shrugging. Hell, if you shrug one more time, I won't be responsible for my actions. Just tell me, are you okay? And is there anything I can do to make you feel better than you are right now?"

I chewed my lower lip as tears filled my eyes. "No. I'm not okay."

"Lisa—"

"The first guy that's interested me in a few years just so happens to be my professor. I don't know who the hell he is, other than, apparently, he needs security and doesn't actually work as a professor year-round. Oh, and the best part? I got attacked by some creep who probably saw a picture of me in Victoria's Secret and thought I was easy, so decided to hop on for a ride. So am I okay?" I laughed bitterly. "No, I'm not okay. I probably won't ever be okay. There will never be a time in my life when I don't wake up in the middle of the night freaked out that maybe someone's in my room. And this probably won't be the last time some creep thinks he has a right to grope me just because I made money taking my clothes off and walking down a runway. No, Tristan. I'm not okay."

Except for the sound of the heat coming through the vents, the car was silent.

With a curse, Tristan made such an abrupt turn I almost

banged my head against the door. He didn't say anything, just drove like he was in a car chase with the cops. We went toward East Denny Street then followed it around to Madera Avenue. I knew the houses there were right by the water with killer views and ridiculously expensive zip codes.

The car pulled up to a modern-looking house with four stories. It had huge windows and the look of a beach house; you know, if a beach house cost a few million and had a security gate in front of it. When we pulled through the gates, he stopped the car and sighed.

"I can handle a lot of things..." Tristan glanced over at me. "...but knowing you'll be scared tonight is not one of them. So, I'm going to show you to my guest room. I'm going to call Wes and Gabe, make sure they know you're safe, and tomorrow I'll take you back to school."

"Would that be before or after class?" I tilted my head mockingly.

"Before." He grinned. "You know how I feel about students being late."

I nodded and broke eye contact. "Will you get fired because of me?"

"Of course not." He shrugged it off completely. "Because, Lisa, there is no you and me... I don't know how else to say it. You're beautiful... but you're not my beautiful."

What did that mean? Rejection hit me square in the chest. It was hard to breathe, but I was able to nod, too embarrassed to argue my case, to throw myself across the console and explain to him that he made me want again, made me desire. That his kiss healed things I never knew had needed healing. But instead, I was brave.

I was so very tired of being that girl.

The brave girl who pretended like everything was fine.

All the while, the guilt, and fear continued to pile onto my shoulders, making me slump under the pressure. I couldn't help but feel like I deserved it. I'd had my part in the past, and now I was dealing with the consequences. Apparently, not being happy in any sort of relationship was one of them because I highly doubted I'd have that same reaction with any other guy.

"Pajamas?" I asked, trying to distract myself from wallowing.

Tristan smiled. I felt it all the way to my toes, almost looked away, but tried to hold his gaze. "I'm sure we'll figure something out."

"Well, at least I know you won't seduce me!" I opened the door and slammed it behind me, then adjusted my dress, only to feel Tristan's hands on my hips and his lips on my ear.

"I don't believe I ever made that promise."

THIRTEEN

"Come on," I pleaded from the hospital bed. "It will make me feel better."

"But it's wrong." She shook her head. "Tay, that's so wrong. Why would I do that? To anyone!"

"I'm bored," I huffed.

She hesitated, and I used that hesitation like a pro. I knew she would cave; she'd do my bidding. Eventually, she nodded, and I told her the details of who the target was and how she was going to shame him — the video would go viral like my videos usually did, and I'd once again have the upper hand. I controlled her, and I needed her to remember that even though she weakened me, I still had control. And she was mine. Forever. She was mine. —The Journal of Taylor B.

Tristan

The lights turned on automatically once we entered the house. It felt weird, bringing a woman home since I typically didn't do that type of thing — too afraid of the scandal it would cost the family. I'd always dated women my family approved of, women who ran in the same circles and knew how important image was. If we met, we met at hotels owned by my father. If we were going to the same room, I had a drink in the lobby while she took the elevator. Ten minutes later, I'd follow, and we'd repeat a similar process the next time. My security tailed anyone suspicious, and it was an enjoyable time for everyone.

Nothing scandalous. Nothing improper. And less-than-stellar sex. After all, what's so scandalous and arousing about planned sex and meetings? About hooking up with a woman I'd known since childhood?

Speaking of, I glanced down at my phone and grimaced. Seven missed calls. She could wait; he could wait; they could all wait. They knew I was taking a break, and that meant from everything, them included. I'd done my family duty by attending the benefit, and now… now I was going to try to pretend I didn't have one of the sexiest women alive alone in my house.

"Wow." Lisa performed a slow pirouette. "You have four floors?"

I nodded. "A view from each room."

"Gabe would love this place." She sighed out loud, then ran her hand across the granite countertop leading into the kitchen. "He has a thing about houses."

"I know." I followed her into the kitchen. "Ever since the death of his fiancée and her obsession with living in Seattle."

Lisa's face froze, her fingers tapping against the counter. "How long have you known Gabe?" Her shoulders were tense.

"Not long," I said quickly. "I've known Wes, however, my entire life."

She turned and smiled weakly. "So that makes you safe?"

"No," I answered honestly. "Probably not the safe you're thinking about." I circled around her. "Safe from any sort of harm? Absolutely. But safe? What is safety?" I grinned innocently. "And do you truly want to be safe all the time, or only in certain circumstances, ones where you know you don't have the upper hand?"

"You're a little too philosophical for my tastes."

The light still wasn't in her eyes. I felt like I needed to fix it, fix her, fix what had happened between us, even though I still didn't know what the hell I was doing. I'd told her she wasn't mine, not my type of beautiful. Because I knew, damn, but I knew, she'd been his. And taking her? Truly taking her? Right now? Seemed wrong. It was wrong. And suddenly, I wasn't okay with the plan I'd put into place. If I could go back in time and talk to myself, I'd probably shake some sense into the old me and get over it, maybe call her and ask her what happened, but I sure as hell wouldn't have hidden my identity, stalked her like a total freak, and then seduced her out of her mind.

Then again, that last part was a total accident.

One I wanted to repeat the more I was around her.

"Are you tired?" I exhaled and went over to the fridge and pulled out a carton of orange juice, then followed it with cups from the cabinet. In my experience, women were more emotional if they were hungry or thirsty. I filled both cups with orange juice, slid one over to her, then put the carton back in the fridge. I pulled out some cut up grapes and apples and a few slices of gouda cheese.

When I had everything arranged the way I wanted, I moved the plate toward the middle of the breakfast bar and looked up, offering it to her with one raised eyebrow.

Lisa was watching me, her blue eyes flashing with amusement. "Do you label your underwear, too, or just the food containers?"

Heat blasted into my cheeks as I looked down at the container with *cheese* printed on the front and the next that read *grapes*. With a chuckle and shake of my head, I scooted them away. "Wouldn't you like to know?"

"Oh, I would. I'm seriously curious now. A bit OCD, are we?"

"You have no idea." I sighed. That was the last thing she needed to know. The last thing I wanted to talk about. It would remind her of him, too much of him, and I'd already decided I couldn't do it. I couldn't ruin her more. I just didn't know what that left me with except morbid curiosity and a need to know if it was the same diagnosis.

"So—" I popped a grape in my mouth. "—I think you should eat some food. After all, I am a doc—"

"Professor."

I held out a piece of cheese to her and lifted my eyebrows. "Doctor."

She rolled her eyes and took it between her teeth, making me want to throw the food against the floor and take her across the breakfast bar. My body tightened, letting me know it was liking the idea more and more as I watched her chew.

Food. I needed to eat before I devoured *her*. I popped two more grapes in my mouth just as she asked, "How old are you?"

In the middle of swallowing, I damn-near choked to death. I banged across my chest and reached for the orange juice, already picturing the headline: *Westinghouse Heir Slain by Grapes*. Fantastic, that's just what my father needed; then again, he'd probably be able to run for president after such high approval ratings. Imagine, his son, taken so young.

"Old," I finally managed to croak out. "Like a gross old man. You're lucky I stopped kissing you when I did. Don't want my arthritis rubbing off on you."

"First off," Lisa said, holding a grape in the air. "Gross. Second, you can't be that old. You went to school with Wes, right?"

"Twenty-seven," I answered before I lost the nerve. "I graduated from high school early. Wes is younger than me, but our families vacationed together a lot. We attended the same private school. Even went to the same crappy summer camp."

"You and summer camp." Lisa squinted. "I can't picture it. That must have been horrible for you, all those labeled clothes jammed into a suitcase… spiders, ants…" She shivered. "You poor thing."

"Have I somehow given you the impression that I'm unable to survive outside?" I teased, leaning in so I could be closer to her.

"The labels." She shrugged one shoulder and popped another grape into her mouth. "Kinda killed the whole alpha-male thing you had going for you."

"I like order," I argued, placing both of my hands on the counter so that I was as close to her as possible without actually jumping over the counter or pulling her down with me.

Lisa tilted her head as if assessing me. "You like control."

Well, that was blunt.

I opened my mouth but shut it again. "In some areas, yes, though in my experience, too much control could be a bad thing."

"Yeah." A shadow crossed her face. "It really can."

I knew I'd touched on her past, knew it by the lost and guilty look on her face.

"More grapes?" I held up the plate like I had the social skills of a seven-year-old and didn't possess a doctorate degree.

"No." She placed her hands on her stomach. "I think I've had enough food and drama for the night. Maybe I should just go to bed."

Bed.

Satin sheets.

Red sheets.

Hell, no sheets, just the floor next to the bed, the wall, the stairs, anywhere I could take her — I wanted her writhing, shaking, moaning, licking? Too many verbs, too many actions I was unable to fulfill as my body grew hotter and tighter with the need to peel the dress from her body and touch her skin. My body leapt to attention at the mental image — any minute, and I was going to start panting.

I was probably going to go to hell for all the images flashing through my brain, images of me doing things to her that no professor — teacher, instructor — should ever want to do to his student. Yet, there we were on my desk naked. In my shower? Naked. On my yacht? Naked.

Groaning, I abruptly turned away from her and tried to calm my body down. She probably thought I was pissed — far from it, just so damn tired of being the perfect son, of doing the right thing. I wanted her. It wasn't right; it was wrong, and for the first time in my life, I wanted the wrong. I wanted the bad. I wanted it more than truth. Give me the lie. Just give me her.

I was going to have to take a cold shower, maybe three. I was her professor. Her teacher. An instructor. At least for the semester. Sharing a bed? Not happening. And even if I wasn't? She'd hate me for it. I'd hate me for it. And I could only imagine what my father would say if he ever discovered what I was truly doing back in Seattle.

I cleared my throat and turned back around. I grabbed the containers and shoved them back into the fridge before offering my hand. "Sounds like a plan. Let me just show you to your room."

FOURTEEN

"Did everyone see?" I smirked as Mel leaned forward, her face pale with worry.

"Yeah." Her lips were even white. "It got the most hits out of all of our posts on the website. The guy was completely horrified. He even called the police. His parents freaked, and…" She shivered. "Why? Why him?"

"His life needed more excitement." I felt satisfied that I'd ruined another life, satisfied that I'd used Mel to do it, though she didn't seem happy about it like she used to. That's how bad choices start, though. Do you truly think a homicidal maniac wakes up and goes, hmm… think I'll kill someone today? Hell no. It's the tiny choices. The small things you think don't matter. Stealing candy from a store, lying to your parents, stealing money, doing drugs, kicking a dog, drowning a turtle… what–the–hell–ever. It's the small insignificant choices that lead to life-altering decisions. She had no idea when she said yes to that one dance with me that I was going to alter her — and now, she had no way out. —The Journal of Taylor B.

Lisa

It was awkward and tense, walking up the stairs to the second floor. Each click of my heels was another reminder that we were alone, just me and Tristan, or Mr. Blake. I wasn't even sure what to call him, how to address him. On one hand, I was fiercely attracted to him; the other part of me was horrified that I'd just done something so stupid that he'd rejected me yet offered me protection, something I'd shamelessly taken without arguing. That's what fear does. It leads you up the stairway into the unknown with a sexy man following your every move.

When we reached the top of the stairs, I stopped, unsure of which way to turn. Two rooms spread out in front of me. To the right was the edge of a balcony overlooking the kitchen, and a few chairs pointed toward the large bay windows. A fireplace sat square in the middle. I wanted to be as far away from that balcony as possible.

I'd hated heights ever since that night.

They made me want to puke. As it was, my hands were shaking.

"Left," Tristan whispered, and his hand grazed my lower back, just enough to let me know he was still there. My knees knocked together as I turned and walked in the direction he'd instructed. I tried to keep my head high. A few more steps and I could lock myself in the room and pretend that his touch didn't affect me, that his kiss wasn't still buzzing across my swollen lips.

"Here we are." He stepped out from behind me and walked to a door, then pushed it open.

The guest room was huge. A large king-sized bed dominated the middle. The wall facing the water wasn't solid but made of glass from floor to ceiling. The windows allowed the moonlight to shimmer inside the room, casting a comforting glow on the white fluffy bed and matching white leather chairs. Clearly, the guy had a thing for the modern look.

Black-and-white pictures lined the walls, and a few candles were scattered around in organized chaos; either he had a heck of a decorator or had an eye for style.

I turned around the room then faced him.

Tristan was busy turning on the switch to the fireplace that appeared to also be visible on both sides, leading into the bathroom. When he turned to face me, his face had become indifferent once again, impossible to read. It made me nervous because I'd known a face like that, one that was emotionless.

I took a step back and tried to appear nonchalant, but my heart was giving me away, beating so rapidly against my chest I could have sworn he could both hear and see it.

"You'll be safe here, Lisa." His voice was smooth, his lips full against his careful smile. "I swear it."

"Safe from the boogeyman." I nodded and offered a shrug. "Thanks for that..." And the kiss, and the night of escapism.

Tristan hesitated, his eyes searching my face. My body heated as his hungry gaze devoured me from head to toe. He took a step toward me, and then another. My hands clenched at my sides as I waited. My breathing slowed. Everything in the room slowed by his fluid movement.

Once he was inches from my body, his hands slowly rose to my shoulders, then caressed down my arms, resting at my wrists. With a shudder, I bit my lip as he lifted both hands to his lips and bestowed a kiss on each one.

Dropping my left hand, he kept my right, flipping it over until my palm was facing his delicious mouth. With a wicked smile, he kissed the inside of my wrist and then my palm, his breath hot against my skin. My body was full-on trembling, unable to decipher if he was safe or dangerous.

"Goodnight, Lisa." He released my hand. "Sweet dreams..."

It took me a second to catch my breath, and when I did, my voice was hoarse. "You too."

"I can promise you…" His eyes traveled from my head all the way down to my toes. "…I will."

With that, he left the room, shutting the door silently behind him. I staggered toward the door, nearly face-planting against it, then turned the lock and leaned against the cool wood. Whimpering, I slid down until I was on the floor and let my head bang back against the door a few times, trying to lodge something logical into my brain.

He wasn't for me.

He was my teacher.

My teacher!

Granted, he was also a sexy piece of man who was also clearly just as important as Wes and Gabe, but that made him even more off limits. I had to stay out of the limelight, at all costs, because I knew if I did… what had been promised to me would finally come true.

He'd ruined my life, my career, everything that night, and I knew my only saving grace was disappearing, pulling out of the public eye and pretending to be something and someone different.

He couldn't hurt me if I was Lisa.

But as Mel?

I might as well have jumped off that bridge with him.

I squared my shoulders and forced the morbid thoughts out of my head. Tonight I was safe, but that didn't mean I wasn't going to check under my bed, in the closet, and also make sure my phone was right on my nightstand just in case.

Feeling silly that I'd locked the door from the one guy trying to protect me, I unlocked it just before slipping out of my dress and crawling under the covers.

The mattress was like lying on my own giant goose, you

know, minus all the internal parts. I sighed longingly into the fluffy pillow and let myself sleep, knowing I wouldn't have to worry about creepy packages being sent to my dorm or opening mail...

But tomorrow? Tomorrow was another story completely.

Tristan... I smiled when I thought of his kiss. For one night, it was nice to escape... one forbidden night.

FIFTEEN

Videos of shame were my idea, my golden child. I'd started it in order to entertain myself. It quickly turned into a blog, and I gained a following so quick it was near impossible to run on my own. I needed recruits. Needed people willing to do the dirty within the circles of the rich and famous. Because this website? It wasn't about picking on the strong, but picking on those who came from money, those who could take it, those who thought the world owed them something just because of who they were. Sound a bit hypocritical? Oh you have no idea. I needed someone sexy, someone who knew how to get people to do things… someone who was just as bored as I. When she walked into the room that night, eyes distant, heart heavy, I knew I had her. Besides, what's the best way to nurse a broken heart? Revenge. It's always revenge. —The Journal of Taylor B.

Tristan

I was a complete jackass. Touching her hadn't been part of the deal. Hadn't I not but a few minutes ago decided to just leave her alone? Why couldn't I make that choice and stick with it? I'd always been solid with decisions, able to will myself toward any choice, and do it without emotion. Apparently, that's what made me… what? Sick? In need of medication? And apparently, it's what had killed him, that same side of me that was able to totally separate emotions from decisions.

If dead men could tell tales, I wondered what his would be

about… his emotions? All I had was the journal; all I had was the sneaking suspicion we were exactly alike — cold, ruthless, easily able to manipulate to get what we wanted. It made me a damn good businessman. But when it came to relationships? Not so much.

But with Lisa? I truly had no control; the madness she created in me stirred parts of my soul that I hadn't even known existed until now. What the hell was I supposed to do? Leave her alone? Kiss her? Walk away?

I was stuck.

Walking away meant I'd given up a few months of my real life for nothing. It also meant giving in to my absolute worst fear. It meant not avenging his death. It meant too many horrible things.

But staying? Staying meant I'd be fighting my carnal nature every step of the way. It meant every time she smiled, I'd have to ignore the way it stirred me. It meant that, when she entered the room, I had to ignore the fact that her perfume practically choked me into submission.

I tossed and turned in bed as my clock mocked my inability to fall asleep. Around two a.m. I almost went downstairs to make coffee.

Instead, a scream jolted me fully awake.

My heart thumped against my chest. Was it my imagination? I waited, the sound of crickets the only noise until another scream of terror erupted.

I flew out of bed and ran down the hall until I reached her door. When I pushed it open, Lisa was tossing in bed, her short hair spilling across the pillow and her face scrunched up in fear. Tears streamed down her face, but her eyes were still closed.

"Lisa?" I whispered.

Another tremor hit her body. She jerked in her sleep, then started hitting the pillow with her hand. "No, stop, don't jump. *Please* don't jump."

My balance took a hit as I gripped the wall to keep me steady. Was this another piece of the puzzle? Was she talking about him? Or was it just a dream?

"No!" she wailed. "Stop! Please stop!"

Not able to take it anymore, I made my way to the bed and gently sat down next to her shivering body. Speaking in as calm a voice I could manage, I said, "Lisa, you're having a nightmare. It's okay. Wake up."

She jerked in her sleep again, whimpering as if she was getting beat. She covered her face and then started full-on sobbing.

I gripped her hands and pulled them free, and braced myself for impact, knowing full well she'd probably attack me as she woke up.

"Lisa!" I shook her wrists. "Wake up!"

Her eyes jerked open; they were so wide they could have swallowed me whole. With a cry, she lunged for me and threw her weight against me.

Cursing, I fell off the bed, Lisa on top of me, her legs bracing me on either side.

"Lisa!" I tried shaking her again.

She shook her head. A frenzied look crossed her face, and then she slumped against me. Recognition flashed quickly, followed by embarrassment. "Oh, my gosh! I'm so sorry! I'm so… I normally don't make habits of assaulting people in my sleep!"

I smiled, even though the last thing I was feeling was amused. More like extremely hard-pressed not to flip her onto her back and kiss some calm into her. Then again, *that* wouldn't calm me and would probably earn more terror on her end. "It's fine." I let out an exhale of relief. "I don't normally make a habit of barging in on my guests. It's just… I thought there was an intruder."

She grinned, the tears streaking against her smooth cheeks. "And you normally make a habit of attacking intruders in your black silk boxers?"

My body demanded I respond to that particular statement. Instead, I winked. "Yeah, well, my labeled bat was downstairs, so I figured scaring them with my expensive boxers was the next best thing."

She pulled away, still straddling me, placing her hands on her hips and looking down. "Absolutely terrifying."

"Yeah," I said gruffly, telling my body to calm the hell down. "Glad I served my purpose."

Every muscle was taut, so much so that it was hard to breathe. I doubt she realized her eyes were still trained on my abs. I thanked every lucky star I had. Black silk boxers didn't exactly cover a multitude of sins.

"If we're going to stay on the floor all night, the least you could do is toss me a pillow," I joked, though my tone was anything but playful.

Her eyes heated for a second before she scurried off me.

My body flat out demanded I pull her back and keep her there. The loss I felt at her leaving was nothing short of ridiculous, but there it was.

Lisa sat on the bed and wrung her hands together while I stood and tried to hide the fact that her mouth was so damn arousing I was having trouble remembering all the reasons I couldn't have her in the first place.

"Is there anything I can do?"

Lisa looked down at her hands and smiled. "You offering to sing me to sleep, Tristan?"

I sat down next to her. "You offering to let me?"

"That depends. How good of a singer are you?"

"Horrible," I admitted with a soft chuckle. "But it may scare the bad dreams away."

"And the girl too." She nudged me with her elbow.

I full-on laughed. "Right, most likely send her screaming into the night. If it isn't the label maker, it will most definitely be the hoarse singing."

Lisa bit her lip and peered up at me through her hair.

I tucked it behind her ear, unable to stop my hands from moving before it was too late.

Her breath hitched; instinctively, she wet her upper lip. I leaned in, my mouth hovering over hers.

"This is a bad idea," she whispered right before our mouths met.

I could taste her — taste all of her — and we hadn't even touched yet. "Well, clearly, it's been a night for bad ideas, bad nightmares, and potentially bad singing. What's one more thing?"

Her entire body tensed, and I knew, once again, I'd lost her, lost her to whatever demons plagued her and, by association, plagued me.

With a lazy smile, I pulled back and whispered, "Try to get some sleep, and in the morning..." I shrugged.

"In the morning things will look better? Is that what else you were going to say?"

I pressed forward, my lips grazing her ear. "Things rarely look better in the morning, but at least you have more energy to deal with them. Sleep." Not kissing her was one of the hardest things I'd ever done as I retreated and repeated again, "Just let go and sleep."

"'Kay." A shiver raced through her slender body. "I'll try."

"If you scream again, me and my boxers will be waiting." And many other things I didn't care to mention.

Laughing, she crawled back under the covers. "Well, if that doesn't set me at ease, I really don't know what will."

"Security system." I winked and made my way toward the door. "State of the art. The only person getting in your room is me, and that's only if you scream again…"

"If I scream, you come?"

I fought back a groan of frustration as I gripped the door handle, nearly pulling it free. When I turned, her smile was flirtatious, almost inviting. Damn it. Sinning never looked so good.

"Sure." I tried to match her smile with one of my own. "Think of your scream as a bell… ring it, and I'm here." Really? That was all I had in response?

"Thanks…" She lay down on the pillow. "…for everything."

Guilt stabbed me square in the chest as I gave a curt nod and shut the door behind me.

What the hell was I doing?

I had no flipping clue.

SIXTEEN

"He tried to commit suicide," Mel said numbly the next day.

I'd just been discharged from the hospital, and she was driving me to my penthouse, the one place I'd let her see that wasn't owned by good ol' Dad, though he'd paid up-the-ass for it to keep his dirty little secret happy.

"So?" I shrugged, tossing a pain pill in my mouth. "That's not the first time it's happened. Surely won't be the last. Think of it as us helping groom him for life."

"Tay!" Mel shook her head. "We can't — I can't… I can't keep doing this. It's not fun. I mean, can't we just do normal things like go to the movies?"

"What's really bothering you?" I asked, finally turning toward her ghostlike face.

She chewed her lower lip and looked down. "I got in."

"What?"

"I applied to college, Tay. I got in." —The Journal of Taylor B.

Lisa

rubbed my eyes and gripped my cell phone. Blurry vision and caked-on mascara, not a good combination. Finally, the fuzziness of the screen dissipated, and I was able to see the time.

Six in the morning.

I set the phone back on the stand and groaned. The last thing I wanted to do was get out of the most comfortable bed I'd ever slept in and take the walk of shame down the hall and let my professor — ha! — my sexy professor — drive me to school.

I groaned again.

He'd been right. The morning hadn't made it better, but I did feel like I had a bit more energy to tackle the day. I sent a quick text to Gabe, so he knew I was all right and slowly rose from bed.

Yawning, I padded over to the door and quickly peered into the hall to see if I could hear any movement or indication that Tristan was up.

Nothing.

Just as I was about to go back into the room, I looked down. A pair of jeans, white T-shirt, and TOMS shoes were sitting in a neat pile on the floor; a yellow knit cap topped off the pile with a note attached:

For you.

That was it. Just… *For you.* Cryptic, even though I knew they couldn't be from anyone but Tristan. When I went to pick up the pile, I noticed a toothbrush stashed beneath the shirt, along with some toothpaste.

The guy was either used to one-night stands or… yeah, that was all I had, used to one-night stands. People didn't look like Tristan Blake and not have one-night stands. Besides, clearly, he was important, had loads of money, and lived in paradise.

I lifted the clothes to my nose to make sure they didn't smell like some other chick's perfume, only to get caught by a throat clearing.

"Have I somehow given you the impression that I'd give you someone else's clothes?"

Slowly I lifted my gaze. Tristan stood in front of me, holding a cup of coffee and wearing nothing but a pair of gray track pants that rode low on his hips. He blew across the cup. My knees again decided it would be a good time to shake a bit as I took in his perfectly sculpted chest and abs.

"Coffee?" He tilted his head and handed me the other mug.

"Yeah." My voice was hoarse. "Thanks, and sorry. I was just making sure—"

"You were just making sure they weren't some other girl's clothes that I'd stashed after a cheap one-night stand and forgotten to return." His smile was one of amusement, not irritation. "Do I really look like that type of guy?"

"Yes." I gulped. "Sorry, but you kind of do."

"I guess kissing you didn't help that particular assumption." He grinned, then stepped toward me until I could feel the heat of his body and almost taste the coffee on his lips. "But I think you'd be surprised to know it's only two."

"Two?"

He flashed a grin. "Figure it out."

With one last teasing wink, he spun on his heel and walked down the hall, calling behind him. "Shower and meet me downstairs for breakfast. Pretty sure you have a class in a few hours, and the last thing you want to do is piss off that prick professor of yours... again."

Heat invaded my entire face as I leaned against the door frame. Awesome. Good to know I told the actual professor that I thought he was an ass to his face and then kissed him.

I was so getting kicked out of school.

Either that or… I don't know, going to hell?

My eyes strained to see Tristan as he rounded the corner to his room. If I was going to hell, I'd at least get an eyeful on the journey.

By the time I managed to make myself presentable, I already felt like I was running late. Something about Tristan's controlling demeanor had me rushing through the shower like I was going to get scolded if I didn't dress fast enough.

"Bacon?" his warm voice asked the minute I stepped foot into the kitchen. "I assumed you'd want more coffee, but I wasn't sure what you normally eat for breakfast, so I kind of fixed everything."

A white towel was on one shoulder while he hovered over the stove. His back muscles flexed through his crisp white shirt. My eyes lowered to his tight dark-wash jeans and just stayed there for a minute, not necessarily staring, more like… okay, so I was staring. It was weird. I'd never been the type of girl to check out a guy like that. I'd been surrounded by beautiful all my life.

But Tristan was a different type of beautiful. He was controlled, orderly, yet, at the same time, chaotic. Yeah, it made no sense to me either.

"Lisa?" Tristan looked over his shoulder.

I jerked my gaze up and felt my cheeks blush again. "Yeah?"

"You didn't answer."

"I was, um…" I chewed my lower lip. "Thinking about class."

"Which class?" he teased, his eyes scanning my body heatedly before returning my gaze.

"Yours." I swallowed and regained my confidence as I took a seat at the breakfast bar. "Ever since getting scolded, I'm super paranoid about being early."

"Scolded." Tristan handed me a plate and started piling bacon and potatoes onto it. "If I was scolding you, you'd know it."

"Why do I feel like that's a double meaning?"

He shrugged. And that was it. No flirtation. Nothing.

We ate in silence.

And I wish I could say it was awkward. But it wasn't. He read the newspaper; I asked him random questions. We both drank our coffee, and, once I was finished, I loaded the dishes in the dishwasher — even though he'd tirelessly asked me not to help. By the time I knew what was happening, we were driving toward school.

Nervousness attacked me the minute we pulled into a parking spot. I had a half-hour to go back to my dorm room, grab my stuff, and go to class. His class.

"Lisa," Tristan turned off the car and stared straight ahead. "It was fun but—"

"But you're my professor. I know."

"Right." He drew out the word slowly. "I just…" His face scrunched up with what I could only assume was anger; a muscle in his jaw jumped. "I'm a bad idea."

"So it's you, not me?" Smiling, I kept my voice light, trying to bring back the playfulness and ease of the morning.

"Yeah." He nodded curtly. "That's a good way of putting it.

Our relationship is best served as a strict teacher-slash-student relationship. Hell, it was a bad idea even coming down here in the first place."

"To the party?"

"To the school." He sniffed and pressed his lips together in a firm line. "You should get to class."

"But—"

"Lisa." He finally turned, his face indifferent. "We're done here."

"Excused like a toddler." I nodded, hurt that he would treat me that way after holding me last night, kissing me, making love to me with his mouth. Teacher or no teacher, I still deserved some respect, right? "You treat all your one-night stands this way?" Maybe that was too far, but whatever.

"Had you kept your mask on, that may have happened, but now that I know who you are…"

His voice trailed off, and I couldn't help but finish it with "What you are." Guilt and shame hit me square in the chest, replacing the irritation I'd initially felt. He didn't need to know the details. It either scared guys away or made them think it was an invitation for something more.

I opened my mouth to speak but had nothing. I was hurt, angry, feeling a bit rejected… a *lot* scolded. And the worst part was I knew he was right. He didn't owe me anything. But I wanted him to; I wanted him to say that that one night was enough to make me like a drug to him. Enough to make him want to break rules.

But I knew that wasn't my reality, not my life.

Guys didn't do that for girls like me; they never had, never would. It sucked because I'd seen guys like Gabe and Wes ready to fight wars for the girls they loved. Music and

TV would have you believe that every girl has a hero; she just needs to find him first.

It was not true.

It would never be true.

"Right." I bit my lower lip to keep it from trembling and unbuckled my seatbelt. When I slammed the door behind me, I fought tears the entire way to the dorm. Confusion was at the forefront of my mind. He'd kissed me with passion. I knew he felt what I felt, that weird unexplainable pull. But that pull isn't ever enough, not when you have the entire world stacked against you.

Not when your dead ex-boyfriend still mocks your every waking moment and nightmare. Not when his voice is all you hear when doubt creeps in.

"*Never enough,*" *he whispered.*

"*I own you,*" *he taunted.* "*Who would want you anyway? You're damaged, so damaged you're lucky I even touch you.*"

I shuddered as the voice got louder and louder, the laughter more menacing. "*Even in my death, you'd be mine. Every time a man touches you, you'll think of me, of what we shared…*"

Tremors wracked my body, and by the time I reached my dorm room, I was ready to puke.

I ran up the stairs and pulled out my key, only to find that my door had been broken. I pushed it open and gasped.

The word *Whore* was spray-painted across my wall… and on the table was a dead rose. With trembling fingers, I picked up the note next to it. Black angry block letters were scrambled across the white paper.

Now your shame will be broadcasted for all to see.

I dropped the note like it was on fire and backed into the

couch, bumping my knee and nearly falling over.

"Sucks," a voice said from the door. I looked up to see my RA standing there, arms crossed. "Sorry, Lisa. Someone called the dorm last night to say you were staying somewhere else, so we weren't concerned for your safety. But it still sucks. You up to file a report? Campus police want to know."

"Yeah," I croaked. "Just let me get my bag."

SEVENTEEN

I never went to college. Didn't want her to go either. It meant she was finally thinking of a life away from me, even if she didn't admit it. It meant it was almost time for my grand finale. Funny, in that moment, I wasn't even pissed! I was excited, so excited to put my plan into place. The plan I'd carefully constructed since the beginning. It was going to be epic. Too bad I wouldn't be around to see it — then again, people would eventually find out why. Find out that my death? Would be on her hands. —The Journal of Taylor B.

Tristan

The black, angry writing stared back, mocking me. My lesson plan was in English — after all, I'd written it, but nothing looked familiar. It may as well have been crisscrosses and smiley faces.

Getting Lisa out of my head wasn't working. I hated that I'd hurt her feelings, hated myself for getting involved. What the hell had I thought would happen? I'd teach for a semester, find out what I came to find out, apologize while still gaining revenge for his death, and move on? I'd never been heartless, but during all the planning, the reading, the scheming, I'd never added her into the calculation.

I'd assumed she'd be different.

Not perfect.

Not absolutely, mind-blowingly perfect from her teasing nature to her addicting lips — damn. She could be my poison, and I'd drink from her cup, embracing sweet death if only for another taste.

Shaking, I pulled out my prescription and took the daily amount, pissed that I had to, pissed that it controlled my life — pissed that I'd let it.

I checked my phone. Father had called and, of course, her. I'd catch up with them later on in the week. Right now, it would be impossible to mask my emotion. My father would think I was off my medication, though I'd never given him any indication that I was the type to stop taking my meds. I was the good son, the perfect son. The one who crossed his *Ts* and dotted his *Is*; the son that was groomed for bigger and better things.

The son he'd actually wanted.

As opposed to the one he'd damned to hell.

EIGHTEEN

"What?" Mel asked. "You're really quiet."

I shrugged. "Well, it's just... it's funny, I guess, that they would want you... I mean, you have shit grades, and, let's be honest, you're not that smart."

Mel's eyes filled with tears before looking away. "I got a really high score on my ACT."

I laughed out loud. "Well, that explains it."

She grinned. "I studied really hard."

"No." I shook my head at her innocence, at her trusting nature. "I mean, clearly, they messed up and swapped your scores with someone else's. It's the only explanation." —The Journal of Taylor B.

Lisa

By the time I filed a report...

I was late. Of course, I was late! To the one class I wasn't supposed to be late to. My RA had taken pity on me, and the campus security had written me a note, but I was still nervous about barging into Tristan — Mr. Blake's class, feeling his heated gaze, knowing I'd be in trouble... again.

Gaining confidence, I opened the door to the classroom

and stepped in. All eyes darted in my direction. The flame of heat burst across my cheeks as I slowly approached Mr. Blake.

His face was stern; his mouth formed a straight line as he put his hands on his hips and looked down, literally looked down at me. "Lisa? What time is it?"

I paused and looked down at my feet, note clenched in hand. "It's nine forty-five, but my room was—"

"What?" he addressed the class. "Your room was dirty, and you had the sudden inclination to do a bit of spring cleaning before coming to class?"

"No, but—"

"Do you truly believe I care what you do during your personal time? And should that personal time directly affect your ability to be at class at the scheduled hour?"

Shaking my head, I found my voice. "No, my personal time isn't important, but if you would just listen—"

"I think we've all heard enough. Now, if you're done giving me excuses and interrupting my time, the time I use to teach, you can find your seat. If this truly is becoming your habit, then you're more than welcome to find the door."

He dismissed me with his hand, just as I was trying to set the note on his desk. It fluttered to the ground. Instead of picking it up, I turned on my heel and went to the closest desk possible so I could disappear. Tears burned the back of my eyes, but I kept them in. For the next hour, I kept them in and took notes, never once looking up from the desk.

When class was dismissed, I grabbed my bag and bolted for the door. A hand gripped my arm.

"Rough." It was Jack, and his easy smile put me at ease. "The guy really hates you."

"Wow, that was encouraging," I murmured. "Thanks."

"Tell you what." Jack fell into step beside me. "Let me buy you coffee, and I'll walk you to your next class."

"Um, I don't really think that's a good idea. I don't want to be late to another class and—"

"Coffee?" His brown eyes twinkled. "I swear, nothing more. You can even take the coffee and bolt, but you look like you could really use it, and I'll let you in on a little secret." He leaned in and whispered, "I work at Starbucks, so I have the power of the employee discount."

At that, I laughed. "Wow, you're like the president."

"Only better looking." He winked. "So what do you say? And before you answer, just remember, nobody should ever say no to coffee. It's a crime punishable by law." He nodded and took a step back. "Okay, your verdict?"

I took in his gray hoodie and fitted jeans. He was cute, a boyish cute, his hair dark and messy. Something about the way he smiled made me think I knew him, which probably meant I'd seen him around campus and never actually seen him.

I checked my phone and nodded. "Fine. One quick cup, but we need to go fast."

"I ran track for four years in high school... My middle name was Flash."

"Seriously?"

"Not an athletic bone in this body," he joked. "But I figured you were one for playful banter, so I went with it. Good move?"

I laughed with him. "Good move."

NINETEEN

She didn't stay at my penthouse that night... pretty sure she went home and cried.

When I checked the website, I noticed we'd gotten a surge of hits over the last week because of the guy I'd embarrassed. What a loser. The guy had pulled his Facebook profile, Twitter account — everything. After a few quick empty searches, I felt confident I'd at least embarrassed him enough to get him to stay away from Mel. That had been the number one reason... competition, well, that and boredom, but it was the fact that he'd stared at her. Granted, she'd rejected him, but still. Nobody touched what was mine. Ever. —The Journal of Taylor B.

Tristan

Classes were grueling; my focus was completely off. By the time I was finished teaching for the day, all I really wanted was to escape. I lifted my briefcase from the floor and frowned. A white slip must have fallen off my desk.

When I picked it up, I felt my entire body shake with rage. It was a note of excuse from campus security — on Lisa's behalf.

Cursing, I stomped my way across campus until I reached her dorm. When I noticed that the door was still broken and just wedged shut, I went from angry to full-on pissed.

I knocked loudly. Twice.

When the door didn't open, the rage was replaced with sheer panic that something had happened to her.

I was just getting ready to break down the door when it swung open. Gabe stood on the other side. His eyebrows shot up in surprise. "Tristan, what up, man? You make house calls now?"

"Not exactly." I tried to calm my breathing. "There was a slight misunderstanding in class, and Lisa—"

"Slight misunderstanding, my ass," Gabe said under his breath. "Look, I know you have to draw that teacher-slash-student line, and I respect you for it, but could you be any more of an ass? Seriously."

"Are you telling me how to do my job or just insulting me?" I asked, dumbstruck that he'd said that to my face.

Gabe crossed his arms. "Both."

"Listen—" I leaned forward, trying to use my weight to push past him. "—I just want to make sure she's okay."

"She has me." Gabe pushed back. "I'll decide if she's okay or not, and didn't you say something about what she does in her personal time not really mattering to you? So, why don't you go have a heart elsewhere? We're full-up on assholes here, and I really don't want to have to see my own face on the six o'clock news because I kicked your sorry ass." His eyes narrowed. "Besides, what would Daddy say?"

With that, he slammed the door in my face.

Deserved. Well played and totally deserved.

I pressed my fingers to my temples. It was tempting to hack the freaking database just to get her cell number. I wanted a damn smiley face or something — something that said she was fine, something that—

Inspiration struck. I didn't need to hack anything. I had all of the students' contact numbers, as well as their emails, back at my house.

I ran down the hall and drove like a bat out of hell. I'd email her. It would be less personal, and what girl ignores email from a professor? Especially one who was paranoid she was going to fail his class?

TWENTY

I used to count cuts instead of sheep. I made small cuts down my arm, but the pain didn't make me feel a damn thing. Mel came over a few nights before I was going to put my plan in place. I was the perfect boyfriend. I cooked her dinner; I rented a movie; we talked; we laughed. I wanted her to remember the good times, so when I hurt her, I'd be able to pull that string again. That's the thing about controlling others. During the good times? That's all they focus on. They focus on good because focusing on bad just makes them feel like less of a person. "See? He really loves me? He really cares!" Bullshit. She was a means to an end... my end. I was going to live forever — or maybe the right word is haunt? —The Journal of Taylor B.

Lisa

"Who was that?" I asked on my way out of the bathroom, towel-drying my hair. Gabe had insisted that he hang out at my dorm while waiting for the maintenance guy to come fix my door.

What I thought was him babysitting ended up turning into a circus show as a few security guys showed up and put cameras and an alarm in my room. I'd asked if it was legal.

Gabe's answer? "Wes Michels." That was always the answer when it came to being allowed to do anything.

Granted, I was pretty sure that the university wouldn't

even blink since the Michels had basically donated enough funds to keep it running most of the year.

"A real live ass." Gabe shrugged. "I told it to get lost. Didn't budge at first, almost pulled out a shotgun, but, low and behold, it finally left before any violence ensued."

"You talk a really big game for a guy who has trouble hitting a baseball, let alone a person."

"Ouch." Gabe grabbed his chest and winced. "That was a deep one. You owe me free foot massages for a week."

"You have a wife for that."

"I lost all massage privileges for a week after I forgot to empty the dishwasher."

I grinned. "Sucks, but, sorry. I'm on her side."

"Everyone's on her side," he grumbled.

"So? Seriously?" I plopped down on the couch. "Who was it?"

"Guess," Gabe swore and ran his fingers through his golden-blond hair. His many tattoos moved across both arms as he flexed his muscles and put his hands behind his head.

"Publishers Clearinghouse?"

"Close."

"Wes?"

"Huh?"

"You said close." I laughed. "He's like his own bank."

"Fair." Gabe nodded. "An intelligent answer." He leaned down and pulled a cookie from the plate. "And now you get a prize."

"For guessing well?"

"And being the cutest cousin ever." He pinched my cheeks.

"Gross." I pushed him away. "So?"

"The man in the black mask." Gabe sighed. "Also known

as asshole-of-the-day. Swear, I'd get him fired if I had that type of power."

"Don't you?" I asked, kind of perplexed that Gabe wouldn't have that kind of power; I mean, it was Gabe we were talking about. He snapped his fingers, and the faculty basically panted after him. Not to mention being best friends with Wes basically meant if they wanted to run the free world, they wouldn't have a heck of a lot of people saying no.

"You have no idea," he grumbled under his breath, then stood. "Let's not discuss him. He said he wanted to see if you were okay, whatever the hell that means. Please tell me he's not one of *those* guys…"

"Huh?" I was still processing the fact that Tristan had stopped by my dorm. Wouldn't that look suspicious? "What guys?"

"The type of guy who verbally abuses a girl to feel powerful and then sweetens them up with nice words, only to repeat the process again." Gabe's face turned serious. "I think we both know that—"

"I don't want to talk about it."

"Lisa." Gabe reached for my hands and pulled me to my feet. "Remember the warning signs, okay? If he's hot and then cold, that's not good. You don't need that again. I don't need that again. This world doesn't need that type of monster again, just…" He tilted his head, creasing his brow as he sighed, seeming more helpless than I'd seen him in months. "…be careful."

I shrugged. "He's just a professor caught in a rough position. Besides, he doesn't want me." And he'd certainly made *that* abundantly clear. Heat began in my neck and seeped into my face.

Gabe released my hands and laughed. "Which is why you've always been so innocent. Believe me when I say that man, your sexy little professor, wants you so damn bad he can't even see straight. Just… keep him at a distance and call me if he gets handsy."

"He's old," I argued and then snorted. "Besides, he was only handsy when he didn't know who I was."

"So he got scared."

"You defending him now?"

"Hell, no!" Gabe held up his hands in surrender. "Just explaining the complicated male psyche to my confused female friend."

"Pizza!" a voice called from the door. Wes appeared on the other side with Kiersten and Saylor in tow. "And can I just say I'm-the-bomb-dot-com?"

"We discussed your usage of that phrase," Gabe growled. "Twice."

"Just like we discussed your inability to spell Seahawk correctly… twice."

"Just throwing it out there," Gabe said defensively. "I was confused about part of it."

"It's Sea and Hawk," Wes shook his head. "Spaces confuse you?"

"So pizza?" I interrupted their tense discussion. "I'm starved!"

Kiersten winked and handed me the box with the smiley face drawn on it. I was the only one in the group who liked my pizza completely plain, cheese only. I took the box, opened the lid, and inhaled.

"It's like her drug," Gabe whispered in an awestruck tone.

"Hey!" I set it on the table and pulled a piece out. "After

getting my dorm room broken into, I kind of feel like I deserve this."

"And having your professor hit on you then treat you like shit then hit on you again then treat you like shit in front of the class, only to come and apologize…" Gabe nodded solemnly.

"My fault." Wes winced and shuddered. "Sorry, Lis. I really didn't think he'd react that way. He's usually… more relaxed."

"The man's so uptight he probably shits diamonds." Gabe tilted his head back and laughed.

"And once again, awesome dinner visual," Wes commented, saluting Gabe. "Thanks, man, for that."

"I'm a giver." He winked and bit into the pizza while Saylor scurried to the kitchen to find napkins for everyone.

"So…" Wes looked around the room. "…who has first watch?"

"First watch?" I echoed, following his glance. "What do you mean?"

Kiersten snorted and threw her hands into the air. "You don't really think we're letting you stay here by yourself… do you?"

"Guys!" I pleaded, injecting a whine into my voice. "I'm totally fine. Besides, Gabe put up those expensive-looking cameras." I pointed at the corner of the room. "And I have weapons of mass destruction—"

"Also known as a pink Taser and Mace that she still doesn't know which direction to point." Gabe rolled his eyes. "Do continue."

I stuck out my tongue. "And I won't have you guys forever."

The room fell silent. Gabe looked down. Wes's eyes were sad. Kiersten placed a hand on my arm, and Saylor sighed loudly.

It was something I'd always thought but never really voiced aloud. They had their own lives. I loved them; they were like my family, but it wasn't healthy, them always protecting me, hanging out with me. They should be doing things with each other, starting families. I don't know. Just... not babysitting a girl who didn't even have a steady boyfriend.

Gabe was the first to speak. "Lis—"

"Forget it." I forced a smile. "I'll stay tonight by myself and have you guys on speed dial. If I get freaked, I'll pack a bag. Now, let's eat!"

The room was still filled with tension, but they all ignored it, just like I did. My heart was sad, and, for some reason, I still couldn't get the fact out of my head that he had stopped by.

To apologize?

Scold me more?

Or... I shook the thought out of my head. It couldn't be for any other reason. That side of our relationship was officially non-existent.

"Hey." Kiersten nudged me. "You okay?"

"Yeah." I forced another fake smile. "Totally. Just really tired."

She wrapped an arm around me and pulled me in for a tight hug. "Well, let's get you fed so you can go to bed then."

Great. Bed. Just another reminder that I was in mine... not his.

TWENTY-ONE

"No man will ever love you as much as I love you," I whispered in Mel's ear when she was fast asleep. Time to put part of my plan into action. I went to my computer and started putting my journals into personal files. One copy sent to someone I'd never met, and the other copy? To the person who was going to carry out my revenge — again. The best people to pick on? Ones who wanted revenge, whose hearts were broken. I laughed at my own brilliance. I would probably still be laughing from hell. Most people want to leave behind a legacy, and that's exactly what I was doing. —The Journal of Taylor B.

Tristan

Finding her email was easy. Sending the email? Not so much. I started typing then deleted the entire thing. With a growl, I typed again then deleted. I repeated this same process until finally settling with...

> Tristan.Blake@uw.edu to LC@uw.edu
>
> Are you okay?
>
> Dr. Tristan Blake
> UW Psychology Department

I waited for about a minute before refreshing the page. When nothing happened, I freaked out over what I'd said. Should I have apologized? I'd rather do that to her face. With a groan, I wiped my face with my hands and started getting ready to turn in.

I hit refresh a few more times before finally giving up. With a sigh, I crawled between the sheets and reached for the journal by my lamp.

The Journal of Taylor B.

It was the thing of nightmares. My nightmares, most likely hers. It was also such an addicting read I didn't know what else to do. I'd only been halfway through it when I'd decided to make the trek across the country and take a semester teaching. The first few chapters had convinced me, and now the story of his insanity called to me. It called to that part of me who understood him, who understood that type of madness. I wasn't sure what was so horrifying. The fact that I got it or the fact that I could end up just like him.

My cell rang, jolting me out of my dark thoughts.

It was my father. I couldn't ignore him forever. With a curse, I picked up and barked a hello into the phone.

"Well, that's a nice greeting." He chuckled. "Any trouble with the benefit?"

A vision of Lisa in her black mask caused my body to tighten. "Nope, no trouble at all."

"Erica's been asking about you." He coughed and then sighed. I could picture him now, sitting near the fireplace, cigar in one hand, whiskey in the other. "You ignoring *her* phone calls too?"

"I've been busy. Companies don't run themselves, you know. Besides, I'm teaching this semester."

I could practically feel his scowl over the phone. "I told you it was unnecessary to stay that long away from everything.

So, she wants to marry you, wants to move forward, start your life together. Instead, you run away with your tail between your legs." He sighed. "You aren't off your meds, are you?"

"No." I ground my teeth. "And you've always pounded it into my head that no decision is to be taken lightly. Think of my time away as my doing that, looking at every angle."

Another sigh. "As long as you're back for Christmas."

"I will be." It was a lie. A total lie. The last thing I wanted to do was go back to him, back to that life, back to the life he'd built for me.

"Fantastic." He sniffed. "I'll talk to you later this week. Don't forget to check in with the board every once in a while. I know you run a smooth ship, but I still worry."

"Always." There he was; in the end, it was always about money, about making more of it. And I'd had the Midas touch. I'd turned his multimillion-dollar empire into a multibillion-dollar empire. I could have done it in my sleep. Because that's the thing about madness... it breeds brilliance. For others? Like Taylor? It breeds death. Absolute death.

TWENTY-TWO

It took me a few days to put the chess pieces into place. To make sure all parties knew what their task was, to make sure she was broken enough to snap. To make sure it would happen exactly as I'd predicted. —The Journal of Taylor B.

Lisa

I ignored his email.

And got to class fifteen minutes early.

Part of the reason was because I hadn't been able to sleep worth crap the night before and figured I may as well get a head start. Better to shock him to death than walk in a minute late and earn another scowl.

"Hey." Jack plopped down next to me. "You're early!"

"I am." I returned his smile. He was easy, no pressure, kind of like Gabe. Not that I had any interest in him, but he was… nice to me. Unlike Tristan, who, by the looks of things, wanted to set me on fire with his eyes.

Jack touched my arm. I looked up to see Tristan's gaze trained on my arm and then narrowed in on Jack's fingers.

I pulled away and tucked my fallen hair behind my ear.

"We're two weeks into the semester." Tristan started pacing

in front of his desk. "I want you guys to start thinking about your first big project. Since this is Psychology of Emotion, I want you to pick an emotion to study. It has to be one of the four emotions. I'll give you two minutes to pick a partner. Then I'll give the rest of the instructions."

"Partner up, cowgirl," Jack whispered next to me. "You in?" He held out his hand. I shook it and gave him a firm nod.

"What do you want to study?" I asked, pulling out a fresh piece of paper.

"Anger." He'd said it with an edge in his voice, but when I looked up, his face was its normal goofy self. "That okay with you? It just seems the most complex. I mean, think about what anger entails? Revenge? Bloodshed? Wars?" He grinned. "Sorry. I'm a guy. I can't help it."

I waved him off. "It's fine. Anger, it is."

"Now that you have your partners and most likely your idea of the project," Dr. Blake continued. "I'll be passing out the instructions. Please listen as I start explaining." He cleared his throat while his TA started passing out the worksheets. "You'll use a personal experience to describe this emotion. Please write it in first person, no less than three pages. I'd like you to research instances when this emotion has helped people in history and when it's hindered. You need to find pictures and attach them to your story and include nonverbal cues as well as verbal cues to identify this emotion. Think of this project as taking one emotion and getting to know it so well…" His voice trailed off as his eyes found mine. "…that it defines you."

Shivers ran down my spine. The last thing I wanted to explore was anger; it reminded me of his personality. It was way too close. Taylor had been a bomb just waiting to set off.

Only he was the only one with the timer.

"Hey." Jack touched my arm again. "You okay?"

"Yeah." I was going to hate this project. "Fine."

I couldn't help but think about the angry notes I was still receiving and the fact that someone was clearly angry with me, so angry and hateful that they destroyed university property on my behalf. I swallowed the fear and focused on the project at hand. By the time class ended, both Jack and I had adjusted our schedules so that we could work together for the rest of the week.

"Lisa," Dr. Blake barked just as I stood from my desk. "A minute."

Jack swore under his breath. "Damn, it's like he can't help but pick on you. If it helps… I know what that's like." His face was shadowed. "If you want me to do something—"

"No," I shook my head and laughed to put him at ease. "It's fine. I'm fine."

Jack nodded slowly. "Just be careful. Crazy comes in all forms, even ones who look completely harmless."

"Noted." I swallowed and turned toward the front of the room.

Tristan was stacking papers on his desk. When the last student exited the room, he walked to the door, locked it, and pulled the blinds down.

Nervous, I shifted on my feet. "You going to scold me again?"

Tristan's entire body tensed as his face searched mine. "I was actually planning on apologizing, but if you'd rather have a punishment."

Curse him for making my entire body tremble! And it wasn't with fear. The way he looked at me, the way he said things, it just… it did things to me, things I wanted to punch him for, because he was just like Gabe said, hot, then cold, then hot again.

"Dinner," he said, interrupting my thoughts. "I want to apologize and take you to dinner."

"Are you planning on rejecting me afterward?"

He went very still, his eyes meeting mine, looking straight into my soul, into every insecure part of me. "No, Lisa. I'm not going to reject you afterward."

It was hard to explain the way he spoke to me; at times, he was flirtatious and well… happy. Other times? It seemed like he was fighting another side of himself, one that was more reserved, uptight, controlled. And if you were to ask me which side scared me the most? I'd say both. Because both sides were dangerous to me — both pushed a person like me past the point of no return. His seriousness made me curious; his flirtation made me want more.

"Just dinner?" I asked. "Isn't that against the rules?"

"Yeah, well…" He glanced down briefly before flashing a sensual smile, his eyes dilating. "…it seems to be an impulse I can't really control around you."

"Control's overrated, you label-making fool."

At that, he laughed a rich chuckle that had my entire body relaxing and heating at the same time. I took a step toward him and smiled. "So, rule-breaker, where are we going?"

He grabbed his messenger bag and keys. "You'll see."

"Cryptic." My eyebrows arched as I crossed my arms over my chest. "This isn't going to turn into one of those six o'clock news things where the crazy professor takes the girl out then buries her in the woods, is it?" I tried to sound like I was joking, but the minute the words left my mouth, it was no longer funny. Suddenly, I realized how stupid it would be to go with him. I knew nothing about him, nothing at all!

He smiled, tilting his head toward me. "Why am I getting the sudden urge to pull out a list of character references?"

"Because I just scared myself," I admitted out loud.

"You want my social security number?" He winked. "Credit score? First-grade class photo? Oh, and by the way, in first grade, I was nominated most likely to own a pet store... so, if you aren't okay with that, we probably shouldn't continue this."

"This?"

"Dinner."

"Because you liked pets?"

"I wanted to own a lizard farm."

I covered my mouth with my hands and nodded solemnly. "All little boys have dreams."

"A bully crushed mine when he told me lizard farms don't exist." He shook his head. "In second grade, I was voted least likely to succeed, on account that I didn't speak for the entire year."

"Why's that?" I took another step toward him.

He took another step in my direction and shrugged. "It took me a while to get over the lizards."

"So, you stopped speaking?"

"It was more of me trying to make the public aware of my outrage."

"Ah, like lizard strike."

"I made shirts."

"Tell me, professor, is that when the label-making started?"

"No." He nodded toward the door and started walking. I followed, genuinely interested in what he was going to say and hating that it was possible he was stringing me along only to go all cold-crazy-psycho on me again. "That was an entirely different situation." He pulled the door open.

"What? No more stories?" I asked.

"Dinner." He shrugged, his eyes a stormy gray. "I'll tell you at dinner."

"Bribery."

"My trump card. Label-maker stories. You know, I do actually know how to romance a woman."

"Well..." I cleared my throat and broke eye contact. "... since I'm your student, I'll just take your word for it."

"Right," he said quickly, then repeated, "Right, shall we?"

"Lead the way." I forced a smile and tried to remember that this was dinner, nothing romantic, just my very sexy professor once again apologizing for being a jackass during class.

The halls of the building were pretty empty. As it was, I should probably have been walking a bit faster, considering I still had a class to get to.

When we reached the end of the hall, where we'd most likely part ways, I felt someone watching. I turned around. Nothing. But the feeling remained. Fully creeped out, I fell into step beside Tristan and turned around again. Only he'd stopped, meaning I tripped against him and almost had a really embarrassing incident where my lips met his — by default.

"Whoa!" He didn't push me back, just braced my shoulders and gazed at me with those gray swirling eyes. "Are you okay?"

"Yeah." I shook my head. "I was just... sorry, I thought I saw something."

Slowly, he released his grip and stepped back. "So tonight? Six?"

"Yeah." I nodded. "Sounds good. Should I meet you there?"

"I'll pick you up."

"But won't that look... bad?"

"A student eating with her professor? I'm sure there are worse things for the faculty to be gossiping about than a professor taking a student out to dinner to apologize for being an ass. You know, school shootings, drugs, rapes, things like that."

My edgy feeling continued, but I found myself nodding in agreement. "You're right."

"Wow." He smirked. "I imagine those aren't words that pass those lips often."

"Talking about my lips is definitely off-limits."

He stared directly at my mouth, then outlined his lips with his tongue and whispered, "Now, that really is a pity." He'd so done that on purpose.

"So, six." I stepped back and coughed, trying to distract him from the heat I felt on my cheeks. "Great, awesome. I'll just be waiting outside... my... dorm, where I live, because that's where..." I held up my hand to wave — yes wave — upon my departure and ran smack-dab into Jack as he came out of the guys' restroom.

"Whoa there. Guys' restroom. No girls allowed." Jack winked then nodded to the professor. "Everything okay?"

"Great!" My voice was too high-pitched to be convincing. "Gotta run. Bye!" I ran down the hall and out of the building. It was already too late to go to class, so I cut my losses and went to the student center to check my mail. I'd been having a hard time remembering my PO on account of having to change everything so often. By the time I scrolled through my notes on my phone, I'd been standing in front of the stupid boxes for ten minutes. Finally, I went to the correct one.

I reached in and pulled out a bit of junk mail, an announcement about a party on campus, and finally, a black-and-white picture.

Of me and Taylor.

Taken two years ago.

I dropped it to the ground, terrified to look at the picture, so damn scared that Taylor was going to jump through the picture and hurt me again. Seeing him was like seeing the boogeyman in real life or chanting *Bloody Mary* in the mirror.

Swearing, I picked up the picture, planning to rip it up and toss it in the trash, but as I grasped it and began tearing the damn thing, I noticed handwriting on the back. It was the same black block lettering I'd seen before.

It's almost time. Did you think I'd stay dead forever?
I own you.

A cry rippled from my throat, and I dropped the photograph into the trash. Without a backward look, I ran straight to my dorm, my body numb the entire way.

TWENTY-THREE

The thing about leaving a legacy? It's not truly a legacy unless you affect the maximum amount of individuals. Why in the hell would I go to all this work just to hurt one person? Do I look like an idiot? I work tirelessly because it has to be perfect; everything has to be perfect. The best part? The players don't even know they're in the game. —The Journal of Taylor B.

Lisa

I locked my door and slid down, hands shaking. I tried to get my breathing under control. I'd run the entire way back to my room and then hesitated even going in. What if a crazy person was waiting for me?

Clearly, the hair hadn't thrown off the stalker.

Which meant someone from my past, someone — someone I'd hurt — knew I was here, knew I was going to school, and knew my connection to Taylor. The worst part? Just thinking about all the people who were negatively affected by him. I shuddered; the list was long. So long.

"You can do this," I whispered to myself. "You aren't Mel anymore. You're Lisa."

The familiar taste of metal entered my mouth, quickly followed by knife-sharp pain as I bit down hard on my tongue. Fear wrapped itself around me like a blanket, and I let it because

I was so tired of fighting. It's sad — no, it's actually pathetic when what you fear most becomes an object of comfort. When fear actually turns into a friend. When you open your eyes, and all you see is the dark because it's been so long since you've seen the light. I'd been under that type of cloak for a while. Meeting Kiersten, having had her as a roommate last year, had helped; and then, of course, meeting Wes, the guy was like a walking inspirational quote. And then there was Gabe; for a while, we had carried the burden together. But now? It wasn't fair to ask that of him.

Which just left me.

I took another deep breath and slowly rose from my position on the floor, and walked over to my computer. I clicked the mouse to wake it up and, with shaking fingers, typed in the one website I swore I'd never revisit, the one place that still gave me nightmares.

Videos of shame popped up right away. Millions of hits, millions of followers. I had no idea who had taken over since Taylor's death, and I didn't want to know. I'd had my parents email the site to take down all the videos I'd been involved in, but once something was on the Internet? Yeah, it's pretty much there forever, and in the end, because I'd willingly participated and apparently been one of the founders of the website, there wasn't really anything they could do.

Thus, changing my name and taking on a new identity.

Only the victims knew it was us.

And the really horrible part? They were always convinced, you know, after the shameful video was posted, that we wouldn't stop shaming them until they signed an NDA, meaning they couldn't expose the masterminds behind the website.

Protecting us, or so I thought.

The home screen had ten different featured videos of the day, a little kid picking his nose and getting caught by his twin brother, then telling the girl on camera and showing the picture to her. Silly stuff. At least it wasn't as bad as what it used to be.

I scrolled through more of the videos. They were embarrassing but mostly funny, not something that would cause a kid to commit suicide or want to start a school shooting.

The last video was titled, *"Revenge, a Dish Best Served... Late."*

I clicked on it.

And almost threw up.

They were pictures of me.

Pictures of me in class, pictures of me at a bar, pictures of me two years ago with Taylor, and pictures of me and Taylor kissing and then...

My entire body went rigid as I watched the video go live...

"Just take it," Taylor whispered. *"It will make you feel good."*

"You promise?" I swayed a bit, already drunk. *"It will help my stomach cramps?"*

"Totally." He winked. *"Would I ever steer you wrong, babe?"*

I rolled my eyes and took the pill; he handed me a beer, and the video continued with us talking. I had no memory of staying that night, no memory of even drinking.

And that's when the video took a dark turn. I stumbled into Taylor's arms, slurring my words. "I f-f-feel funny."

"Probably tired from the pill." He waved to some of our friends. *"Let's go lie down."*

"'Kay." I snuggled into him and sighed happily.

The camera shook a bit as it followed us closely behind. At one point, Taylor turned around and winked straight at the camera.

"Come on, Mel, let's get you comfortable."

He proceeded to strip me of all my clothes.

I should have hit stop on the video. Black censor marks covered my nudity and his, but you could tell what was happening by the fact that I was murmuring stop, *by the fact that my body was completely limp, and by the fact that Taylor said directly into the camera, "Revenge, my friends, is a dish best served... late — are you watching? I know you are... I knew you would be." He dropped my limp body to the ground and strutted toward the camera, then whispered, "I. Own. You."*

I slammed the computer shut and stumbled backward. I didn't know who to call, who to tell, what to even do! It was so long ago; could you even report a case like that? Plus, he was dead? Right? He was dead? I watched him die, watched him throw himself from the ledge.

I ran into the bathroom and puked, then slumped to the floor again. I didn't want Gabe to know, not now, now when he was so happy and done with drama. Besides, what could he possibly do? Tell the police? Arrest a dead person? Take down a video that I'm sure would just be put back up the next day? Because that's the thing about the website; Taylor had specifically filtered it through a different country, so even if we did have some crazy person filing against the site...

We'd block their IP.

Keep it up.

And keep running.

The video was there to stay — forever, I was one click away from turning into an E Hollywood story.

It was like Taylor was haunting me from the grave. How would he even know? He'd always said he owned me, and he'd been right.

And now.

Even in death, he owned me.

"Well, congrats, you sick bastard," I mumbled. "I feel…
owned."

TWENTY-FOUR

Making someone feel, making someone care, making someone experience emotion when your whole life you've been numb to it? It's like fireworks going on all around you. It's so loud, so damn loud it deafens. And then there's the light, so brilliant it blinds; it scorches your retinas. And you take it as long as you can until you have to close your eyes, plug your ears — until all you want to do is scream. Mel was my fireworks, my everything, and because of that, she needed to be punished the way she was punishing me. You see, she made me human, and the last thing I'd wanted was to be something I wasn't. She spoke calmly to the beast; she did my bidding. She was going to have to pay for that. I'm not sorry. I'll never be sorry. The story is halfway done. —The Journal of Taylor B.

Tristan

I was about fifteen minutes early to Lisa's dorm... I decided that leaning against the wall looked odd, and sitting in my car made me look like an absolute predator, so I went into the lobby and sat on the couch. UW was so big I knew people wouldn't necessarily recognize me, especially considering I was only wearing jeans and a T-shirt, meaning I looked a lot younger than I typically did in the front of the classroom.

By the time 6:15 rolled around, I'd started getting nervous. I had to laugh. Was the girl ever early? Maybe that was just her thing, being late? With a growl of frustration, I went over to the elevators and pressed her floor. I hurried down the hall, hoping we hadn't just missed each other, and knocked on the door.

No answer.

I guess I deserved to be stood up.

Then again, what if something really was wrong?

I knocked again.

The door swung open. Lisa stood there in the same clothes as earlier, her eyes were puffy from crying, and her hair was a mess.

"What happened?" I cupped her face and examined it for any hint of injury. Finding none, shifted my gaze, and quickly scanned her body. "Are you okay? Did someone hurt you?"

I kicked the door shut behind me and walked her backward toward the couch. I sat her down and gripped her hands with mine as I knelt in front of her. "Lisa, talk to me."

"I—" she croaked, her eyes glancing at the computer and back at me. "I…" She started shivering. "I can't tell you."

"What *can* you tell me?" I was going to go crazy. Her tears were like tiny knives driving into my skin by force. I wanted to fix it; I had to fix it.

She shook her head, tears streaming down her face.

"Are you physically hurt?" I asked calmly, even though I was ready to run my fist through whoever had made her cry.

"No." She sniffled.

"Did someone try to hurt you physically?"

She nodded her head slowly and then shook it like the question confused her. But she cried harder, so something had happened.

"Lisa." I sighed heavily. "Let me help you, let me take care of you."

"Oh yeah…" She rolled her eyes and sniffed. "The professor that hates me so much he can barely look at me wants to suddenly take care of me? Sorry if I'm not so keen on trusting you at this point."

I reared back, eyes searching her face. She was right, completely right, but she had no idea the real reason. Why I did what I did, what drove me to treat her like she was nothing when really I knew in my soul she was an everything girl, the type of girl that guys hold on to. Hell, I knew that firsthand because she'd been the one to drive him to madness. And I knew I'd follow happily in the same footsteps, even having proof that I could end up the same way, and I was ready to pack my suitcase and jump along for the ride.

"I'm sorry," I whispered. "Sorry for the way I addressed you in class, sorry for not listening to the real reason you were late, and sorry that you're crying, that someone's hurt you so deeply that you feel the need to waste tears on them." I tilted her chin toward me again. "But I won't apologize for kissing you, for thinking about you every night, for wanting you when I know I shouldn't. I can't apologize for that. I won't."

Her sharp intake of breath was all it took for me to move. My mouth met hers, and I knew, in that instant, in that very second… madness for her? Was something I would choose.

No going back.

Her fingers tangled in my hair, and then, just as quickly as the kiss had started, she pulled back and quickly covered herself with the pillow, blocking me from reaching her.

Chest heaving, I held up my hands. "Sorry. I'm sorry, no touching."

She shook her head again, taking her lower lip hostage as fresh tears started pooling in her eyes.

I sighed, feeling completely helpless, totally unused to the foreign feeling that there was no one I could call to fix it, nobody I could pay to make her tears go away. "Are you hungry?"

She sniffed then looked away. "A bit, but I don't want to go out. I'm sorry I lost track of time, and then—" She paled even more.

"No problem." I shrugged. "There's always pizza."

Her watery smile had me reaching for my phone before she said yes. Her fingers grazed my arm, and I paused.

"Cheese," she whispered. "I want extra cheese."

"My five-year-old self would have played with you on the playground solely based on that pizza preference," I teased, trying to cheer her up.

"Good to know at least your five-year-old self approves of me," she said, though at least she was smiling.

"Yeah, I imagine my five-year-old self would kick my ass or at least push me down into the mud for the way I've been treating you."

"Maybe later." Lisa's eyes locked on mine.

"Later you'll kick my ass?"

"Later I'll push you in the mud."

"Join me, and we'll talk."

"Order pizza, and I'll think about it."

Grinning, I pulled out my cell and whispered, "I think I like taking orders from you."

"Don't tempt me."

"Why?" I searched for the closest pizza place, hit call, then glanced up at her pretty blue eyes. "Just think of it as returning the favor."

"Pizza Palace!" A voice said, interrupting our heated

exchange. I turned around and started firing off instructions, all the while feeling Lisa's gaze burn a hole through my body. When the call ended, I turned around to see Lisa staring at the floor. All teasing had dropped from her face. She looked lost. Not the type of lost you see on people when they're in a new city; the type of lost you see on a little kid when she thinks her parents left her at the store.

She was the type of lost I had felt on the inside when he'd died.

Hopeless.

Withdrawn.

Angry.

"Pizza will be here in a few minutes," I said casually, though I felt anything but casual… worthless was more like it. I was a fixer, and I was used to making things right. It was in my blood, but I was unable to do anything but sit there and order her pizza while she stared blankly at the wall. "Do you maybe want to watch a movie?"

"You don't have to stay." She shrugged; her voice was weak. "You came, you apologized, you bought me food—"

"I'm staying." I placed my hand on her arm. "Besides, I ordered two pizzas. Can you really eat two pizzas all by yourself?"

A small smile formed across her lips. "Right now, I don't even think I could eat one slice."

"We'll go easy." I moved toward her. "Bite by bite."

Her head jerked up. "Is there a reason?"

"What?" I asked, completely confused.

She sighed. "A reason that every single thing you say to me, when we're alone, when you're not pissed or acting like an ass, is dripping with sexual innuendo."

And… officially called out. Words jumbled in my head — big words, great explanations, excuses mostly, but what came out was, "You're beautiful."

Her smile grew.

"And…" I sat down next to her and slowly raised my hand to caress her face. "…it seems, I just can't help myself. When I want something… I want it. I'm selfish like that. I want to take it. I want it to be mine, nobody else's. I never did share well as an only child."

Her eyes flickered with something. Hesitation? Amusement? I wasn't sure. "Who said you had to share me?"

"Off-limits." She was like a drug; even her eyes drew me in, made me want to kiss her again, made me want to absolutely lose myself in her. "And a student."

"If I put my mask back on, will you kiss me?"

"No."

She tried to pull away, but I had a solid grip on her body as I pulled her across my lap so that she was almost straddling me. Her eyes were uncertain as they looked from my lips to my eyes then back again.

"No masks this time." I lowered my mouth to hers. "No masks."

"No masks," she repeated, her tongue sliding into my mouth.

And just like that, I sealed my fate.

And signed my destiny right along with his.

Cheerfully.

TWENTY-FIVE

I hated her so much... I wanted to strangle her as much as I wanted to kiss her... I wanted her to feel pain the way I felt pain — raw, uncontrollable. The more I think about what she did to me, what she made me feel? The more angry I become... I am anger, and she is my catalyst. — The Journal of Taylor B.

Lisa

His kiss was slow; he tasted like mint as his tongue flicked mine, then went deeper into my mouth, exploring me as much as I was exploring him. A part of me — you know, the sane part — was totally freaked, but something about his touch, about his kiss, calmed me, made me think that maybe, just maybe, he was safe.

I needed safe.

He deepened the kiss, his hands moving around to my hips and pulling me against him. With a moan, I tipped my head back as his lips moved away from mine and found places on my neck no guy had ever, ever taken the time to find. I closed my eyes in ecstasy as his hot mouth devoured, infusing his touch and scent into my memory.

"You're beautiful," he said gruffly, his lips still teasing my neck. His mouth moved to my ear. His kiss was wet, hot, as he whispered in my ear, "You are absolutely beautiful."

I wrapped my arms around his neck. I didn't want to talk. I wanted to be the girl that could make out without puking, the girl who could ignore the fact that my ridiculously sexy and mysterious professor had just ordered me pizza and was making out with me on the couch.

But most of all? I wanted to ignore the fact that my life was hanging on by a thread… a thread Taylor still held. Heck, he held both thread and scissors.

"Lisa…" Tristan's mouth covered mine again, heat soared through my body. "…before…" He finally pulled back and looked directly into my eyes. "Tell me, tell me what happened."

I froze. My hands clenched his shirt so tight it was going to permanently wrinkle it where my fingers had tugged.

"You can trust me," he whispered.

"I can't," I said honestly. "At least not yet."

"Okay." He sighed. "Okay, then it seems I have a lot of work to do."

"You're leaving?" Rejection slammed into me.

His eyebrows shot up. "Does it look like I want to be anywhere, but here?"

Confused, I shook my head. "But you said work—"

"Work on your trust," His eyes narrowed. "Do you really have no idea the effect you have on me? On possibly the entire male population, including the blind?"

I laughed and rolled my eyes, trying to pull away from him as a blush crept up my cheeks.

"No." He held me firm in his lap. "You are magnificent." He kissed me softly on the lips. "Anyone who says differently is clearly insane."

"Says the guy who let me get out of his car."

He nodded. "Says the guy who let you walk away… once."

"Twice."

"Class doesn't count."

"Oh?"

"And I won't make the same mistake three times."

"We'll see." I touched my tongue to my lips. "Won't we?"

With a grin, he set me away from him and leaned back on the couch. "Ask me anything."

"Anything?" I pulled my knees to my chest. "Anything I want?"

He laughed; his smile was beautiful. "Well, within reason."

"Reason? What's that?" I teased.

"Cute." His eyes narrowed.

"Okay." I popped my knuckles.

"Whoa!" He chuckled and held up his hands as if to shield himself. "Preparing for a fight?"

"Just getting my question ready."

"With your fists?" He scooted away. "Just to be safe, you understand."

"Please, like I'd actually beat my professor."

"Stranger things have happened." He dropped his hands into his lap. "So, question? You get one question before food arrives, then I want to see you eat at least three pieces."

"What is with guys making girls eat all the time? We're either too fat or too skinny." I rolled my eyes. "And, for the record, I normally love eating and have an appetite that would put Gabe to shame."

"Gabe..." Tristan repeated the name. "...threatened to kick my ass."

"He's a good friend."

"Good to know if we were in a duel, I could count on you," Tristan said grumpily. "I'm going to put a time limit on the question if you don't hurry up."

Panicked, I searched my head for the right question, one that would give me more clues to who he was.

Meanwhile, Tristan hummed the Jeopardy theme.

"You're right." I laughed. "You can't even hum!"

"I did warn you." He continued humming.

"Okay, okay!" I held up my hands, happy he was here, happy for the distraction. "So, you're the CEO of a huge company I have yet to do an Internet search on, but Wes made it sound like... I don't know like you were really important."

"Do I not look important?" he asked in a serious tone, his eyebrows pinching together.

My smile fell.

"I'm kidding." He smiled. "So I'm the CEO, yes, but the board mainly runs a lot of the company now, and it's expanded so much that... well... I'm able to take time off and not worry too much about us going under."

"What type of company?"

"Is that your question?"

I chewed my lip. "For now."

"Companies... real estate investments, which is kind of boring and... um, pharmaceuticals."

Wow, not what I expected. "So you're a legal drug lord?"

He burst out laughing. "Sure, I'm part of the US drug cartel, also known as prescription drugs."

"What type of drugs?"

"All drugs."

"Meaning?"

"Our specialty is... psychotropic drugs." He coughed into his hand.

I nodded slowly. "Psychotropic? So drugs for mental health."

"Exactly." He looked away and shrugged. "All very boring to you, I'm sure."

"That's why you're so rich." I hadn't meant to say it out loud, and by his stunned expression, it was completely possible I'd just crossed a line. "I'm so sorry. I didn't mean to offend you…"

"No." He ran a hand through his hair, his T-shirt lifting enough to give me an awesome view of his lower abs. "It's true… that's the society we live in, right? Have a headache? Take this. Have a pain? Take this. Have a heartache? Here, this will make you happy again." His tone became more and more bitter as he talked. "We mainly deal with research drugs, ones that help people who have mental struggles. We've made strides for those with bipolar disorders, and we've failed in other areas…"

Fascinated, I couldn't help but ask, "What areas?"

He swallowed. "Schizophrenia, dissociative identity disorder, anti-social personality disorder, to name a select few."

"What's—"

A knock sounded on the door, interrupting all train of thought. I jumped to my feet just as Tristan rose to his and gently pushed me back on the couch. "My treat. You sit…"

"Sitting." I held up my hands in surrender.

With a smile, he bent down and kissed me briefly across the lips, then went to the door and opened it.

"That'll be—"

The voice stopped talking.

I leaned back and nearly choked on my tongue.

Jack. Jack was delivering pizza to me and my professor. Oh. Crap.

"Dr. Blake?" Jack scratched his head and weaseled his body halfway into the door. "Lisa? Is there a class party I don't know about?"

"Actually…" Tristan looked ready to confess.

"I needed help—" I said quickly. "—with our new project, and, after being so late to class, I wanted to meet with Dr. Blake to go over ways I could earn some extra credit, but I almost passed out because I forgot to eat, so he ordered me pizza… so basically—" I shrugged. "—he just wants to make sure I'm alive so he can torture me some more."

"That right…" Jack grinned. "Well, far be it for me to stand in the way." He took the bills from Tristan's hands and nodded. "We still on for tomorrow, Lisa?"

"Tomorrow?" I squinted.

"Our project?" His eyebrows shot up. "Wow, you really do need food. I see what you mean."

"Sorry." I covered my face with my hands, praying I didn't look like I'd just been making out with Tristan. "I'm lethargic."

"No sweat." He shrugged. "Let's just meet at Starbucks."

"'Kay." I nodded and waved goodbye.

It wasn't until the door closed that I remembered he worked at Starbucks — at least he said he did, right? So what was he doing delivering pizza? Did he have two jobs? I mean, that was completely normal for some students, but how did he find the time?"

"You didn't have to do that." Tristan leaned against the door then finally turned to face me, pizza in hand.

"Do what?" I lifted one shoulder and let it fall.

"Protect me."

I sighed. "Consider us even."

At his confused look, I kept talking. "You saved me from crying myself to sleep tonight, and I save you from getting fired, but that also means I deserve another question."

"Fine, shoot." He placed the two boxes onto the table. "But make it fast. You need food."

"Who's your dad?" I blurted.

He cursed under his breath before turning away and whispering, "Pretty sure if you look up Mark Westinghouse, Jr., you'll get that answer."

Stunned, I could only stare at him open-mouthed.

"Plates?" He went into my tiny kitchenette and started rummaging through cupboards.

I heard things slamming, but my entire body felt like it was paralyzed with shock.

"No paper towels?" He sighed. "Such a college student."

When he returned, he dished out pieces of pizza and handed me the plate. "What? You don't need Google?"

"I have a brain," I whispered. "And if it's working correctly, that means your dad's the Secretary of State..."

"Yeah." Tristan cursed. "Fourth in line for president. So, pizza?"

TWENTY-SIX

I took another pill, then another, they weren't working like he'd promised; in fact, it felt like they were making the dreams worse, making the itch to do something stupid damn-near impossible not to scratch. When she came over that night, I barely even looked in her direction. Maybe I was still pissed she'd applied to college. Maybe, just maybe, that feeling that wouldn't go away was jealousy. Pure and simple. Jealousy that she'd get a chance — and even more determined to be the one to take it from her. —The Journal of Taylor B.

Tristan

I didn't want to look at her; I knew what her face would tell me. Her eyes would be wide, her mouth slightly ajar, and then she'd either snuggle up closer to me or push away like I was a disease. Most women were either so power hungry they could barely see straight or terrified that they were going to be on the FBI watch list by association. Knowing she could be either one of those or both? It bothered me more than it should. Bothered me so much that my appetite was basically gone.

With a grimace, I looked down at the pizza. The clock ticked in the background, and still, Lisa said nothing.

Finally, a painful five minutes later, she reached into one of the boxes and grumbled, "They still never put enough cheese on mine."

I jerked my head up and stared at her. "What?"

"Cheese." She scrunched up her nose and piled two pieces onto her plate. "I ask for extra, and I think they assume I'm a toddler because they never, ever give me extra. It's almost worse to say you want extra, I think." Sighing heavily, she lifted the slice to her lips, inhaled, then took a huge bite, sauce getting all over her lips. I licked mine on impulse, imagining licking hers until they were clean until the pizza was forgotten, and it was just me and Lisa.

"Sorry," I croaked. "That sucks."

"Yeah, well." She took another bite and winked. "Can't win 'em all."

I shrugged and took a bite out of my own piece, hoping to God that the rest of the evening wasn't going to be filled with the sound of both of us chewing and nothing else.

"So..." she asked, placing the piece of pizza on the plate and reaching for one of the dishtowels I'd brought over. "...you know tae kwon do?"

"What?"

"Fighting." She grinned. "To protect yourself from terrorists."

"Very funny."

"Come on, tell me. I know I don't get any more questions, but you have to know some sort of self-defense. Let me guess. They kicked you out of karate class because you were too serious." She tapped her chin. "No, wait! I've got it! You refused to break the board in half because you were afraid to hurt your hand, so they made you sit out. Bummer."

A grin spread across my face as she kept guessing. She

concocted a story about me being afraid of breaking a toe, hitting the wrong dummy because it wasn't labeled correctly, and somehow, by her weird math and powers of deduction, that meant I was afraid of all things without labels.

"No," I finally interrupted. "No, no, and no. I didn't have a pet cricket like Mulan, and I don't have a crazy grandmother with a cane that I know of. A dragon would be awesome, but I'm pretty sure now you're just pulling from the movie, and if I did have to become a geisha, I'd be badass at it because I think we've established what a perfectionist I am in every aspect of my life, both personal and professional. And to answer your first question, before you decided to Mulan me to death, no, I don't know karate. But I can shoot a gun; took mixed martial arts for a few years, back when I was young enough not to care that my nose might get broken a few times. And yeah, it's true. When I was six, I could do the splits. Happy?"

Lisa burst out laughing then gave a little bow. "See? I knew I could figure you out."

"Right, Mulan-loving badass with a heart of gold. You were so ridiculously close that I got chills. Look, right there. Hairs standing on end."

"Hmm…" She reached across the couch and placed her warm hand directly on my arm. "Yeah, I see what you mean. Disney gives you chills, who knew?"

"Right." I leaned forward, so I was inches away from her face. "Let's blame Disney."

"Well, it's not the pizza."

"Or the crickets."

"Geishas?" She moved closer.

"Negative."

"Extra cheese dirty talk?"

"Close," I whispered, my lips almost touching hers.

"Well!" She jerked back. "Then, I'm out. I have no idea what it could possibly be."

I let out a low growl and narrowed my eyes. "Teasing the professor may gain you a bad grade."

"And what? Kissing your student gets you promoted?"

"I bet Gabe doesn't win any argument with you, does he?" I joked, looking away so I wouldn't be tempted to grab her by the shoulders and kiss her again.

She shrugged. "Sometimes I throw him a bone."

"How horrifyingly degrading."

"Put that in your label maker and smoke it."

I rolled my eyes and picked up my plate. "You have an oddly strange fascination with my label maker. Maybe next time you come over, I'll let you have some alone time, just you, the maker, and some wine." Standing, I held out my hand for her plate and waited.

Lisa handed me her plate but didn't release her grip right away. "Sounds like a dirty fantasy to me, Professor."

"And there it is." I jerked the plate away and fought the urge to laugh out loud. She brought that out in me, the temptation to laugh, to forget responsibility, to just be normal when I knew I wasn't anywhere close to being able to own up to that particular word and the meaning behind it.

"So…" Lisa placed her hands on her hips while I put the dishes in the sink. "…Secretary of State, huh?"

My hands shook as they gripped the edge of the counter. With a curse, I bit my lip and stared her down, trying to read her expression, but it was blank, emotionless like she didn't give a damn who I was or who my father was.

"What?" Her eyebrows furrowed. "I figured you didn't

want to talk about it." She tucked her hair behind her ears then crossed her arms. "Besides, I imagine that's why you liked the mask."

"Mask?" I rounded the corner back into the living room. "You mean the party?"

She gave a quick nod. "At the party, you could be whoever you wanted to be. For a while, you weren't a CEO, you weren't the son of a really powerful man, you weren't even a nerdy professor."

I smirked.

Her smile grew. "You were just you, and sometimes, well, sometimes it's nice to remember what that's like, right? To just be you and not have to worry about anything else in the world."

"Right." I couldn't take my eyes off of her. "There's something about... being anonymous, not having to worry about others."

"I know." She swallowed convulsively and looked away. "Believe me, I know."

Did it make me a total ass that I knew more than I let on? That for a minute, I was actually judging her for judging me when really I'd been doing nothing but passing that same judgment over and over again until my head spun.

On impulse, I held out my hand. "So come with me."

"What?" Her eyes darted to my hand. "What do you mean?"

"Anonymous..." I was flirting with danger. I could feel it in the way my body heated at the word, the way my blood roared to life. "Tonight, come with me."

Her breathing turned ragged as she clenched her fingers around my hand tightly. "Where?"

I tugged her in against my body and wrapped my arms around her waist. "That's just it, wherever we want… anonymous, right?"

Lisa tensed beneath my arms. "Is that what you're offering me? Just another night, full of masks, full of dancing under the stairs, stolen kisses, and pretending not to know each other the next day?"

I tilted my head and examined her expression, the way I could see her pulse pick up in her neck, the way her body continued to arch toward mine, even though her eyes were unsure. She wanted it; she was just afraid to take it. "Yes Lisa," I finally said. "That's exactly what I'm offering. No strings, no commitment, no promises. Just… right now."

"And tomorrow?"

"It always comes, doesn't it?"

She nodded, nibbling her lower lip between her teeth. "Even when we're afraid of what it may bring."

"I promise to keep you safe… you'll be with me, no stalkers, no break-ins, no crying… just us."

"And if I fall for you?" She looked directly into my eyes. "What then? Who's going to pick up the pieces?"

"I never thought you'd lie to me." I searched her gaze. "There won't be any pieces to pick up, Lisa, because you won't trust me enough in the first place to give anything, let alone leave it in my hands."

She gasped.

I kissed her hard on the mouth, backing her toward the door, tangling her hair in my hands, gripping the silk, my tongue exploring her mouth like it was made for me and only me.

"Okay." She broke away the kiss. "Okay."

Little did I know that one more night with her would seal my fate forever… would align our destinies in a way I couldn't possibly fathom.

But that's what happened when you were blinded by your own attraction. Your own emotions, they rule you. So when you walk by someone taking pictures of you from the shadows… when you hear cursing from the dark corners, you don't pay attention — because you're blinded by your lust for her. And that's where I took my first stumble, not knowing I was taking her with me.

TWENTY-SEVEN

"So…" I licked my lips and waited. "…when do you leave?"

Mel looked up, her eyes wide. "Not for another month or so… but, I mean, it's not finalized. I still have to…" Her voice trailed off.

"Don't lie, Mel." I shrugged. "Guess I'll have to find a replacement for you, huh?"

Her face fell. "I'm not abandoning you—"

"Let's call a spade a spade." I flicked my cigarette onto the pavement. "You're abandoning me, but don't worry, I'll always be here." I tapped my fingers against my head and laughed. —The Journal of Taylor B.

Lisa

The minute we got into his car, I knew I'd made a mistake. What had I been thinking? After finding out who he really was, what his family was associated with, I was literally the last person on earth he should be with.

Next to murderers on death row. And even then, well… I shuddered. Did he even care about his image? The thought hit me square in the face: of course, he didn't care. He was teaching. At a university. For a semester.

"When do you leave?" I asked, too curious to keep my mouth shut, even though I knew it was what was best.

"What?" His voice was so smooth it made me forget that he was a bad idea, that we were a horrible idea. "What do you mean?"

"You're not taking the whole year off."

He shifted in his seat, a part of his demeanor revealing a bit of nervousness before he straightened up and shrugged. "Christmas. It's a big deal in our family now that—"

The car swerved.

"Now that?"

"What?" Tristan glanced over at me and raised an eyebrow. "Sorry. I didn't mean to say that. I was distracted by the, um… raccoon."

I smirked. "Wow, must have been a pretty raccoon to get you to swerve this nice car."

"I'd probably label it," he joked. "It was that pretty." Tristan turned his head to the side, his smile brightening up the mood in the car.

He was clearly unaware of what that smile did to a girl; he shouldn't be flashing it all over the place if he truly wanted one night of no commitments where I kept my hands to myself rather than running them through his hair.

I cleared my throat and tapped my fingers against the side of the door. "So, where are we going?"

"Do you have to know everything?" He grinned, taking a turn down a road I didn't recognize.

"Yes?"

"You plan," he stated calmly. "I may label things, but you plan, don't you?"

I coughed into my hand and tucked my hair behind my ear, then tried to offer a noncommittal shrug. "Who doesn't? I'm a college student. I'm basically forced to plan."

"Not normal things," He shook his head slightly, taking the next left. "You plan everything, don't you? Not just your classes and your major, but your life, each month, down to what you're going to wear the next day on the night before. Tell me you don't pick out your entire outfit with jewelry before you go to bed at night. Tell me your toothbrush isn't thrown away every thirty days so you can replace it with a new one," He reached for my hand. "Tell me you wash your jeans."

"Wh-what?"

"They aren't supposed to be washed." He brushed a kiss across the inside of my wrist. "But you plan, and you like things to be… orderly, so you wash them, just like I'm sure you don't own a pair of white sneakers for fear they'll get dirty."

"Well, white's stupid." I jerked my hand away and crossed my arms like a toddler. "And I don't wash all my jeans."

His eyebrows arched even though he didn't look at me.

"Okay, fine. So I wash them after wearing them even for half a day. Not a big deal. And really, isn't this just calling the kettle black? I mean, you label see-through plastic containers. Uh, I think we know they're strawberries."

Tristan burst out laughing. "Fine. You've got me there."

"I do." I nodded sternly. "So we both have… issues."

"Which makes my idea for tonight perfect."

"Oh yeah? Why's that?"

Tristan put the car in park and turned off the ignition. "Get out of the car, and I'll show you."

I looked around the empty parking lot. We were at a pier I didn't recognize. "The parking lot's really dark."

"Anonymous," Tristan whispered. "You thought that meant crowds?"

"Well, no." But really, I hadn't thought parking lot either.

He opened his door. "You can either follow me or stay in the car, but I imagine your curiosity will get the best of you. Another weakness."

"That isn't attractive." I scowled. "Pointing out all my weaknesses."

"It's only fair that I point yours out since mine are so obvious." Tristan eyed me up and down.

"Name one."

His whisper was so low I almost didn't hear it. "I'm looking at her."

The door slammed behind him.

Without another thought, I rushed out of the car and fell into step beside him. I gripped his hand so tightly it almost hurt.

"Knew you'd see it my way."

"You're really controlling."

"And a compliment." The moonlight washed over his features, making him look like an angel. "Careful with your pretty words. Don't want to harm my ego."

I rolled my eyes. "Your ego is just fine, I'm sure."

"Always." He smirked. "Now, up you go."

"Up? Up where—?"

"There." He pointed to a dock, where just beyond was a small houseboat.

"It's like *Sleepless in Seattle*."

"Rules…" Tristan stopped me on the middle of the pier, his hand brushing my lower back. "…for our night of anonymity."

I looked up into his eyes and tried desperately not to get lost in their gray depths, but how was I supposed to keep myself from leaning forward when his body was so warm? His expression both dangerous and inviting. "I'm listening."

"No phones." He slid his hand around my backside, carefully lifting my phone from my back pocket, his fingers brushing bare skin across my back in the process.

Goosebumps broke out on my flesh, and I fought the urge to let out a little moan. "Fine." My confidence was wavering already.

"No pictures."

"Kinda hard without my phone."

"True." He squinted at me and crossed his arms. "No promises."

I about choked on my tongue at that one. No promises. Neither of us could make a promise. For some reason, it reminded me of the games Taylor used to play with me, the twisted ones that ended up hurting other people and me in the process. I'd always been powerless against them; it was a reminder of my old life, a reminder I didn't need in an abandoned parking lot. I shivered. "Fine, no promises."

"And finally..." Tristan leaned forward, his body towering over mine. "...to keep things interesting... absolutely no touching."

With that, he walked past me and into the house, leaving my body hot, my heart hammering against my ribs, and my mind whirling as to what the heck he had planned other than a mean game of checkers.

Against my better judgment, I followed him into the dark house and shut the door behind me.

TWENTY-EIGHT

Take a pill — feel better. Take a pill — feel worse. Take a pill — feel nothing at all. Regardless of the pill, you take it to gain some sort of reaction. In a way, the website was like another type of pill for me. It gave me the reaction I needed to keep going... until one day, it just didn't. That was the day things fell into place for me when the plan was finally set in motion, the stopwatch clicked on, and I finally felt at peace. –The Journal of Taylor B.

Tristan

The house was completely dark. All I could see was the outline of the path to the kitchen, and only because the blinds hadn't been pulled. The door shut softly behind me.

I knew it was Lisa, knew that she had followed me, not knowing what I had planned for her went for longer than just one night, but several nights. Because I'd already decided with my own sick justification to have her, even if she wasn't mine to have, even if he'd had her first, even if he'd destroyed a part of her, I'd probably never be able to get back.

The room was so charged with sexual tension, it was almost hard to breathe, and when she stepped up behind me, her clothes brushed my back. I almost slammed her against the wall and just said, screw it. It's not like my moral compass had been actually working as of late. And she woke up something primal in me, something that I hadn't ever felt. I think I despised it as much as I craved it.

Sighing, I hung my head and let the seconds of charged silence trickle by.

"It won't be easy," I whispered. "Letting you in."

"It won't be easy," she repeated. "Keeping you out."

With a smile, I turned and looked down at her wide blue eyes, the same eyes that had seen tragedy at his hands. Pain, ruin, shame. The only thing I could do was be the exact opposite of what he'd been to her.

But it meant fighting against every urge I had to selfishly take what I wanted and leave come Christmas.

If I did that, I'd be just like him, and I wanted to be different. It was so tempting to burn that damn journal. To throw away my past, to live the lie, to make it so she never discovered the truth. Hadn't I lived my entire adult life in that way? Right along with my parents?

What was one more dirty secret between lovers? Friends? Enemies?

Maybe if she let me in, she'd divulge the information I needed anyway. It was always the fear that kept me pursuing the truth. The fear that I would end up like him, the fear that in some ways, I was him. The Jekyll to his Hyde.

"So, this rule…" Lisa folded her arms in front of her and leaned forward. "…does it apply to objects?"

"For not being such a rule follower, you sure are eager to learn what they are," I said smugly.

"For being such a controlling tight-ass, you sure don't seem to be in a rush to explain them."

I smirked. "You think my ass is tight?"

"No." She swallowed and looked down.

"Denial's so sexy…" I teased. "It's okay to look all you want, Lisa. You just can't touch, remember? A night of being anonymous… a night where it's just you and me. But technically, we're strangers and things…" I leaned in so close I could almost taste her. "…are about to get very intimate." Taking a step back, I lifted my shirt over my head and threw it onto the ground, then turned away from her and slowly slid out of my jeans. At her gasp, I made my way over to the fridge, where I knew I'd find some chilled wine, and pulled it out. I placed two glasses on the counter, then I turned to face her.

Her eyes were wide. I loved that look on her face, the desire evident in her heavy breathing. So I did what any logical man would do: I poured us two glasses of wine, brought her one, and whispered, "Strip."

She reared back as if I'd just asked her to jump into the Sound naked. Then her eyes narrowed. Slowly, she took off her shirt, followed by her jeans. I tried not to appear aroused, but the woman had hands-down the sexiest body I'd ever seen in my entire life. Blood roared in my ears as she finally faced me in nothing but a lacy black bra and fire engine panties with the words *Selfie*, on them.

"I wish," I murmured, looking down, arching my eyebrows.

It was too dark to see if she was blushing, and honestly, if she were, I would be shocked. After reading some of the things in that diary of Taylor's, it was hard imagining her blushing or getting embarrassed.

"Let's go." I nodded toward the fireplace and carried the wine bottle with me.

She followed, not speaking.

I flipped the switch on the fireplace, causing it to roar to life, then grabbed a few blankets from the couch and positioned them on the floor. I carefully wrapped one around her, careful not to touch her, and then sat down next to her.

"I'm confused," she said. "I thought—"

"You thought a night of being anonymous meant moonlight and masks…" I interrupted with a shrug. "But being anonymous is so much more than that. Clothes have a way of masking us, defining us, making us appear sheltered, unequal, depending on where it was bought. Tonight, you're in your most vulnerable state, next to being naked, with an almost-complete stranger. We're going to be intimate without touching, but only with each other, and when the night ends, we'll go our separate ways with no regrets."

"Because we didn't sleep together?"

"Because regardless of how naked you get, Lisa, your shield will always be up until you choose to take it down. Sleeping around, partying, drinking — they're all forms of protecting yourself. It's not freedom. You are never your most vulnerable until you've removed every lens you allow people to see you through. Some have one. Others have several."

She took a generous sip of her wine and laughed, but it was fake. "And what makes you think I have so many lenses, oh wise one?"

"Did I say you did?"

She was silent.

"And I think it's probably time we talked about that elephant in the room."

"What?" She snorted. "Me, being almost naked, having wine with my professor on a Monday night?"

"Oh that," I teased and gave her a wink. "We're anonymous, remember? Nobody knows we're here."

"True."

"I told you a secret… now it's time to trade."

The glass shook in her hand.

"Why were you crying tonight?"

"Stress."

"Fine. I'll ask differently." I shifted, so I was closer. "I'm sitting with Lisa right now… the first lens… the one that's strong, late to class, great kisser, hard worker…"

She stared hard at the flames in front of her.

"So let's try a different angle… the girl you used to be, Melanie Faye, why was she crying tonight?"

And just like that, I was given a vision of what Taylor had become so obsessed with, what had enraptured his attention and completely destroyed his sanity. Instead of being afraid, Lisa tilted her head to the side and narrowed her eyes. The light that had once been there — completely gone. And in its place utter darkness. Sweet, beautiful, addicting darkness.

I'd been wrong.

It wasn't the light that had drawn him.

But the beckoning call of the dark.

And like an idiot, I'd fallen before I knew.

"I would say screw you, but I imagine you'd just think it was an invitation, you sick bastard."

"You resort to name-calling when you get cornered?"

"Depends. Do you resort to seducing your students when you don't get what you want? I knew it was you, the guy I bumped into at the student center. You called me Melanie then. You've known this whole time." She leaned forward, the blanket dropping from her body, giving me a tempting view of her breasts.

"I was always curious." I changed the subject and looked

away, hoping she'd drop the fact that I'd called her Mel the first time I saw her; it was out of shock. "How does one compartmentalize so well?" I glanced back at her. "They don't. They just repress until the other part dies. You know it's similar with dissociative identity disorder. Shrinks used to suggest that each of the personalities decide who the strongest would be, and then, in what they thought was a stroke of genius, had the strongest personality kill the rest of them, leaving only one."

Lisa's eyes flashed.

"Funny how that never works." I sighed. "Just like repressing the person you are never works when you try to replace it with someone so out of this world vanilla and boring. I imagine you're both things... weak and insecure, paired along with being sexual and demanding. Your greatest fear is letting go. Am I right?"

She tried to stand, but I held up my hand. "Sit."

She sat, her jaw clenched tightly.

I continued, "At least for tonight, be both people."

"No."

"Yes, damn it," I growled. "Or are you that afraid of your past?"

"You know nothing about my past!" she screamed, her voice almost rattling the windows. "Stop psychoanalyzing me! It's bullshit! You know nothing!"

"So, tell me something."

Her chest heaved; she glanced at the fireplace and shook her head. "When you spend your teen years being so horrible, so terrible, so... bad..." She flinched. "...the last thing you want to do is be anything like that person you were or even the things associated with it."

I nodded. "You don't really want to be a teacher, do you?"

She said nothing.

"What would you do with your life if you have a choice?"

"Who says I don't?" she snapped.

"You do," I argued. "So tell me, what would you do?"

"Everything." She sighed longingly. "I'd do everything. I'd live. Drive fast cars again and forget the bad memories with them... maybe that's it. I'd do every single thing I did when I was younger, only I'd make it better so I wouldn't associate everything that used to be fun with pure evil."

"You've come to the right place."

"Real life isn't a movie, and I think we already established you aren't part of Mulan's family, so I highly doubt that means you hail from the good fairies."

I watched the torture flicker across her face. She was a girl who used to push limits, just like Taylor, only he'd ruined every single thing that could have been good. I had a vision of him finding joy in that. He always did find joy in the perverse of taking something so pure and tainting it. With Lisa, I was sure he'd seen the dark and thought... *finally, someone who can join me in my misery, someone I can alter forever.*

And he had.

"One thing," I asked. "Name one thing that was ruined for Melanie that Lisa wants to do."

"Drive a Ferrari," she said quickly. "You're not Obi-Wan. You don't get to know why. Just know... it was... ruined." Her face paled. "But driving fast used to be one of my favorite things to do. It felt... free."

"I'll toast to that." I lifted my glass and clinked it to hers.

Her eyes narrowed. "Don't tell me." She took a slow sip of the wine. "You have a Ferrari."

I leaned forward, so tempted to lick the liquid from her

lips. "If I didn't, I'd buy one just to see you let go."

"Is this about me or you, Tristan?"

I smiled — a genuine smile. "It's always been about both of us, Lisa. I'd think you'd know that by now. Besides, I was always the good son, remember? I've never even gotten a speeding ticket. I think it's about time."

"How?" she whispered, her lips pulled tight like she was trying not to reveal any sort of emotion. "How do you see so much when I try so hard to hide it?"

I wanted to tell her the truth right then, tell her I knew more than I'd let on, tell her I was sorry and ask her point-blank what she knew. Maybe she'd forgive me; maybe we could move past the pain together. I glanced up at her again. She was shivering even though she was in front of the fireplace.

Gaining her trust was the only way to gain her knowledge.

Falling for her hadn't ever been part of the plan, but I imagined it was too late. I was caught in the spell of her. She intrigued me, like a puzzle I was struggling hard to figure out. I knew once I did, I'd be rewarded with knowing the most amazing person in the world.

So I answered as honestly as I could. "Madness…" My voice dropped low. "…recognizes madness."

She gasped, her eyes narrowing. "I'm not crazy."

"Crazy people think everyone else is crazy, and they're sane. Believe me when I say I know you're not crazy. I'm talking about a different type of madness. The kind that follows you into your dreams, only to haunt you when you're awake. A madness that sucks joy out of every good thing in life and makes you feel guilty about smiling. Madness…" I repeated slowly. "…in its definition, is going in circles, repeating the same process over and over again, knowing you're going to get the same result but refusing to stop anyway."

"But I did," she argued. "I stopped it."

I was silent and then whispered, "But at what cost?"

TWENTY-NINE

He was so pissed that I'd called him. After all, I'd helped ruin his life, but in that moment? On the phone with him? I was like a god. Not only was I going to offer him his manhood back, his confidence, his life — but revenge on a silver platter. Funny, I was sacrificing the only thing I'd ever cared about, which oddly made me feel sad and angry all at once. I knew I was doing the right thing because she made me feel, and I had no business feeling in this world. I didn't want it, didn't have time for it. Not anymore. No, not anymore. — The Journal of Taylor B.

Lisa

"**Y**ou know," I said, forcing a smile. "You could have just seduced me instead of giving me a free shrink session. I would have been just as happy."

"No, you wouldn't," Tristan said quickly, leaning in until his face was inches from mine. "You don't want seduction."

I arched my eyebrows and let the blanket fall again, then met him halfway, almost brushing my lips against his. "I don't?"

"No." His gaze flickered to my lips, then back up to my face as he tilted his head. "A good seduction is wasted on a girl who wouldn't enjoy it enough to let go."

I gasped, half-tempted to slap him. "Is that your way of

saying you're crap in bed? Well, why didn't you just tell me? I would have understood."

He grinned. "Guess you'll never find out, and since I can't touch you, I can't really kiss you into submission." He blew against my mouth. "Pity." The sweet taste of wine lingered on his lips. "Because I imagine the best thing for you right now would be a good punishment… maybe a firm hand." He smiled, then blew against my mouth again. "A night of recklessness…" He jerked away and shrugged. "Yeah, it's really too bad I can't touch you."

I was frozen in spot. Why did it feel like he'd just spent the last hour seducing me? Why did it still feel like he was seducing me? Not with his hands, but his words.

"You're too beautiful to frown." Tristan reached behind him and pulled a down feather from one of the pillows on the couch.

"So you're going to tickle me to death?" I joked, though my mouth was completely dry, and I was afraid to move for fear I would give myself away. The anticipation was killing me.

Tristan grinned.

The man needed to stop looking so gorgeous and perfect. It was like the more I looked at him, the sexier he became, and he'd already started at a ten. Now? He was more like a twenty. So controlled yet taut, every muscle in his chest flexed as he twisted the feather between his fingers. My body hummed with pleasure just watching him. There had to be something seriously wrong with me.

He slid the white feather between his two fingers, back and forth a few times. "I wonder how much of your body would feel like this feather, soft… tempting… so damn alluring I just want to touch, caress…" He turned to me. "…kiss."

I gulped.

Tristan's eyes hooded as he moved toward me and slid the feather down my face, then slowly trailed it between the valley of my breasts. "I may have made a mistake when making those rules..."

"Oh yeah?" My chest heaved as I gulped for air. "Why do you say that?"

The feather dropped from his fingers. "Because not touching you tonight has been one of the hardest things I've ever had to do, especially considering..."

The room was silent except for the crack of the flames.

"Especially considering what?" I leaned forward, hanging on his every word.

"How damn tempting that mouth of yours is." He growled and reached toward my face but stopped just short of touching me. "Think of me tonight..."

"That's it? We get naked, you psychoanalyze me, find out I like to drive fast cars, and you just drop me off at my dorm?"

"Of course not." He quickly pulled back and stood, then offered his hand. "I'm going to help you up, the one and only time I'll touch you tonight, and slowly walk you to the bedroom, most likely watching the sway of your hips the entire way. And when I've gotten my fill, I'll imagine kissing you... everywhere, and then, I'll let you go to sleep and, well, lock my own door just in case you get any ideas."

I burst out laughing. "Afraid I'm going to take advantage of you?"

He pulled me to my feet with a jerk. "It's not fear that has me locking the door..." He turned around and began walking toward the stairs.

"What is it?" I asked as we made our way up.

He stopped, his hand pausing on the rail. "Necessity."

"You really think I can't help myself?"

His entire body tensed as he continued walking. "Not after tonight. I imagine you feel exactly like I do right now, left completely and utterly wanting."

Yeah, that was true, not that I was going to admit it to him.

He stopped at the second door on the right and pointed. "Your room."

I walked past him, knowing he watched me and shivering under his gaze.

"I'll wake you up for breakfast and drive us back in time for you to get ready before your first class. Besides, I think you have an early meeting with one of my other students tomorrow for the class project."

Groaning, I banged my head against the door. "Moment ruiner."

"Lisa?"

I turned.

He grinned and took two steps forward. He dipped his finger into my mouth, then pulled back and licked that same finger, his eyes closed in ecstasy. "Just like I remembered."

"I thought you weren't going to touch me."

"All men lie." He smirked. "Now go to bed before I decide to really have a taste."

"And if I tell you I want you to?"

His eyes went completely black. "Then I'll have to say no… even though I would really want to say yes. Go."

When I didn't move, he physically turned me around, pushed me into the room, and shut the door behind me.

Too stunned to do anything, I almost didn't register that I was spending the night again with him. But not *with* him, with him. I was more like a roommate that he liked around. I was thankful, nonetheless, because that was one night I didn't want to be alone.

And I knew that with Tristan, even though he seemed dangerous, he was safe. He wasn't Taylor. Not at all. And it wouldn't be fair to compare him to Taylor, even though I'd done that with every other guy.

It was finally time to move on.

And I thought I knew exactly who I wanted to do that with.

THIRTY

He'd almost agreed to do it after I explained things my way, and when he was still hesitant, I offered him one more thing I knew he couldn't refuse—wouldn't refuse. Her. —The Journal of Taylor B.

Tristan

By the time morning rolled around, I was one giant conflicted mess. My father had called and asked about business — the typical conversations usually lasted around three minutes. *Was he still rich? Was I keeping my nose clean?* Whatever the hell that meant. Had I ever let him down? Even once in my life? And the last, my personal favorite... *have I returned any of Erica's calls?*

Yes, yes, and no. But I'd said yes in hopes it would appease him. Talking to her seemed about as fun as calling Gabe and having him run me over with his car.

I woke Lisa up. She was quiet, pensive. I imagined I'd given her too much to think about. With a wince, I let her have her silent time. I knew I'd probably pushed her boundaries a bit, but I didn't want casual, not with her. She had to know that about me. Casual was meant for women I'd once met at my dad's hotel. Casual and Lisa did not fit in the same sentence. If we did this, if she truly let me in, I'd be hers forever, but I refused to let her think I was like him, so I'd pushed. I wanted the real her. Not the one I read about every night in his journals, but the one, the *girl* who had come out of that. The only problem? She didn't know who she was.

In fact, she had no clue.

She was afraid of the darkness he'd brought out in her almost as much as she was afraid of the light that she was still unable to reach. I halfway wondered if that hadn't been his plan all along. Self-doubt and insecurity make a woman lean on a man in ways that brainwash to the extreme. She becomes so dependent, so lost in the definition of who she is with that person, that when that person finally leaves, no matter how good or horrible he was, the memory is there forever, imprinted in her consciousness.

"Thanks." Lisa opened the car door but hesitated. Finally, she turned around, a blush staining her cheeks. "Thanks for a night of letting me be myself."

"Anytime." I held out my hand. When she'd taken it, I kissed her wrist and released her, even though I wanted to drag her across the center console and then pull her into the back seat. Acting like a caveman wouldn't get me anywhere, but it sure as hell would stop the constant ache I had to have her.

But sex wouldn't be surrender to her.

It would be submission.

And until it was something more, I refused to push that limit. Especially considering she wasn't anyone harboring dangerous secrets. I just wasn't sure anymore how or when I'd reveal mine.

The more time I spent with her, the more I refused to

acknowledge that I'd come there for a reason.

I watched her hurry into her dorm and made sure that the door closed behind her before I drove off.

Not really paying attention, I almost ran over a kid on a bike in front of me. He turned and glared.

It was Jack. My stomach knotted, but I had no idea why my body would react to his presence; he was just a student in my class. Just… something about him bothered me.

The minute he saw that it was me, his eyes narrowed. I had sunglasses on, and my windows were tinted, but I was probably the only professor on campus who had an array of cars from a decked-out Ford truck to a Tesla — and I just happened to be driving the Tesla.

I sped by and decided to run home and switch cars. I needed to anyway if I was going to follow through with my plan.

Operation Save Lisa.

Funny how it had started as Operation Redeem Taylor.

Funny how one person can change your mind, your heart, your soul so completely that you forget what you were fighting for in the first place. Consumed with thoughts of her, I sped all the way home with a smile on my face. It wouldn't be subtle; then again, that word had never really been in my vocabulary.

THIRTY-ONE

"You know I love you, right?" I whispered into her ear.

She shivered in response and tried to pull away. "Yeah."

"No, really." I tugged her closer.

She fought me. Her body was tense, but it was always tense.

"Let me show you how much."

I tried to remove her shirt. She stiffened at my touch, and I was so damn angry. I'd done that to her, but it was her fault for allowing me to. It was her fault for being so weak. It was my fault for being so strong.

"Lie down," I barked.

And just like that, she submitted. And the world was right again.

—The Journal of Taylor B.

Lisa

I barely had enough time to shower and get ready for the day when a knock sounded at the door. I grabbed my bag and keys and made sure my straightener was off, then ran toward the knocking.

"I'm coming!" I shouted. Geez, if it was Gabe, I was going to kill him.

I swung the door open. Jack stood there, leaning against

the doorframe. "So…" He tilted his head. "How was sleeping with the professor?"

I rolled my eyes. "Don't be an ass. I didn't sleep with anyone."

"You didn't come back." Emotion clouded his eyes, almost like he was hurt. "Last night, I mean, I was worried, so I came looking for you."

"Worried?" I walked past him and locked my door. "Why would you be worried?"

"One." He held up a finger. "Because I heard about your break-in. Actually, I think the entire campus heard about your break-in. And two." He held up two fingers. "One of the guys I worked with at the pizza shop totally got the shit beat out of him last night outside this dorm."

"What?" I stopped in my tracks. "What do you mean?"

His eyebrows furrowed together as he allowed me to go into the elevator first and then followed. "I mean, a guy who I worked with got his face smashed in and is in ICU."

My ears felt like they were filled with cotton. What if the attacker was the same person breaking into my apartment? Sending me hate messages? I shivered and suddenly felt better that I had my Taser with me.

"Hey, you okay?" Jack put his arm around me, but it felt all wrong like forced.

I don't know how to explain it; I just didn't like it, so I shrugged away.

His eyes flickered with a bit of irritation, and then he leaned back against the wall of the elevator.

"You know…" he said slowly. "…flirting with the professor isn't the smartest thing you've ever done."

"I'm not flirting," I lied. "And since when do you work at a pizza place? I thought you worked at Starbucks?"

"We live in Seattle." He rolled his eyes as the elevator dinged open. "I have to have three jobs to even afford my books and enough umbrellas to get me through the day."

I smiled. "It doesn't rain that much."

We stepped outside into a nice morning mist, and I'd officially forgotten my jacket.

Jack smirked and dug an umbrella from his shoulder bag, holding it over my head. "You were saying?"

"Shut up."

"I know I'm an hour early, but what about we get something to eat at the coffee shop, and we can go over our plan for the project?"

I sighed. I really wanted to make it early to class to impress Tristan, but two hours early did seem a little overkill. I stifled a laugh; he'd probably have a stroke if I was that early. If he was even at his desk. Then again, it was Tristan. I imagined he was the type that was an hour early only so he could prove a point.

"Fine," I relented, sending a sideways glance at Jack. "But I want to be early to class."

"Ah, so that's how it is." He nodded knowingly.

"What?"

"You and the professor. Keep getting in trouble, and he's going to keep making house calls. Smart."

"I'm not—" I shook my head. "Whatever. Let's just talk about the project."

"Sure." He grinned and held the umbrella higher over me. I ducked farther under it and collided with his left hand; the umbrella teetered a bit, so I steadied it with my right, gripping his hand in the process. I felt cloth and grimaced.

A large bandage was covering his entire hand and knuckles;

it was an ace bandage, and I hadn't noticed it before.

"What happened?"

"Pizza ovens." He shook his head, then winked. "Don't try to fight them. They fight dirty, and apparently, I lost."

I scrunched up my nose. "Sorry. Burns suck."

"Pain sucks." He shrugged. "But sometimes it's absolutely necessary."

"Except for this time," I corrected.

He swallowed convulsively, his eyes darting back and forth before he offered a kind smile. "Except this time."

The rest of our walk was easy. He talked about himself, and I listened while I tried desperately not to think about Tristan. I think I did a good job nodding my head and smiling. But my thoughts were consumed with the previous night, with what he'd said, how close it had hit home. How had he seen what Gabe even had trouble seeing? That just breathing in and out was hard for me, that I tried so hard to compartmentalize the person who I was, with the person I am. It was exhausting, not to mention stressful, since my past seemed to keep haunting me at every turn. I still had that stupid website to worry about. I just hoped people wouldn't recognize me in it, though I didn't think they would. I mean, who would imagine a normal girl like me starring in my own sex tape? Then again, you can't really be starring in something if you aren't aware it's happening.

He'd ruined sex for me.

He'd made it painful.

He'd made me want to vomit every time he touched me, but the guilt had been worse than the sex, the guilt that I'd been a horrible person to him, the guilt that he would take more pills if I didn't do what he wanted.

Tristan might be right about me trying to fight who I was, but if he truly knew how horrible I'd been, he wouldn't be encouraging me to try to discover my true self. No, he'd be helping me bury that demon or, as he'd said last night, kill off that personality for good.

"So, anger…" Jack sat opposite me in the booth and shook the rain from his jacket. "Why don't you write out different facial expressions while I go grab us some coffee and food?"

"Okay." I pulled out my notebook and went to work cataloging things I'd learned in class, like tight lips, narrowed eyes, clenched jaw — things that usually revealed a type of anger or repression. Funny, I had those memorized because Taylor was rarely happy. Anger was his companion. Then again, most of the time, he was so numb I wondered if he ever truly felt anything; I wondered if he ever wanted to.

"No," Jack said after reading my list. "Some of these are wrong."

"Well, according to the Internet and our textbook, they're all right."

"Wrong." He leaned back and folded his arms across his chest. "Anger can be a smirk, sure… but I think the most intense anger is the type of anger that people rarely see on the surface. It boils beneath, getting hotter and hotter until finally one day—"

He slammed his hand against the table. I almost spilled my hot coffee.

"—they just explode."

"So…" I swallowed and suddenly felt very uncomfortable that we were some of the only people in the coffee shop. "How would you describe that, then? In a nonverbal cue?"

"You can't." He leaned forward. "Because anger has too

many faces, too many masks. This type of anger is the kind you don't recognize until it's too late." His nostrils flared as he brushed hair away from his face.

The movement was familiar, oddly so. I narrowed my eyes, truly looking at him, examining Jack, because something about him didn't make me feel safe; it made me feel… wary, afraid.

"What?" He smiled, his big toothy grin making me feel a bit better. "You think I'm speaking from experience?"

"Are you?" My throat went dry at the question.

"Maybe." He nodded slowly. "Then again, how would you know?"

I reached into my satchel and gripped my mace tightly with one hand.

"And that…" he chuckled and took a sip of coffee. "… is my point. Geez, stop looking so serious. I just want an A, okay? And if lover boy wants us to dig, then we should dig, cool?"

I released the Mace, feeling a bit stupid. My spider senses had always been off when it came to people. I mean, Taylor had been Exhibit A, so I really shouldn't suspect a guy like Jack was anything but nice and studious.

"Right." I took another sip of coffee, feeling better. "Let's do it your way."

His eyes crinkled as he smiled. "I like the sound of that."

We worked for the rest of the hour, and then I made an excuse about needing to stop at the mailroom before class.

I still had an hour, but I wanted to check and see if I had any more threats. My hands were shaking by the time I turned my key and unlocked the little box.

Nothing but spam.

I released a tense breath I didn't realize I'd been holding

and quickly shut my box.

"Boo!" Someone gripped my shoulders.

I screamed and reached for my Mace again.

"Whoa!" Jack reared back. "Was totally not planning on you getting ready to karate my ass!" Laughing, he shook his head. "I think my stories about pizza wars and coworkers getting beat up are going to give you nightmares. You just forgot your notebook, that's all." He held it out.

"You could have given it to me in class." My heart was still hammering against my chest when I took the notebook from him and shoved it into my bag.

"Right." He winked. "Maybe I just wanted to see you again."

I gave him an annoyed look.

"Or maybe I want to get impaled by one of your sharp nails." He grimaced. "Alright, see ya later!"

He ran off.

And I was tempted to slump against the wall. He was right. I was being ridiculous and jumpy, and it wasn't his fault I'd left my notebook.

With a huff, I vowed to go decaf for the rest of the week and slowly made my way toward the social sciences building.

I made it to class with twenty minutes to spare. When I walked into the room, Tristan was already sitting at the desk reading some brown book. He still hadn't looked up, so I slowly made my way toward him.

The book appeared to be a journal. It had angry red writing on the pages, and a few things crossed out. There were pictures, but I wasn't close enough to see what they were of.

"Didn't take you for the type to read your own diary," I joked.

Tristan swore, dropping the journal to the floor, then bent and picked it up and shoved it into his desk. "You scared the shit out of me!"

"I would apologize, but I kind of like the fact that I caught you unaware and out of control."

His sexy grin had me wanting to both retreat and maul him.

"Lisa, if you want to see me out of control, all you really need to do is crook your little finger. I'll be at your mercy in seconds."

"Is that a challenge?"

"Hell yes, it is."

"I never back down from challenges."

"I hoped you'd say that."

"I could lock the door."

"I'd really appreciate the door being locked."

I grinned as he took a step toward me. The room was thick with tension. He held out his hand. I took it.

"Then again, if we leave the door open, there's always that rush you get when you think about getting caught."

"You want me to get fired over you?"

"Like they'd fire you." My smile was so wide it hurt. "My guess is your company donates just as much money as Wes's does."

"Ah, and she puts puzzles together well. Damn. I love that smart mouth of yours. The mind's not so bad either." He tilted my chin toward him. "But, sadly… now we only have fifteen minutes." He released me from his hold and stepped back. "And I would really hate to rush anything that has to do with my mouth on your body."

I gasped.

"You're not shocked." His eyes narrowed. "But I can damn-well tell you're a bit excited, which, in turn, gets me way too excited if I'm supposed to be talking about sociopaths today."

I giggled.

He reached into his desk and pulled out an envelope. "Open it after class when you're by yourself."

"What's this?" The envelope wasn't really heavy, but there was something rattling around in it.

"Guess you'll find out after class." He nodded. "Now go find your seat. It seems today you're so early you can get a head start on pulling out your notebook. I imagine it's the first time you've had that exciting feeling."

"I'm seriously shaking with nerves at the thought," I said dryly.

"Me too…" He winked. "But it was a different thought."

THIRTY-TWO

I had a month before she left. A month to damage her life, a month to plan. Then again, I'd been planning for a while. So really, all I had was a month to enjoy her before things went black. It honestly pissed me off — you have no idea how much it pissed me off, that tiny sliver of a feeling that tried to push through the darkness. I think it was guilt? Or maybe just a bad case of indigestion. I ignored it and pressed on. Funny, because if it was guilt, it just made me that much more determined to ruin her, to ruin a life that had such a bright future, whereas mine had been damned the very second I was born to the wrong family. Dad had called that day, asking about which pills I was taking. Honestly, they all ran together. I wrote down any physical symptoms, like getting a rash on my ass, as well as if they made me feel suicidal. Actually, every pill I was prescribed made me feel suicidal, but that feeling was always paired with what I'd like to call a god-complex. Yeah, I may want to die, but, man, in my death, I'd still be a god. I was untouchable. Totally untouchable.
—The Journal of Taylor B.

Tristan

I didn't realize how hard teaching a class would be with Lisa being that attentive. She'd dropped her pen twice and stuck it in her mouth at least a dozen times. Her tongue had popped out, touching the tip, and my entire body tightened at the sight. I literally had to teach from behind the desk because

I was afraid that the students would think talking about mass murders and sociopaths was a turn on for me when, in fact, it was the exact opposite.

This was the lesson I hated.

Because it was too close to home.

I knew more than I'd like to know about the topic.

"Sociopaths," I said in closing, "are usually well-liked, good-looking people. They're people you trust, people that seem like Good Samaritans. Take, for example, Ted Bundy. I think the misconception, especially with TV these days, is that if someone looks harmful, they are harmful. What about a stranger, someone you see on the street? Their hair is messy, they're talking to themselves, and they're waving their hands all over the place. They wave a gun in the air, and you immediately think they're going to start shooting."

I shrugged and glanced around the room, making eye contact with a few of the students without really seeing them. "Take a similar situation: a nice-looking doctor pulls out a gun and smiles. Are you going to immediately duck? Or will you think, *wow, is he protecting me from something?* Science has proven you're more trusting of those who appear to be trustworthy, which means those intelligent, attractive people who are, most likely, well-spoken. It's why you can't ever base your judgment on someone solely on his looks or what you perceive her intellect to be. You don't know their stories, and, for some of these cases you'll be reading about, the victims didn't know until it was too late. I'm not saying this to freak out the entire sophomore class."

Chuckles followed.

Good, I was still reaching them. "But I think it should be fair warning to look beyond the masks and into the person's soul. Study the nonverbal cue charts, and let that be what you put your trust in. Subconscious movements don't lie."

I checked my watch. "Alright, looks like we're out of time. Be sure to look over the human emotion study sheets. We'll be having a quiz tomorrow."

The sound of scraping chairs and talking filled the room. Lisa was rooted to her seat, her eyes glazed over like she was in another time, another place.

Jack waved in front of her face, then shrugged and walked off.

Students piled out of the room.

And finally, it was just me and her.

When she didn't move, I got nervous, so I shut the door to the classroom and slowly made my way to her desk.

Her eyes were wide, her mouth tight, jaw clenched.

"Lisa?" I whispered. "Is everything alright?"

"No," she said quickly. "But it will be."

In an instant, she was out of her seat and in my arms, her mouth pressed hotly against mine. I wasn't ready for her attack, so I almost fell backward. Gripping her shoulders, I tried to brace myself, but she held on to me for dear life.

She kissed me hard.

But not with passion.

No. Her kiss tasted like fear.

So, I kissed her back hard enough to gain the upper hand, then slowly retreated my mouth so that I could nibble on her lower lip. When she let out a whimper, I rained soft kisses on her cheeks, and finally her forehead, then pulled her in against my chest. "Whatever it is, you can tell me."

"No." She shivered. "I can't. It's just... maybe one day, but that day isn't today. One day I'll be brave enough to throw all those masks at your feet. I just don't think I'm ready yet."

"Kissing me won't make it go away." I sighed. "Not that I'm complaining at all about your methods."

She sighed, her hands wrapped tightly around my waist. "I'm sorry. It just seemed like a good idea at the time."

"Kissing…" I pulled back and gave her a soft smile. "…is always a good idea."

She flushed. "I should probably go to my next class."

"You can open it." I nodded to the envelope. "Now that the classroom is empty."

A look of pure joy crossed her face before she reached for the envelope and tore it open.

The key dropped out with a note taped to it.

"From Anonymous," she read aloud. "Hmm… wonder who that is?"

"No clue," I said seriously. "Some people like to keep their identity a secret just in case the gift receiver isn't happy with the gift."

"So, a key?" She lifted it into the air. "Is my gift?"

"Let's just say the experience is the gift." I shrugged, hoping she would get the hint not to make a big deal. Then again, if buying you a car gets me in your good graces, I'm all for it."

"A car?"

"Look closer."

She brought the key closer to her face and squinted at it. "Holy…" Her eyes flashed to mine, filled with a hundred questions.

"*Vroom, vroom?*" I smiled and leaned closer. "Oh, and you're going to love this part."

"What part?"

"The shopping, of course." I grinned, satisfied with her

stunned expression. "Now get to class. I'll text you later."

"But—"

"You know how I feel about being late."

Rolling her eyes, she put the key in her back pocket, grabbed her bag, then reached up and kissed me on the cheek. "Thanks for the surprise."

"Don't thank me yet."

She laughed softly, and damn-near skipped out of the room.

THIRTY-THREE

"I have a secret," I mused, drawing circles in my journal, feeling marginally better since my asshole of a father had given me more pills. "Wanna know?"

"What?" Mel asked, her expression shuttered.

"I'm going to die." I shrugged. "Just thought you should know since it's going to be your fault." I held up a piece of fruit. "Hungry?" — The Journal of Taylor B.

Lisa

I think in all my twenty-one years of living, I'd skipped once, maybe twice. And both times, I was probably in pigtails. But he made me want to skip. A Ferrari? I knew he was extravagant, a bit crazy, but I felt… special, like he'd really listened to me.

By the time I skipped back into my apartment, the easy, happy-go-lucky feeling was gone.

Both Wes and Gabe were waiting inside, sitting on the couch, looking pissed.

"Is, uh, everything okay?" I dropped my bag onto the floor and crossed the room.

Gabe looked up first, his eyes menacing. Wes put a hand on his shoulder as if to keep him from lunging at me.

"Is everything okay?" Gabe asked, then turned to Wes. "Oh, I don't know, what do you think, Wes? Do I look okay? Does it look like sunshine's sprouting out of my ass?"

"I'm not looking at your ass." Wes rolled his eyes. "And stop being so dramatic."

Gabe's nostrils flared, and he locked his eyes on me. "Your professor."

"Which one?" I bit my lower lip and stood behind a chair, just in case I needed to throw it down and run away while Gabe tried to tackle me to the floor.

"Ha!" Gabe clapped slowly. "Hilarious. Which one, which one, which freaking professor? I seriously can't have kids, man." He looked at Wes again. "No seriously, if girls are going to pull this type of shit, I'm out. Give me boys, you hear that, God?" He started pointing at the ceiling. "I know you can hear me because you saved Wes's life, so listen up, no girls! NO girls!"

I looked over at Wes and raised an eyebrow. "Is he losing his mind?"

Wes groaned into his hands while Gabe shot to his feet and charged toward me. "Making out with your professor *on* school property *in* your dorm? Tell me you aren't that stupid!"

"I'm not…" I swallowed and averted my eyes. "I'm not stupid."

"I'm not calling you stupid."

"You're accusing me," I snapped and pushed against his chest. "Same thing."

"Mel, swear to all that is holy if this has gotten any further—" Cursing under his breath, he turned away and tugged at pieces of his blond hair.

Gabe only called me Mel when he was pissed or when he forgot that I was supposed to be Lisa. He knew it made me insecure and upset. He knew the name brought back too many horrible memories.

Sighing heavily, Wes stood and marched over to Gabe, then shoved him toward the couch. He roughly pushed him down.

"Okay…" Wes's eyes were wide. "Let's try this my way before Gabe has an aneurism." He tilted his head to the side and flashed his typical Wes Michels' I-can-get-anything-I-want smile. "I thought you and my friend were just… friends, especially after discovering each other's identity. I mean… it's not like I threatened him or anything, but I did tell him that dating a student would be a bit frowned upon."

"We aren't dating."

"Shit." Gabe whistled. "He's dead. I'm calling in a favor. Wes, I'm sorry, but we're killing your friend. Clearly, he's seducing her!"

Wes rolled his eyes. "Watch the footage again. I think you'd be surprised who seduces whom."

I felt my cheeks blush, and then anger boiled up inside. I'd forgotten those damn cameras. "What the hell, Gabe! You were watching the tapes? Like a psychopath? And why come to me now, guns blazing! You should have called or something!" Security footage? My stomach heaved at the thought of Gabe and Wes watching me make out with Tristan like some horny teenager. Pretty sure at one point I was straddling him or was he on top of me? I was going to start sweating any minute. Heat blasted into my cheeks as I tried to recall just exactly what had happened.

"Wes had a game," Gabe said through clenched teeth, interrupting my thoughts. "And I was in Portland at a freaking meeting. Believe me when I say I came as soon as I saw the…"

He shook his head. "…whatever. It's like you don't care that I'm the only person who's protecting you from crazy stalkers and would-be assassins!"

"Assassins?" Wes repeated, his lips forming a smirk. "Good one."

"You know what I mean." Gave waved him off. "And it's not like I put one in your bathroom. I'm not that much of a paranoid control-freak. You know they've been on. You knew about them, Lisa. Hell, you saw them get installed. Why are you so surprised I'm checking up on you? It's not like I can move in and sit at your door with a gun!"

"Though, he would if he could." Wes nodded. "Just saying."

"Ass," Gabe said hoarsely. "You're supposed to be helping."

"This is me helping." Wes shrugged and faced me again. "Look, it's not a good idea. You and him…" He lifted his hands in the air and pushed them together and apart and then shook his head and walked off. "Just kidding. I'm not helping. Gabe, you're up."

Gabe shot from his chair. "What Wes is trying to say is sleeping with the faculty, though guaranteed to give you an A, isn't the way to start your sophomore year if you plan on graduating or keeping the guy from getting fired. Besides, his father would freak if he knew—"

I reared back, colliding with the chair behind me and then the table. The candles flipped out of their holders, rolled off the table, and hit the floor with a bang.

Tears threatened to escape.

"Aw, shit." Gabe reached for me. "I didn't mean that, Lisa. You're fine. It's not you."

"But it is." I nodded as a lone tear escaped and rolled down my cheek. "Isn't it? If his dad or family find out he's dating a girl who's to blame for someone killing himself… what then? Right? If they find out that the girl was involved in one of the biggest bullying sites on the Internet? If they find out a girl like me was freaking raped in one of those videos! But the video made it look like I asked for it? What would he do? Fourth in line for president! Right, gotcha, I need to stay away because I'm a disease, and it's only a matter of time before I spread."

Wes and Gabe both fell silent as more tears streamed down my face.

A soft knock sounded at the door.

I stomped over and yanked it open. My jaw dropped as I came face to face with Tristan. He stared at me for a split second, then pressed his lips into a hard line and pulled me in for a hug.

Warmth surrounded me as I returned the hug, pressing my face against his firm chest.

He nudged me into the room and kicked the door shut. When I pulled back, his gaze was murderous, though not directed at me, but Gabe and Wes. With a curse, he lifted his hands and wiped some of the tears from my cheeks with his thumbs. His jaw flexed as he shook his head and then narrowed his eyes at the guys.

"What's going on?" His voice was hard, and even.

"You tell me." Gabe crossed his arms.

I stayed in Tristan's embrace. I felt dirty, used, spoiled, like I wasn't even good enough to fight for. It was stupid for them to argue because, in the end, Gabe had been right. I know he hadn't intentionally tried to hurt me, but hurt me he had because he'd reminded me of what Taylor had told me right before he died.

"You're used goods. Trash. You think a guy would touch you

if he knew the things you've done with me? You think a good guy would even kiss those dirty lips of yours? I own you. Body and soul. You're bad, like me, and the worst part is, you won't even own up to it... at least I do. At least I know I'm bad."

I hugged Tristan tighter, turning my face into his chest. I listened to the rapid beating of his heart and tried to match my breathing to the thump, even though with each second it was increasing.

Wes spoke up first. "We put cameras in the room... for her safety."

Tristan tensed and then swore under his breath. "And you saw us kissing?"

Gabe's voice cracked. "Yeah, we watched the PG-13 pizza party without sound, though, so don't get too pissed off."

"So..." I glanced up just as Tristan's jaw clenched. "...let me get this straight. You decided to confront Lisa, by herself, without anyone to defend her, especially the guy who was just as guilty, and then made her cry, thinking that would actually help your case?"

Gabe closed his eyes and sighed. "I hate Lisa's tears. She should know that by now. I live for her smiles. That's it. I love her. She's like a sister to me... I'm protective, yes, but she's been getting threats."

"Threats?" Tristan repeated, his face falling. "You mentioned something about threats at the benefit, and she did get attacked."

"She hides them from me."

"I'm right here!" I snapped, irritated that even Tristan was stepping into protective mode yet wasn't even asking me how I felt about three men charging around my room stomping and roaring.

Gabe kept talking. "But I'm not stupid. She gets them in her mailbox, switches mailboxes, but they keep coming. Her dorm's been broken into, and the website—"

"Gabe, that's enough!" I shouted. "Just leave it!"

"Website?" Tristan repeated in a low, intense voice. He settled his stare on me. "What website?"

"Gabe!" I begged, breaking free of Tristan's hold and running across the room. He didn't know what I'd just found on that site, and he was about to reveal it to the one guy I liked. "Please, please don't, please." I clawed at Gabe's chest, pulled at his shirt, trying to get him to look at me so he could see the absolute terror on my face. When he finally made eye contact, I knew it was pointless.

His eyes were sad, heavy with guilt. "Lisa, he has to know. If he's invested, he has to know. If he isn't… then he isn't worth your time."

My body began to shake… he would know. He would know everything, and he'd leave before I ever got the chance to kiss him again or feel his protective arms around me once more time. He'd been the only guy in years I could kiss without feeling sick to my stomach, the only one who had challenged the old me and the new me. Gabe was taking that away from me.

The thing about your past… it never stays there. We just think it does until the time comes for it to reveal itself in all its gory shame. And there's nothing, absolutely nothing a person can do, but watch.

The world turned to slow motion for me when Gabe walked over to the computer and started typing. My body felt too heavy; my head pounded as blood rushed to my temples. The website would still be saved in my search history because

I'd been looking at it last night.

He must have noticed because he cursed under his breath. I knew the rules, knew Gabe didn't like me digging up my past ghosts. When the webpage popped up, I groaned, swaying on my feet.

Tristan was at my side immediately, tugging me toward the monitor, toward the sickness. I watched like I wasn't actually part of the nightmare in front of me. When Gabe clicked on the video, I almost puked. And when the talking began, when I heard Taylor's voice, I finally caved.

I burst into tears, ran into the bathroom, and lost everything I'd eaten that day and then some. When my stomach was empty, I lay down on the cold floor and sobbed.

All good things… really do come to an end, don't they?

THIRTY-FOUR

I truly believe all good plans take time and strategy... this will be my last entry. If you're reading this, know that you were chosen for a reason beyond getting insight into the mind of a madman. I chose you. I chose you just like I chose her. I bet you're curious. I bet you wish you knew why I chose you. Two copies of this journal exist in the world. You have one, and another chosen person has the other. You should thank me for allowing you to see part of my plan, for allowing you to see what others can only dream about. Don't worry... we'll meet again, even if it's just in your nightmares. –Final Entry — Taylor B.

Tristan

I was battling between chasing after Lisa and listening to what Gabe had to say because he had the look of a guy trying to help... or maybe he just looked helpless. But I knew enough about him, about Wes especially, that they would never hurt their friend intentionally. And I had a sinking feeling in my gut that this had everything to do with Lisa's past.

I craved the information I knew they had, but I hated myself for wanting it and not being able to ignore the fact that they could have the truth I needed in order to move on.

"The website..." Gabe's eyes clouded with anger.

I could hear Lisa's soft sobs coming from the bathroom.

Gabe swore and kept talking. "…was called Shame."

The website pulled up immediately.

Videos of people embarrassing other people flooded the homepage. Nothing too crazy. More like a glorified YouTube, only it focused on bullying.

"People post anonymous videos… the whole idea behind it was to shame people who deserved it without having to be blamed for ruining their reputations."

"That's messed up," I muttered, wondering if Lisa had been shamed on the site, feeling protective all over again.

I clenched my fists as Gabe shook his head and compressed his lips as if he was struggling for control.

"Look." He scrolled down. "I'm showing you this because you seem to care, but Lisa isn't like you. She isn't like any of us. She's fragile. She's been through more in her short life than I can possibly imagine, and you need to know that she isn't the same person. She was brainwashed… the sick bastard played on her insecurity, played on her desire to get noticed." Gabe swallowed convulsively and clicked on a video, then stood back. "And this is how he thanked her for her loyalty."

The video started. I heard a guy's voice talking, and then I saw a girl stumble forward. I knew what was happening, what would happen. I looked away. "Shut it off."

Gabe clicked the pause button and cursed under his breath. Wes was silent from his spot on the couch.

"Twenty-seven," Wes finally spoke up. "We had to take down twenty-seven videos… She was in all of them, Tristan."

"Getting freaking raped?" I shouted, knocking the chair over with my hand. "Where the hell were you, Gabe?" I lunged for him but stopped because he didn't even lift up his hands. Instead, he closed in on himself and hung his head.

"Here," Gabe said slowly. "I was here. I had no idea it had gotten so bad. I finally got her out, helped her get into school, but by then, it was already too late."

"He did what he could." Wes came to his defense. "The only video we can't take down is that one. For some reason, the new owner of the site is basically unreachable. We've sent cease and desist letters, but it's based outside the US, so we're powerless. The only positive is it's the only one that still plays."

"But it's up," I said quietly. "And it's only a matter of time—"

"Nobody would recognize her... not unless someone tipped off the media."

I looked at the frozen screen, my heart twisting in my chest. The guy next to her was Taylor. The only reason I knew? He'd left a picture in the journal. I wanted to join Lisa in the bathroom in that moment. I wanted to break down, to punch something, preferably the guy who had ruined her.

The guy who had raped her and taken joy in it.

The guy who had manipulated her and relished her pain.

But most of all? I wished he was alive so I could send him back to hell.

"The guy's name," I whispered, needing confirmation of my suspicions.

"Taylor Blaine."

"No." I wanted to avert my eyes but met Gabe's cold stare without flinching. "That's not his name."

He and Wes shared a look.

"It's Taylor Blaine Westinghouse, Jr." My voice shook. "My half-brother."

THIRTY-FIVE

The look of joy on his face right before he jumped made me sick. I called 911 with trembling fingers. When they arrived on the scene, I was already down at the river bank. The EMTs thought I was going into shock over the trauma, when really I felt nothing but relief. —Mel

Lisa

The bathroom door opened and shut. I expected Gabe to slide down on the floor with me, offer his hand, and then hold me while I cried my eyes out.

Instead, it was Tristan.

I wanted nothing more than to grab one of the towels, put it over my face, and sob. I refused to look at him; instead, I looked straight ahead at the brassy gold knobs on the cabinet below the sink. I watched the knobs flicker in the crap fluorescent lights. I watched them like they were my only way to stay sane.

Tristan moved in front of me and turned on the water. His body was tight, every muscle strained. His worn jeans hugged his legs; his T-shirt did the same to his stomach. His back flexed as he shut off the water and then turned to face me.

I averted my eyes again; my own breathing was the only

sound filling the room. My chest felt so heavy I thought it was going to explode.

He knelt in front of me and touched the hot cloth to my face, slowly wiping away what I'm sure what a mess of mascara and tears. His eyes revealed nothing. He continued examining my face, tilting my chin as he washed. When he was finally through, he placed the cloth on the floor.

I waited for the gauntlet to fall — for him to tell me he couldn't see me anymore, couldn't be associated with me, for him to say things like I was a disgusting, horrible person.

Instead, he held out his hand and whispered, "Let's go drive fast."

Gasping, I jerked my head up so I could see the condemnation in his eyes. He was messing with me, right? But his hand was there right in front of me; all I had to do was take it. Take the hand and hope the body attached to the hand wouldn't betray me — wouldn't hurt me — because I was completely broken in that moment, the most vulnerable I'd ever been. And taking his hand wasn't just a physical act, it was an emotional one. I think he knew that because he moved it closer until finally, he cupped the back of my head and used his other hand to brace my hips.

"All you have to do is say yes."

"Yes…" My voice was hoarse from crying. "…is a very scary word."

Tristan caressed my cheek. "But it doesn't have to be, Lisa."

With a deep breath, I reached for him and allowed him to help me to my feet. I started walking toward the door, but he held up his hand and shook his head. Deflated, I crossed my arms to close myself off.

"Shower." Tristan nodded. "It will make you feel better.

Take a shower, put on jeans and a sweatshirt, and in the meantime… I'll wait."

"Right." I swallowed the bitter taste in my mouth. "For how long?"

Tristan's eyes never wavered from mine. "As long as you need."

The door shut silently behind him. I wasn't sure if I wanted to sob with relief or shame. Possibly both.

Slowly, I turned the tap. Water burst from the showerhead, and steam began to fill the room, choking everything in its wake, making me feel the need to disappear in its fog and never come back. I slipped out of my clothes and let them fall wherever they landed, taking care not to look at myself in the mirror. Knowing that if I did, I'd break. My nakedness reminded me of my vulnerability. I gulped for air. Humidity hit my face as I stepped into the shower and allowed the hot water to cascade over me. It combined with my tears. I wasn't sure where my crying began and where the water ended. He was right. It made me feel better, not good enough to laugh, but at least good enough to feel the need to get dressed instead of drowning myself. Ten minutes later, I wrapped a towel around my body and pulled open the bathroom door.

Tristan was sitting on the couch talking to Gabe in hushed tones while Wes stood by the window on his cell.

All of their expressions were grim.

I quickly slipped into my room and tossed on a pair of skinny jeans and a black hoodie, then brushed on some lip gloss.

By the time I returned to the main living area, both Wes and Gabe were gone.

"They left?" I asked, shivering but not sure why.

Tristan shrugged. "They had some business they needed to take care of. Besides, they aren't invited."

I cracked a smile at his haughty attitude.

"Just you and me?"

"Yeah." Tristan nodded slowly, his eyes drinking me in. "Just you and me." There was that stupid trusting hand again. I took it. I gripped it. I embraced it and closed my eyes, trusting him completely and hoping I wasn't making a giant mistake by doing so.

"Alright."

He wrapped his arm around me and kissed my head, whispering, "It's going to be okay. I swear it."

Maybe it made me naïve. But I believed him. In that moment. I believed him.

THIRTY-SIX

They said he was still alive, though his back had broken on impact, along with one of his legs. Freaked out, I watched the EMTs work on him. I heard someone shout that they were losing him, and I did something no human being should ever do. I turned and walked away. —Mel

Tristan

Keeping my hands from shaking was a lot harder than I thought it would be. Every time I saw the look of hurt cross Lisa's face, I wanted to pull the steering wheel from the car and throw it, but who would I aim for? Taylor was dead, and, honestly, it felt like I was too.

My chest hurt with each breath.

For her to go through what she'd gone through.

To even, for one instant, think I could reveal who I was? What I was to her? No. That couldn't happen. My father had had things right when he said it needed to stay a secret. It did. For her sanity, it truly did. I would take it to my grave and feel no guilt whatsoever about keeping the demon in his prison of hell. The only loose end was Gabe and Wes. But it wasn't my own guilt that had me confessing; it was my need to protect Lisa at all costs, even if it meant they had to eventually protect me from her.

I was still worried about what had set him off the edge, worried because I'd been diagnosed with something similar. Then again, my own father functioned just fine, though he seemed to be just as heartless and callous as his sons.

"This isn't a Ferrari," Lisa whispered.

"No." I barely got the words past my dry lips. Licking them wasn't helping; I was a nervous wreck as we turned the corner to my house. "The Ferrari is parked, just waiting for you to take it for a ride."

She didn't smile.

And it killed me, literally made me want to pull over and do anything and everything in my power to get her to smile again. To get her to realize that it wasn't her fault, regardless of her involvement in that stupid website, it wasn't her fault that she'd been taken advantage of. Nobody deserved to be raped.

"Alright." I put the car in park and hit the garage opener. "Now, you are going to have to pick a color…"

Lisa's eyebrows furrowed. "Pick a color? What? Like you have a car lot—" Gasping, she covered her mouth with her hands as the lights clicked on, revealing not one Ferrari, but three — along with a few other cars and toys that I rarely used but had looked nice at the time. Now it all seemed pointless. The money, the lies — all of it.

"Well." I cleared my throat. "What are you waiting for?"

"How?" she rasped. "How do you have three Ferraris? No, scratch that. Why? *Why* do you have three?"

"Too much money." I sighed and tapped the steering wheel. "And too much freedom when I came into it."

"Red." A ghost of a smile appeared on her face. "I think I like the red."

"You can't just pick a Ferrari from thirty feet away, Lisa.

You have to touch it, caress it…"

"Am I buying it dinner later?"

"Hell, no." I opened the car door. "You don't want to make me jealous, do you?"

Her smile fell. Just like that.

As if the idea of me being attracted to her wasn't even a valid one anymore, but stupid, an impossibility.

One I was more than happy to tackle, even if it killed me.

Lisa slowly walked up to the garage and went to the side of the red one. "I think I like this one. Yeah, I want to drive this one."

"Alright." I went over to the spot on the wall where I kept my keys, grabbed them, and tossed them in her direction. "Just one thing before you get in."

Lisa fingered the keys and shrugged, her shoulders slumped. "What?"

"I don't want to get in the car with Lisa."

She stiffened.

"And… I don't want to get in the car with Mel."

Her shoulders slumped even more as her lower lip trembled.

"But you?" I said with a clear voice. "The woman standing in front of me… scars and all… shame… and all? I would really, really love to get in a car with her."

A tear slid down her cheek. "I don't know who you're talking about."

"Let me tell you about her," I whispered, walking around the car. "She's beautiful… like stare-so-hard-you-run-into-a-wall beautiful."

She let out a pathetic laugh and cried harder.

"She's brilliant…"

Another step toward her.

"Has this crazy blue streak in her hair that I honestly think fits her really well. It's a part of her past mixed with a part of the present."

Her clear blue eyes lifted to meet mine from beneath thick black lashes.

"Her lips are an addiction, in and of themselves. One that any man would be insane to give up." I cupped her cheek.

Those beautiful eyes fluttered closed, and another tear escaped. It slid down to meet my palm.

"And she is one of the strongest women I've ever met."

Lisa shuddered. "She's a stranger. I don't know that woman."

"All you have to do is look in the mirror, Lisa, and you'll find her. I think I'm falling for her... this girl I want to take a ride with, this girl I'm trusting my Ferrari with. I want to be with her. I want her to trust me. I want to chase those demons away, and really, most of all, I want to help her discover who she is because I imagine she'll fall in love with that person almost as much as I have."

Lisa's entire body relaxed against my hand. I slipped my other hand behind her head and pulled her in for a kiss, not expecting her to want to kiss me back, expecting her to be timid.

Instead, she launched herself at me. She wrapped her arms around my neck and her legs around my waist. The keys dropped to the ground, forgotten, unimportant as I moaned and opened my mouth to hers.

The kiss was all aggression, all passion, all trusting, and, in that moment, I knew I was never ever letting her go.

Her mouth opened to mine over and over again, giving me intimate access into parts of her I wanted to taste, to explore for as long as she'd let me. My entire body was tight with the need to take her inside. Never had I wanted a girl so desperately. She moaned, tightening her hold around my neck, dipping her hands into my hair and tugging.

I pushed her up against the car, probably scratching it, not caring if it decided to all of a sudden break in half if that meant I could have her right then and there.

She arched her back as I plundered her mouth, my free hand moving from her head down to her sweatshirt. I slowly lifted it so I could expose her skin.

"Thank you," she panted against my mouth.

My hand lingered as I pulled back and looked at her.

"Please tell me you aren't thanking me for kissing you," I teased. "Better yet, prove your thanks and get your mouth back here."

Lisa smiled a real smile and released her legs from my hips, slowly and painfully sliding down my body. "For saying those things... for being you."

Guilt whispered. I ignored it and pulled her in for another scorching kiss. "Anytime."

"Drive." She nodded. "We should drive before—"

"Before I take you upstairs and throw the keys into the lake? Yeah, we should do that."

THIRTY-SEVEN

The sirens were so loud, my head pounded. By the time I reached my car, I saw more cars had pulled up, including a black unmarked vehicle. A gentleman stepped out, dressed in a suit and sunglasses — which was weird. I mean, it was close to midnight. I shivered, my hand on the ignition. If I drove off, I could get in trouble. But I didn't care. He was gone, and I didn't care. I felt nothing. Maybe that had been his plan all along — to get me to turn into an exact replica of him. Heartless, numb. —Mel

Lisa

I hit the accelerator as we turned a corner and gasped as the feeling of adrenaline coursed through me. Adrenaline had always been bad. I'd associated it with the things Taylor had me do.

Because the God's honest truth? When I first met him… it had been exciting, exhilarating. He'd had me start small, little things. It wasn't like he'd just asked me straight up to ruin someone's life. No, it had been small, little justifications I'd made in order to appease him, and after each justification had come an even greater reward. Someone older than me — rich, sexy, dangerous — wanted me and thought I was sexy. I'd never felt sexy. I was always too tall, too lanky, and thin to feel sexy. My body was a mannequin, but Taylor'd made me feel like a goddess when he touched me — when he worshiped me. The least I could do was listen to him when he asked for tiny little favors.

And when I made him laugh or groan with excitement, I, in turn, had gotten excited because I was the cause. Only… after a while, I needed to do more and more in order to have that adrenaline rush. He hadn't warned me that would happen, and by the time I looked in the mirror and hated myself, it was like I no longer had a voice.

"What are you staring at?" Taylor came up from behind and wrapped his arms around my body. "You're beautiful."

"I'm ugly." I averted my eyes. "What I'm doing is ugly."

"Ugly…" Taylor repeated, gripping my chin tightly in his hand, forcing me to look at my own reflection. "…is just a term people use to categorize things they don't understand. Some days you're ugly," he whispered in my ear. "But those are the days I love you the most because you're at your worst. And isn't that what true love is, Mel? When I can look at you in the eyes and say I love you, despite the darkness inside? Despite the ugly? See?" He grinned menacingly. "We're perfect for each other because I get you, and you get me."

I shivered, hitting the brake so hard that the car swerved.

"Lisa." Tristan put his hand on my shoulder. "Sometimes it's okay to go fast…"

"He was so confusing," I whispered. "Like what he said to me always made sense, Tristan. It always made sense. I mean, it was like my brain was cobwebs, and he'd pull a bit away, and I'd feel better — but only for a while. Then the confusion would happen again, and he'd make it better. But it never lasted. And when I finally started questioning him, he turned on me. But it was like he expected it like it was just another stage of our relationship. I felt… manipulated." I shook my head at Tristan. "I don't want to feel that way again like I don't have a voice. Like even my thoughts are being silenced."

Tristan gripped my right hand. "I will never make you feel that way, Lisa. Nobody deserves to be silenced."

My chest heaved like I'd just been jogging.

"Do you want to go back?" Tristan asked after a moment. "Because we really don't have to keep driving fast…"

"He made all the good feelings shameful." My voice cracked. "So no, Tristan. I don't want to go back. I'm going to go forward."

His eyes lit up as he leaned back against the seat. "Then, by all means, beautiful, drive."

All things considered, I'm surprised I didn't get a speeding ticket. By the time we reached Tristan's house, I'd been driving like a NASCAR escapee for the past hour. It had been years since I'd felt so exhilarated, so alive.

I parked the car, hopped out, and grinned, gliding my fingertips along the smooth red fender like it had just given me a gift.

"It's yours." Tristan came up behind me and wrapped his arms around my waist. "Whenever you want to drive it, it's yours."

I laughed nervously. "For a second there, I thought you were giving me a car."

"Oh, I am." He released me. "But I figured you'd say no if I just came out and said, 'Hey, Lisa, take it home.' So you can keep it here, but I think you've left your mark on it as much as it's left its mark on you. It would be a tragedy for me to ever get behind that wheel when it's meant for your body."

Grinning, I turned around and threw my arms around his

neck. "Just because you're rich doesn't mean you should give people things that cost more than a nice house."

He chuckled. "Of course it does. What's the point in having money if you don't get to spend it on the important things in life?"

"I'd be happy with a Ford Focus." I kissed him softly on the mouth.

"Which is exactly why you get the Ferrari." He deepened the kiss, sliding his tongue past my lips, before speaking again. "Because you'd be happy with a Ford Focus or a tricycle, or even a high five... and I think you deserve more than all three."

"Thank you." Heat raced into my cheeks as I stared hard at his chest. "For the ride."

Laughing, Tristan pulled away and shoved his hands in his pocket. "Oh, Lisa, you really don't want to say things like that to me, not when you look that beautiful, and not when my self-control already waved goodbye two hours ago." He jerked his head toward the door. "Dinner?"

I twisted my hands in front of me, excited and nervous at the prospect of being alone with him a few more hours. "That depends."

"On?" His smile was so sexy I almost moaned out loud.

"Your self-control."

That sexy smile grew so wide I darn-near fainted.

"I'll be the perfect gentleman..." He held out his hand.

I took two steps.

And then he added, "...until you ask me not to be."

With a *whoosh*, all the air left my lungs. I took his hand and squeezed. "Overconfident today, are we?"

"Hopeful." Tristan tugged me into his chest. "Just really damn hopeful."

With a lame laugh, I pushed past him, staggering into the hallway, feeling drunk off the looks he was giving me, off the feeling he gave me by just being him. Not caring about who I was then, but who I was now.

"So…" Tristan placed his hands on my shoulders and led me into the kitchen. "…how about I cook, and you tell me one more thing."

"One more thing?"

"That you miss — that he stole from you."

Yeah, I about swallowed my tongue because there were a lot of things he'd stolen the joy from, that much was true; but there was one thing in general that had hurt the most. He'd stolen my pride in myself, what it felt like to feel beautiful to a man. He'd stolen what a guy never had the right to steal — my self-confidence.

Tristan pulled out a pan and began rummaging around the kitchen. I chewed my lower lip while he reached for a knife.

"Sex," I blurted. "He stole sex from me."

The knife in Tristan's hand clattered to the countertop. His entire body tensed as his fingers pressed into the hard granite — knuckles white. He swore violently before finally turning around and facing me. I knew he'd turned because I'd been watching his body — not his face, definitely not his eyes because eyes revealed too much. And to see his pity? Well, I wasn't really sure I could handle that, wasn't sure if my confidence would suddenly crack, and I'd burst into tears.

"Lisa," Tristan barked. "Look at me."

Slowly, I lifted my chin.

Tristan's gray eyes were blazing. I wasn't sure if it was hatred or something else… something far more possessive. "No guy has the right to take that from you."

I nodded, my throat swelling with emotion.

"Just like no guy has the right or power to give it back," he whispered, his voice tinged with a bit of sadness, maybe even regret. "Listen very carefully… you are the only one with the power to take it back, but you have to make a choice."

"I suck at choices." I played with the empty glass in front of me, twirling it between my hands.

"No, you don't." Tristan walked around the bar. I could feel the heat of his body behind me as he placed his hands on the counter on either side of me. His lips touched my ear. "You give power to it when you feed the fear. When you keep his memory alive."

"You think I want that?" I snapped, trying to push away from him. I was trapped by his hands instantly.

"No." He kept a firm hold on me. "I think you believe you can't help it, but you can… you can help it. Don't give him that satisfaction. Don't feed his power by keeping his voice, the voice of a liar, in your head."

Tristan removed his hands and walked back around the counter, and started cooking again while I sat there, stunned, a bit hurt, and confused. Why couldn't he just make it easy and sleep with me? Why couldn't he chase the demons away? It would work. It would have to work.

Then again, what would happen in the morning? When I was all alone again…

I'd hear Taylor's voice.

His scorn, mockery, contempt.

And the fear would be back.

But how did you banish something so cemented in your psyche? It was like he was still alive in my head, regardless of what I did.

"Go for a swim," Tristan said. "Clear your head."

"Swim?" I repeated. "You want me to swim?"

"Either swim or over-think things until you give yourself a headache. Use the hot tub or lap pool. I have spare suits from parties I've thrown, and I'm pretty sure one of them will fit you. Take the trail down to the pool. The bathhouse is on your right... and relax."

"Relax." I almost laughed out loud. "Right."

"Professor's orders."

"To put on a bikini while he cooks for me?"

"Exactly." Tristan flashed me a sideways grin and kept working.

"Fine." I pushed away from the barstool and slowly made my way down the trail. Maybe he was right; maybe it would help.

Besides, the last time I'd swum was at one of Taylor's pool parties; may as well swipe one more thing he ruined off my list.

THIRTY-EIGHT

I drove away that day...from everything. I went home, packed all my stuff, and bought a ticket to Seattle. I didn't even take my car—I'd just buy one up there. I needed to escape so desperately that the money didn't matter. My parents were just happy I was smiling again—which is sad considering someone had to die in order to put it back on my face. —Mel

Tristan

Cutting vegetables while so pissed off you couldn't see straight? Probably not the best idea I'd ever had. I was such an ass, but I'd needed to get rid of her. It was damn-near impossible to hold my anger at bay, and all I really wanted to do was slam my hand against the counter until either *it* broke, or the counter broke.

"Damn it, Taylor." I hated him. I'd never felt such hate for another human being in my entire existence; it was overpowering, exhilarating, terrifying.

I dropped the knife and dialed Wes's number. He answered on the second ring.

"Anything?" I barked.

"Whoa, you alright?"

"Would you be alright?" I turned around as the sound of water splashing hit my ears. At least she wouldn't hear our conversation; at least I'd had her leave before I lost complete control and scared her shitless.

"No," Wes finally said. "I wouldn't be, and sorry, we haven't found any medical records. Nothing. I have my PI working on it. Gabe has his contacts working on it, but... it's like he never existed. Though we did finally catch a break on the website."

"Yeah?"

"Sure. I should have the information to you by tomorrow. Just do yourself a favor."

"What?" My eyes were trained on Lisa's body as she swam across the pool.

"You gotta tell her, man."

"No." I shook my head. "No. I can't."

Wes sighed heavily, the puff of breath amplified over the phone connection. "Look, I'm not saying she's going to take it well."

"No shit."

"But..." Wes continued, his tone making it clear he wasn't receptive to an argument. "...can you imagine if she found out later? If she found out that you kept this epic secret from her?"

"That's what you guys are for... to make sure she doesn't find out. It will only hurt her more, and I'm done with my family hurting her. Done."

"What exactly... are you doing then? Really. I'm curious."

"Giving her exactly what she needs."

"Which is?"

"Healing," I said softly. "Look, I gotta run, but keep me posted."

"Yeah... just... think about it, Tristan. That's all I'm asking."

"I will." I wouldn't. I hung up the phone and stared at the

meat as it cooked in the pan. The past needed to stay buried, and I'd do anything to keep it that way, just like I'd do anything to keep that smile on Lisa's face.

I finished cooking the meat and added in all the fixings for tacos. By the time I'd set the table, Lisa walked in, wrapped up in a fluffy towel, an easy smile across her face.

"Have fun?" I asked, matching my grin to hers.

She wrapped the towel tighter around her and plopped onto one of the barstools. "Your pool has two waterfalls."

"Yup."

"And a slide."

"True."

"And a diving board."

"You gonna tell me all the things my hot tub has too?"

"I mean, a swim-up bar?" she said, ignoring me. "Can I just live in your pool forever?"

"Hmm…" I leaned forward, bracing my hands on the counter. "…that depends. You gonna turn into a mermaid and go topless?"

Her eyes narrowed. "No."

I shrugged. "Sorry, no deal."

"Perv."

"No." I chuckled and pointed at myself. "Honest man."

She laughed with me. "Okay fine. That's a valid point. At least you didn't lie and say it was okay only if I wore a one-piece and sombrero."

"Yes to the sombrero, no to the one piece." I shuddered. "Always no to the one piece."

"Ah, he likes skin."

"Only yours."

I fought to keep my mouth from falling open as she

dropped the towel lower, giving me an enticing view of her skin.

"Only yours."

Her face flushed. She looked at the food and pointed. "So, tacos? Who told you?"

"Told me…" I raised my hands in a show of innocence. "…that you hated tacos? Shit, do you hate tacos?"

She grinned and started piling up her plate. "Nope, I love them. Next to pizza, best food ever created."

"Thank God, you're not a vegan, organic-loving, soy milk drinker."

Lisa popped a chunk of ground beef in her mouth. "Sorry to disappoint you, but I'm more of a cheese-loving, hamburger-eating, whole-milk-drinking, potato chip cruncher."

"Chip of choice?"

"Lay's Sour Cream and Onion." She rolled her eyes. "Like there's any other choice."

I nodded my approval. "And cheese?"

"All cheese. That's not even a real question. You should know this by now."

"Hamburger? With onions or without?"

"With, but I like the little crunchy ones that are fried and tend to permanently find their way onto your hips."

"Yeah, I hate that." I winked.

Lisa rolled her eyes and loaded up two tacos with sour cream. "And you?"

"Doritos… ranch." I rubbed circles on my stomach and lifted my eyebrows in teasing. "Though I'll eat anything with a crunch."

Lisa paused before biting into her taco and chewing. "So you'd eat a crunchy spider or snail?"

"Only if I was dared…" I started making my own tacos. "And only if they had ranch on them."

"Cheese?"

"Gouda."

"Snob."

"You know this about me. Plus, Gouda always has the best labels; all expensive cheeses do."

"Hopeless." Lisa took another bite and wiped her mouth. "What about you? Hamburgers with or without onions?"

"Am I with you?"

"Umm… sure."

"No onions." As Lisa chuckled, her smile had me staring at her mouth for a good few seconds before I responded. "Or give me onions. Since you'll be eating them, it wouldn't make a difference anyway. I'd still kiss you… and I'd still really enjoy it." And that was the truth.

That was the last of the food talk. Lisa averted her eyes and chewed while I tried to wrack my brain for more ideas to keep her with me rather than drop her back at the school.

From her purse came the sound of her ringtone. Damn it. I hated phones. Always interrupting things, interrupting us. I wondered if she'd be pissed if I threw her entire purse into the pool and took her with me, stopping all interruptions for good.

She wiped her hands on the napkin and pulled out her phone. After reading through it, she groaned. "Ugh, Jack."

Every nerve jumped to high alert as I cleared my throat. "Oh?"

"Yeah." She typed something into her phone. "He wants to meet tomorrow morning again about the project."

"Just out of curiosity." I worded the question carefully.

"How often have you guys been meeting?"

"Just twice." She put her phone back in her purse. "I think we have the basis for our project outlined and ready to go… at least I hope so. I hear this professor's a tight-ass."

"How nice of you to notice." I winked.

At her blush, I grabbed the dishes and started cleaning up, needing the distraction that cleaning would give me, so I didn't do something regrettable, like throw caution to the wind and jump over the table and attack her with my mouth.

Lisa started helping me with putting things away.

The kitchen was cleaned up way too fast.

I had half a mind to spill stuff out of the fridge just so she'd stay longer in order to help me clean it up.

"So." Lisa folded her arms across her chest. "What now?"

"I can take you back…" I really hated saying that out loud. "…or you could stay the night."

"Like a totally harmless sleepover?"

"If by harmless you mean we sleep separate and I only think about taking advantage of you, then yeah, totally harmless."

"So honest."

"At least I have that going for me, right?"

"I'd say you have a lot more going for you." Lisa wrapped her arms around my neck and grazed my lips with hers, a whisper of a touch that left me craving something deeper, longer, more passionate. "A lot more going for you."

"Tacos never tasted so inviting." I licked the side of her mouth and pressed another hungry kiss against her lips. Moaning, I lifted her up onto the clean countertop, pulled her legs around my hips, and kissed her from a different angle.

Every angle had a taste.

Every kiss was different.

And every time I touched her, I wanted more.

"Harmless sleepover, huh?" She panted against my mouth.

I took a step back and cursed. "Right, so I'll just lock my door."

"Again." She grinned.

I rolled my eyes and helped her off the counter. "Yeah again." I gripped her hand and led her down the hall into the theatre room. "So what movie?"

"Anything." Lisa yawned and sat down in one of the chairs. "Actually, anything but one of those psychological thrillers."

I winced. "Alright, *Dumbo*, it is."

"Saddest Disney movie ever."

"I think you're confused with *Up*."

Shaking her head, Lisa ignored me. "Those animals were bastards to him!"

"There wasn't even any dialogue, just the old man and woman holding hands."

"And they made fun of him all the time for being different!"

"He never took that trip… never had the chance. Damn mailbox."

"His poor mom!" Lisa punched the chair. "At least he ended up flying."

"And then the little boy ended up saving him."

We shared a look. Lisa burst out laughing and covered her face with her hands. "Okay fine. *Up* it is."

"Now I'm kind of in the mood for *Dumbo*."

Her eyes heated. "Sad, I thought you were going to say something else."

My body hummed to life as I hovered over her chair. "Oh yeah, what's that?"

She leaned up and kissed my chin. I stifled a groan.

"Butter… smothered over popcorn."

"Say smother again."

"Smother."

"Done." I pressed a kiss to her mouth. "You load the DVD of your choice…" I tossed her both movies. "…and I'll go smother your popcorn."

"Talk dirty."

Laughing, I made my way out of the room, thinking to myself how normal it was… not just normal, but how wonderful it was.

My phone buzzed in my pocket.

Erica. Again.

I hit ignore.

If she wasn't getting the hint now… she never would. As I waited for the popcorn to finish, I had a sudden feeling of home. What if I stayed? What if I ran the company from the Seattle office? What if I stayed… for her? What if I stayed?

I wanted to.

For as long as she wanted me, I would stay.

Dread tried to make me doubt that choice because there would always be him in between us. But I wasn't going to let it ruin what could be something so beautiful.

He'd ruined her before, and I'd be damned if he ruined her again.

THIRTY-NINE

I didn't watch the news for fear I'd be on it. The crazy thing? Nobody called me. The cops didn't contact me; nobody did. It was as if that past didn't exist. When I got to Seattle, I had my parents' lawyers work on taking the website down. In the end, it was nearly impossible to get all the videos down. I was surprised the website was even still up, but later we found out it had changed domains to outside the US. I remember shivering, thinking, wow, Taylor really did have it all planned, didn't he? His memory lived on through Shame; it lived on every day through me, and I hated him for it —Mel

Lisa

Colors and characters flashed across the screen as the movie played. My eyes were so heavy it was impossible to keep them open long enough to actually watch what was going on. I startled myself out of a doze probably four times before I finally gave in and snuggled against Tristan's firm chest. The steady beat of his heart was my lullaby. His hand dipped into my hair, twisting and tugging, making me relax even further. Before I knew what was happening, I was asleep.

He woke me up around two in the morning; the only reason I knew was because of the clock on the wall.

"I don't want to move," I grumbled.

Tristan shifted next to me and then pulled me tighter into his lap. "Then stay."

"Ask me again."

"Stay, Lisa…" He kissed my forehead. "…with me."

I sighed happily against him and murmured, "I really like you."

"Yeah, well… I really like you too."

"Should we make necklaces or something? I can wear your tight-ass professor jacket to school… prove to everyone we're going steady."

Tristan's warm chuckle had me smiling. I kept my eyes closed. "It would only make sense."

"Does that mean you're going to label us?"

"Yeah." Tristan tucked my hair behind my ear and kissed my cheek. "I think I'll type in the word *girlfriend* and slap it onto your face. That way, there's no confusion."

"Better put whose girlfriend."

"That's easy…" He hugged me tighter. "Mine."

"Yours." I smiled again. "I like the sound of that."

"Yeah, that makes two of us."

I fell asleep after that, unable to keep my eyes open any longer. The next morning we barely had time to scarf down breakfast before Tristan drove me back to campus.

He gave me a hungry kiss before ushering me out of the car; both of us had meetings, though mine I wasn't exactly thrilled to be having.

"So…" Jack's voice nearly had me tripping over my own feet as I reached my dorm. I turned around and squinted against the sun. "Is it just me, or is our professor taking a really special interest in you?"

"It's you." I rolled my eyes. "I have to grab a few things.

Why are you so early all the time?"

"Part of my charm." He grinned. "Can I come up with you? Sorry, I just really have a headache, and the damn Seattle sun is killing my eyes. Promise I won't make a sound. I just want to lie on your couch and forget the fact that I actually don't need my umbrella today."

I hesitated for a minute, then realized I was being rude. "Um, sure."

"Awesome."

We walked in silence up the stairs and into my room. I pointed to the couch and dropped my keys onto the table. Jack went over and made himself at home, punching the throw pillow and closing his eyes like he really didn't feel well.

"Do you need ibuprofen or anything?"

"Is it laced with opiates?"

"Um, no."

"Then, I'm good." Jack flashed me a smile and closed his eyes.

"Okay, well, I'm just going to hop into the shower really quick, and then I'll be ready."

He lifted his hand into the air, waving me off. "Take your time."

I grabbed my bathrobe and ran into the bathroom. It was weird that he was in my room, but I tried not to overthink it. He'd been nothing but nice and protective, and it was totally wrong for me to assume that he was anything but a good guy.

I showered, dressed, brushed my teeth, ran my hands through my messy hair, put on a baseball cap, and managed to swipe on some mascara — all within fifteen minutes.

"Lisa?" Jack's muffled voice came from the main room.

I shut my bedroom door and ran out. "What's up?"

Jack was completely white like he'd seen a ghost. "I'm not trying to freak you out more, and I'm pretty thankful I'm here right now, all things considering, but I think you should look at this." He held up a newspaper clipping. Angry red markings had been scribbled across it: *Your fault!*

I read the caption, *"Young man jumps off bridge, falls to his death."*

Feeling sick, I took a step back and covered my mouth so I wouldn't puke all over the place. My stomach dropped to my knees.

"Hey, hey," Jack came around and draped his arm over my shoulders, then guided me to the couch. "Sit down, it's okay. It's going to be fine."

"Where…" I croaked. "Where was that?"

"Taped to the inside of your door."

"*Inside* of my door?"

"Yeah." Jack nodded. "I didn't notice it until I looked up from my nap. Whoever put it there…" His voice trailed off.

"I have to move." I shook my head. "I mean, my place has been broken into, the hate mail… I have to move."

"Probably not the worst idea I've heard all day." Jack gave an innocent and semi goofy shrug. "You want to go report it?"

"No." I put my hand on his. "No, that's fine. I'll take care of it." More like, I'd have Gabe take care of it. I was going to give it to him — all the threats, all the notes. I was sick of dealing with it. All of it. I was finally happy, and I deserved to be happy. Tristan had taught me that.

Jack gave my hand a reassuring squeeze. "Then, at least let me buy you a coffee while we go over the project. I promise we don't have to get all crazy with our plans, but let's get out of here because it's kind of creeping me out."

I nodded my head a few times before getting up. When I did, Jack put a protective arm around me and led me to the door.

"I would say to lock it, but—" He shrugged. "—a lot of good it's been doing you."

"That's reassuring."

"Just saying."

By the time we made it down to the coffee shop, I was in a better mood, probably because Jack had somehow managed to turn my fear into hysterics with his crazy stories and antics. I felt guilty all over again for being so suspicious. Especially after he'd bought me another coffee and made me eat a pastry.

"So..." said Jack, pulling out his notebook. "...we're supposed to find case studies. The prof, you know the one you've been riding in that car with..."

I rolled my eyes.

"...he gave us about a billion different links to stories. We just have to click on the emotion and *boom*, pick out five."

"Do you have your computer?" I asked.

"No." He shrugged. "I left it at my place, but I can always stop by tonight and go over them with you. It will seriously only take us like ten minutes or so."

"Okay." I took a sip of coffee. "That's fine, but make it around five because I think I may have plans."

Jack grinned. "Would these plans start with a P?"

"Huh?"

"Never mind." He saluted me. "Five it is. Now run along to class. We both know how the professor gives good grades to those who are early."

"Right." I laughed along with him and grabbed my stuff.

I took the usual route to class, stopping at my mailbox

since I had around twenty minutes before I needed to be there. I braced myself for impact and shuddered when I had one piece of mail.

It wasn't addressed to Lisa.

It was addressed to Melanie Faye.

I swallowed the fear in my throat and closed my eyes. Tristan had said to take control. With a grimace, I opened the envelope and pulled out a slip of paper. All it said was. *Ding-ding… your time is up.*

With a curse, I pulled out my phone and texted Gabe. I grabbed the other notes out of my backpack, stuffed all of them in a large manila envelope, and left it at the post for him to pick up.

The minute the student worker took it from my hands, I felt lighter. I was done. I was so done. For the first time in weeks, I felt a smile grow on my face as I thought about going to class. I wasn't Melanie Faye anymore. I was Lisa. Lisa was strong. Lisa was independent. Lisa didn't get scared when threatened. She didn't back down.

Lisa drove fast.

Lisa liked cheeseburgers.

Lisa liked Tristan.

And Lisa… was here to stay.

FORTY

*The minute I came to Seattle, I told Gabe I'd changed my name...
well, I hadn't really changed it. My name had always been Lisa, but
at a young age, my agency had told my parents to give me a stage
name, something about protecting my identity and all that, so they
did. And I was so grateful they had done that for me because now I
could go back to being normal Lisa, not Mel, the girl with the dark
past and sinful secrets. —Lisa*

Tristan

I hated how close Jack hovered to her. Then again, if I wasn't
teaching the damn class, I'd probably be doing the same
thing. The quiz went by slowly. The clock ticked in the
background, and the journal in my bag may as well have been
screaming at me.

I'd finished it.

And I was more resolute in my decision than ever that
they were the ramblings of a seriously insane individual. I just
wasn't sure if that made me feel better or worse.

Better because that meant that Lisa was innocent.

Worse, because by omitting my true identity, I was
allowing her to live another lie. But if it was to protect her?
Then I would keep lying — I had to.

"Pencils down." I stood. "Pass your papers to the left and

leave them on the farthest desk. Grades will be posted this Friday. Dismissed."

Students filed out.

Jack lingered.

I gave him a pointed stare. Smirking, he lifted his hands in surrender and walked out, leaving just me and Lisa.

"That wasn't obvious at all," she said in a reassuring voice. "Really, I think it went right over his head."

I shrugged. "It's Jack."

"True."

"How was your meeting?"

"How was yours?"

"You first."

She slumped in her seat. "Well, I did get another threat, but," she said quickly, "you'd be proud to know that I handed all pieces of evidence over to Gabe, and I made a big decision today."

"What's that?" I slowly made my way to her desk and sat on the top.

At her grin, my heart almost stopped. Damn, she was beautiful.

"He doesn't have the right to control me anymore. So, whoever's sending me that crap is going to burn in hell or prison, whatever happens soonest. Gabe will turn it over to the police. I'll make a statement, even though it's the last thing I want to do, and things will go back to being boring."

I put a hand to my chest. "Ouch! Are you calling me boring?"

"I really, really like boring."

"Because that makes it better."

Lisa stood and leaned in just as a throat cleared from the

doorway. Jack stood there, holding up his notebook. "Lisa? Sorry to interrupt, Dr. Blake, but I think I accidentally stole her notebook, same color and all."

Lisa blushed and quickly grabbed a notebook from her desk and ran it over to him.

"Thanks." He took it from her hands and sent me a curious look. "See you tonight, then?"

I clenched the desk tightly.

"Sure," Lisa squeaked. "Tonight."

Jack closed the door behind him.

I waited for Lisa to say something.

When she didn't, I walked past her, locked the door, crossed my arms, and asked, "Tonight?"

Lisa crossed her arms, mimicking me. "Jealous?"

"Let's call it mild curiosity."

"Or insane jealousy."

"A twinge of jealousy. Can hardly even define it as jealousy if it's a twinge, right?"

"Does that make you feel better?"

"Immensely."

"Homework." Lisa gripped my hand. "He's stopping by for a few minutes to go over some homework from this really sexy professor."

"Okay, now I'm jealous. You better be talking about me."

"And if I'm not?"

"Then I'm clearly not wearing the right clothes to show off that tight ass you're always talking about."

Lisa burst out laughing and reached up on her tiptoes to place a kiss on my chin. "I think my other professor has gout."

"Sexy."

Lisa kissed my mouth, her tongue slowly dipping between

my lips, touching mine with languid smoothness.

I groaned and pushed her against the door, pinning her arms above her head.

"And after?"

"Wh-what?" Out of breath, she panted beneath my assault as I trailed kisses down her neck.

"After you meet with him?"

"I have a private tutoring session with you?"

"Damn right you do." I kissed her harder. All the passion I felt inside was going to explode if I didn't do something about it. I wanted her so bad it hurt. It hurt to control myself, and I hated that I had to. Hated that she needed me to.

"Mmm..." She rimmed her lips with her tongue when I pulled away. "That felt good."

"Go to class." My voice cracked. "Before I throw you across my desk and take advantage of you."

She winked. "At least I'd earn an *A*."

"You'd earn way more than an *A*." Visions of her body underneath mine plagued my thoughts. Cursing softly, I turned away. "Yeah, you really need to go. I'll see you tonight?"

"Six?"

I still didn't turn back around since I was trying to hide a very physical and obvious reaction to my little image of her on my desk naked. "Yup."

"Thanks, Dr. Blake." Her voice was low, sultry.

I cursed again as her laughter floated out of the room.

FORTY-ONE

Finally, things were normal my freshman year... I'd met Kiersten and Wes, and things felt... happy. So happy that I should have known the other chips would fall. Soon Gabe's secret was out... and then, mine was too. —Lisa

Lisa

For the second day in a row, I skipped back to my dorm. Not surprising, I found both Wes and Gabe waiting for me again when I got to my room.

"Wow!" I shook my head. "Should I just let you guys move in? And where are Kiersten and Saylor? Do they know how much you check up on me? Because I'm pretty sure they wouldn't approve of all the babysitting." I was tempted to text Kiersten or Saylor but knew both of them were super stressed since they'd taken on so many credits to graduate early.

Gabe gave me that look, the one that said he was seriously pissed, while Wes just paced. It seemed, most of the time, Gabe was ready to attack, and Wes was there to make sure he didn't do anything stupid.

"Thirty," Gabe said, tossing the threats onto the table. "How the hell do you have thirty threats without me knowing?"

Feeling slightly guilty, I sat down next to him and stared at all the different pieces of paper; they varied in size and color, not one of them the same. The angry black block letters were always present, though. "You just got married, Gabe. I'm not going to slam you with all this after you just got over Princess's death and moving in with Saylor and — it's just a lot!"

"And me?" came Wes's stern voice. "Why not me?"

I rolled my eyes. "Because I think dealing with cancer and playing for a professional football team should be enough stress to last you a lifetime, not to mention you have a wife too."

Neither seemed convinced.

In fact, it was like the more I talked, the angrier their expressions became.

"Sorry?" I finally offered.

"Damn right, you're sorry." Gabe groaned into his hands. "How can I protect you if I don't know these things?"

"It's not your job."

"It is," Gabe said loudly. "It is my job. I'm your family, Lisa. Me and Wes, we're not going anywhere, and if there's one thing I learned last year, it's that you can't just carry everything yourself and hope it doesn't kill you. It will kill you. I think you know I know this. Now, we have a plan."

"We?"

"Me and Wes."

"And me?"

"You get no vote because you've been like an errant child." Gabe shook his head. "But I think you'll like it."

"I'm listening."

Gabe put an arm around me and sighed. "First things first. Pack up your crap. You're moving off campus."

"To where? Witness protection?"

"Sort of…" Wes and Gabe shared a look before Gabe swore and pulled his arm away.

"Let it just be known that I'm not a fan of this part of the plan, but dipshit over there thinks it's a great idea because of the security. But I swear, Lisa, if he touches you without you as much as begging him to touch you, I'll break every single finger from his hand."

Wes rolled his eyes. "What he means is… if he's anything less than a gentleman, tell us, and we'll move you right away, but because of who his father is…" He nodded. "His security is probably better than mine and Gabe's combined."

"He?"

"Tristan," they said in unison.

I smiled.

Gabe groaned. "Stop smiling."

I smiled harder.

"Don't make me regret this, Lisa. I'm serious!" He pointed his finger at me and stood. "Just pack up enough stuff to stay for the week, and next weekend we'll help you move. I can't today because I'm flying back down to Portland with Saylor for a wedding, and Wes has practice."

"Okay." I stood. "Did you talk to the police?"

"Going there next. Your safety is first. The police tracking this bastard down is second. Just be careful, carry your Mace, and stick close to Tristan."

I smiled again.

At my third or maybe fourth smile, Gabe barked, "And stop looking so damn happy about it."

"Love you, Gabe." I ducked into his arms and sighed as he wrapped them tightly around my body.

"Love you too, Lisa. Just be careful, okay? Not just in

general, but with your heart. I couldn't handle it if it broke."

"Promise." I kissed his cheek and went over to give Wes a hug too. Both guys left a few hours later, after going over more of the plans they were going to put into place around campus, and by the time they left, I was exhausted.

I set my alarm so I'd wake up in time to meet with Jack and fell into a dreamless sleep.

"Don't move," a voice said. "Keep your eyes closed. I like you like that."

Terrified, I didn't move. My heart rammed against my chest. Someone was in my room! Someone was with me in my dorm.

"It's almost time, Mel." The voice was muffled like the guy was talking through layers of clothing. "Almost time… shh… so pretty lying there, so innocent, when we both know you aren't. I'll be back. You can count on that. Scream, and I'll only hurt you. Call the police, and you'll just look crazy. Now keep your eyes closed like a good girl so I can leave."

I squeezed my eyes tighter.

Terrified that if I opened them, the guy would attack me.

When I heard the door shut, I jolted from the couch and ran after the guy. When I opened the door, it was Jack waiting on the other side, raising his hand to knock. "Whoa!" He gripped my shoulders. "Are you okay?"

"A guy—" I choked out the word. "—a guy came into my room, and he — he said things, and… did you see him?" I tried to peer around him, but Jack's expression was furrowed, his eyebrows drawn in.

"Lisa, I'm not trying to be a prick, but I've been standing here for at least a minute. There wasn't anyone leaving your room. They would have run right into me."

"But, Jack, he was here! I swear!"

Jack nodded. "Okay, it's not that I don't believe you, but what were you doing when he came in?"

I backed away. "Sleeping, but—"

Jack shook his head. "Then it was probably a nightmare."

"But he was in my room!"

"Lisa." Jack braced my shoulders again. "You've had a lot of stress lately, with having your room broken into and being romanced by our professor."

Great. He was making jokes.

"Why don't I take you to get some food? I've got my laptop anyway. No need to sit in your creepy room."

"I don't know…"

"Come on." He walked into my room, grabbed my bag, and held it out to me. "Just a quick snack, and, for the love of God, lock your door."

"It was locked."

"You sure?" He nodded to the door. "Looks to me like your intruder has a key then, because if what you say really is true, and you did lock the door, and he did break in… the only way in would have been to use a key or somehow bobby-pin the crap out of it."

Shivering, I folded my arms around myself.

"Food." Jack winked. "Let's go."

I followed him out of the dorm. I was missing something. I had to be! I know what I felt. I mean, I didn't see anything, but I wasn't crazy. It wasn't like I heard voices. I wasn't Taylor. I shivered as the wind bit into my arms.

"Mel," something whispered.

Gasping, I turned around and looked at the building and the trees nearby.

Jack paused. "Hey, you okay?"

"Yeah, just… the wind… my imagination."

"Please tell me you're thinking of moving out!" Jack squinted. "I mean, I think it's probably best considering…"

"Yeah… tonight."

"Where to?"

Yeah, like I was going to tell him that. Talk about getting a professor fired. "Somewhere safe."

"Good." His jaw clenched. "Safe is good."

FORTY-TWO

I tried to flirt with other guys… I pretended to be that girl, the fun slutty one who partied all the time, was too loud, wore her clothes too tight. And it made me feel better for about a minute until a guy took me up on the offer, and I lost my lunch in his face. Kissing wasn't even the same… nothing was. —Lisa

Tristan

I was early picking up Lisa, but after hearing what the guys had told me, there was nothing I wanted to do more than pack her an overnight bag and kidnap her, bring her to my house, and keep her safe.

I knocked on her door. No answer.

I knocked again.

Panicking, I dialed her number just as I heard laughing coming down the hall. Lisa and Jack were talking about something clearly hilarious, and she was standing a bit too close to him, and I… I was caught. Again.

"Dr. Blake." Jack grinned. "Fancy seeing you here."

"Right," I said in a clipped voice. "How was studying?"

"Got a lot done." Jack nodded, looking between the both of us. "And you're here because?"

"Tutoring," I said smoothly. "Sorry, I thought Lisa might

have mentioned it to you. I've been tutoring her for the past three weeks."

"Is that what they call it?" Jack sneered.

"It?" I raised both eyebrows and crossed my arms, knowing I looked intimidating compared to his shorter frame. "Mind explaining, Jack?"

"Whoa!" He held up his hands. "Didn't mean to ruffle feathers. I would really hate to flunk just because I saw something I shouldn't."

"Jack," Lisa warned.

"No, it's cool." Jack shrugged like he didn't have a care in the world. "In fact, it's perfect... too damn perfect. I'll catch you guys later."

He whistled as he charged down the hall, shoving his hands into his pockets like he hadn't just acted a bit off.

"Well, that was fun." Lisa gave me a wide-eyed look and unlocked her door. "Did you know you're gaining a roommate?"

"I may have heard through the grapevine she's really hot." I followed her into the room. "Then again, that means I'll just have to double my efforts to keep myself from mauling her every time I see her."

Lisa froze then turned around. "Every time, huh?"

"Your look of complete satisfaction with yourself isn't helping."

"Should I pack a bag?"

"Thought you'd never ask. Grab what you need, and I'll help the guys pack you up later this weekend, alright?"

She went into her room and returned fifteen minutes later with a large duffel and the rest of her books stuffed into her book bag. I took the heavier one and double-checked that she locked the door behind her, and then we made our way down the stairs. At that point, I didn't even care if other students saw me. Then again, the campus was so big it didn't really matter, and hell, even if someone saw me helping a student move, I'd just deny it, or maybe I'd claim it and quit so I could be with her twenty-four-seven. It wasn't like I needed a cover anymore. It was blown, and I was officially ready to move on.

With her.

"Ooooh, you brought a truck today," Lisa said, running toward my new Ford. "And it's red. I think you like red."

"I like red because you like red, though I got this last year. Now hop in. We're going to get takeout before I take you home."

"Home." Her hand hovered over the handle. "I like the sound of that."

I sighed, wishing I could pull her into my arms and kiss her senseless. "Me too, Lisa. Me too."

Lisa wanted Thai even though she'd had a sandwich with Jack. When I'd asked her why Thai, she'd said it was just another food that apparently Taylor had destroyed. I didn't mean to pry, but honestly, I was curious. Curious about her past, not that it would change my opinion of her. I was pretty sure that's how you know you're falling for someone — when you want the good and bad, when you want everything, regardless of how horrible, how dark. You want it all because, at the end of the day, it's still them.

"Did he kiss you here?" I pulled down Lisa's sweatshirt and placed my lips on her shoulder.

With a shudder, she closed her eyes and nodded.

"Here?" I tapped her collarbone and kissed, lingering against her skin because it felt so good against my tongue.

Another nod.

She was quiet, sleepy. Then again, I'd fed her enough food to put her in a coma. We were sitting in front of the fireplace downstairs in the family room. It was one of the only fireplaces I had that wasn't gas; the real thing was more soothing to me, the sound of crackling wood like my white noise. All the lights were off, but I liked it that way because my focus was totally on her and nothing else.

"Let's just assume…" Lisa shuddered, burrowing her head in my neck. "…that he touched and claimed everything he thought was his."

"So… everywhere."

She said nothing.

"I'll have to fix that." I tilted her chin toward my lips. "I'll have to make new memories with those lips… and make sure that nothing touches your skin that isn't good, that doesn't feel good. And, Lisa, if you ever say no, I'll stop… you need to know that. I want you. I want you so damn bad sometimes I think I'm actually going insane, but… my desire for you will never trump your need for me to go slow. Understand?"

Tears pooled in her eyes as she whispered, "Kiss me again."

I kissed her mouth, then her neck, slowly blazing a trail back down to that shoulder I couldn't get enough of. And when her sweatshirt restricted me, I peeled it off her body, revealing a tight white tank top. With a curse, I sat back and stared. "You're beautiful."

"When you say things like that, and look at me…" She gulped. "…in that way, you make me feel like you mean it."

"I do mean it, Lisa."

Her eyes flickered away from mine as if the topic of her beauty made her uncomfortable.

"Lisa…" I shook my head. "…would I lie to you? To your face?"

A ghost of a smile appeared across her lips. "No, you've been pretty honest."

And in that moment I almost told her everything. Because I had been honest… about every aspect of my life — except one.

"Let me rephrase that." I back-peddled a bit. "Do you believe me when I tell you I find you gorgeous?"

Her eyes met mine. "Yeah. I think so."

"Not good enough." I stood and pulled the shirt off my body, followed by my pants.

"Whoa, what are you doing?" Lisa moved to her knees in front of me.

"Proving a point." I stripped all the way down until I was completely naked. "I can't hide from you." I lifted my arms into the air. "It would be impossible to hide my body's reaction… by just looking at you… I'm like this. By just looking at you, every single muscle in my body is tight. Just watching your smile, concentrating on those gorgeous blue eyes, and I forget everything except you. Your taste, your lips, your mouth." I moved to the floor. "My body can't lie…" I kissed her softly. "And believe me when I say I'm not lying with my words. In here…" I tapped her chest. "…you're beautiful. Out here…" I caressed her cheek. "…you're impossible not to stare at. To me, you're perfect."

Her breathing picked up speed as she leaned in, her mouth barely meeting mine before she whispered, "Show me."

My body about set itself on fire as I met her lips in a frenzy. With a whimper, she straddled me, her body exactly where I wanted her, sans clothes. The kiss was hard, aggressive. Teeth knocked. Tongues collided. I couldn't keep my hands off her as I helped her out of her tank top, even though, somewhere in the back of my mind, I was trying to tell myself to stop.

I couldn't stop.

I didn't want to.

I wanted to exorcise every part of him from her consciousness. I wanted to mark her. With a moan, I slid my mouth down her throat and bit softly where her skin met her shoulder. Her head tilted back, allowing me to trail kisses down her chest.

"Your mouth feels so good." She moaned. "So good."

"Good?" I laughed, drawing lazy circles with my tongue down the center of her chest. "Pretty sure I'd rather be great. Good is what you get for participating in a race you never won… and pretty sure, at the end of this, I don't just want a participation ribbon but a damn trophy." With that, I flicked my tongue across her bra then tugged it off. "Beautiful."

She moved her arms. But I held them firm at her sides.

"No, Lisa. Let me look at you."

She ducked her head.

I stared.

I stared hard and finally realized I'd never get my fill. I tilted my head and plundered her mouth again, this time with such slow strokes — tasting, biting, memorizing. Her lips molded against mine perfectly, making me forget that I was supposed to have control. Making me regret I even knew the word.

"Please." Lisa pressed her mouth together against me as her body shifted against mine.

I reached for her jeans.

My hands hovered across the buttons. And I hesitated. I hesitated enough to allow logic to trickle in.

If she didn't know... and I took this from her...

She wouldn't just hate me. She'd never forgive me.

"We can't..." Who the hell was that lunatic speaking out of my mouth?

Lisa jerked away from me, but I grabbed her arms again.

"Lisa, look at me." I gripped her chin lightly. "Let me earn your trust first. Let me earn more of it. Let me date you. It's been three weeks. I want more than one more week with you or a one-night stand. Let me be the gentleman tonight."

"I don't want you to be the gentleman."

"Yeah, but, Lisa, I think that's exactly what you truly crave. Not the adrenaline soul-pounding quickie in front of the fireplace, but the type of lovemaking that lasts for hours... days. The type you experience only once in a lifetime, only when you truly give yourself over to someone. It's what I want with you."

She nodded her head and slowly got off my lap. I quickly slid on my boxers and put on a shirt.

"Sleep with me tonight," I offered.

"But..." Lisa shook her head. "...you just said?"

"In my room," I corrected. "Like one of our totally harmless slumber parties that ends up being completely acceptable because I don't actually take advantage of you."

"Will you make popcorn again?"

I grinned. "Tell you what. It's a little cold. You know where my room is. Turn on the fireplace, get comfortable in bed, and I'll be up in a few minutes with your popcorn."

"Smothered." She added, pointing at me.

"I remember." I exhaled and looked away. "You're killing me, by the way. I hope you know. Go put a top on before I forget that great speech I just gave you."

Laughing, she nodded and picked her discarded clothing off the floor. "Alright... I'll just steal one of yours to sleep in."

"Do that, by all means. Then I'll just be more turned on by the sight of you in one of my labeled shirts."

"I knew you labeled your shirts!" She pushed against my chest.

I pulled her in for a lingering kiss then slapped her on the butt.

"Ouch."

"Upstairs, go."

"Yes, Dr. Blake."

I groaned aloud.

"Whatever you say, Dr. Blake."

"You fail!" I yelled after her. "Just in case you were wondering."

I heard nothing but laughter, and I knew in that moment I'd made the right choice. But did making the right choice one time with her trump the fact that I was still lying?

Pushing the doubt away again, I made my way into the kitchen to get the popcorn. That I could concentrate on. That I could do.

FORTY-THREE

I pretended, just like Gabe had pretended. On the outside, I was fun and easygoing... and honestly, things were great — until my mask slipped, and then, all of a sudden, I realized I'd been living a lie. —Lisa

Lisa

I made my way into Tristan's room and let out a snort of laughter when I got there. We really were a pair. The guy had his closet labeled *Closet*, really bordering on OCD. I peeked in and was rewarded with labels of different seasons for different clothes. I wanted nothing more than to peel every label and replace it with the wrong one. Give the man a bit of chaos. He could use it.

His shoes had similar labels, and when I walked into his bathroom, I wasn't surprised to find more labels for toothpaste, Q-tips, you name it.

If I hadn't known him, it would probably make me hightail it home, but knowing Tristan just made the whole label thing endearing and so cute, I wanted to keep laughing.

I needed a laugh after the rejection, but in the end, his words had made sense... we didn't know each other well enough. Tragedy had a way of doing that to you, creating a false sense of security with the people you're with, making you trust them all the more. I knew that firsthand, and I also saw the wisdom in what Tristan had said.

With a sigh, I grabbed the remote to his ridiculously large TV and plopped on the bed.

I figured I was lying on his side on account that the alarm clock was there with his reading glasses.

With a smirk, I pulled out the book on top. It said DSM-5 on it and was probably the biggest book I'd ever seen. When I looked at the back, it said a whole bunch of stuff about diagnosing different psychological disorders. Kind of heavy reading, if you asked me. Then again, he did have his Ph.D. in psychology and had mentioned owning that pharmaceutical company.

Shaking my head, I set the book down and noticed a brown worn journal. I didn't really take Tristan as the type of guy to have a journal, and the fact that I'd get to peek into his private life sent a bit of thrill through my body. Then again, it was Tristan. He was most likely labeling more things and making grocery lists, not writing about his deepest darkest fantasies.

Smiling, I opened the book.

My smile fell.

Along with the book.

I heard it tumble to the ground, but I was unable to move… frozen in spot… because the very first page hadn't said Tristan on it.

No, it had said *The Journal of Taylor Blaine.*

It was *his* writing.

And his picture was next to it.

Right along with mine.

Tristan walked into the room, popcorn in hand. "Hey, what's wrong with you? Looks like you've seen a—" His eyes flickered to the floor, then back to me. The popcorn dropped out of his hands as he lunged for the bed.

"No," I said in a cold voice, then louder. "NO!"

"Lisa, I can explain!"

"No!" I yelled over and over again. All I kept saying was no. It was all I could get out, the only word I could actually form without screaming my head off, without bursting into tears.

Tristan knelt in front of me, gripping my hands. "Lisa, I know you're pissed, but you have to listen to me."

I slapped him across the cheek so hard my hand stung.

"Did you have fun?" I spat. Betrayal was a knife twisting in my chest. I was hot then cold all over. "Making fun of me behind my back? Pretending to like me when you knew the truth all along?"

"It wasn't like that." Tristan shook his head. "If you'll just listen, I'll explain everything."

"Yeah, right." I snorted, pushing at his chest. "Explain how you came to have Taylor's journal. The same Taylor who raped me," I rasped. My breath was uneven, like someone had just punched me. I tried to move away from him but fell to the floor, like my legs wouldn't work. I turned around and kept yelling as tears streamed down my face. "The same Taylor who committed suicide in front of me! That's—" I gasped. "—my picture."

"Lisa, calm down. You're hyperventilating."

"No!" I gasped again, my throat feeling like it was closing. "It was all a lie! You lied... you said I could trust you, and you lied!" My vision blurred. "Just like him— I'm so stupid, so, *so* stupid! I keep falling for it, over and over again." Hot tears streamed down my face. "I can't — I can't — breathe."

Tristan rushed to my side. I tried to shove his hands away, but I was too weak, both emotionally and physically. He gently drew me into his arms and whispered, "In and out, breathe with me, slowly…"

I fought against him.

He still held me.

I punched him in the stomach.

But he didn't stop trying to soothe me.

"I hate you…" I wheezed. "…so much…"

"I know."

"You made me believe… you made me believe in love again…" My voice trailed off as my vision turned black. I succumbed to the darkness, praying I'd never wake up.

There were voices in my dreams… they were familiar. I heard Saylor and then Kiersten…

The bed dipped. I curled onto my side, still not opening my eyes as Gabe shouted, "What the hell did you do!"

"She just found it."

"You mean you left it out? You bastard! I should kill you!" Gabe roared.

"Guys." Wes's voice sounded calmer. "Stop."

"Right. I just freaking left out his sick journal, so she'd hate me forever." Tristan matched Gabe's loudness. "Good plan, jackass!"

"I'm going to kill you!"

Tristan was quiet and then whispered, "Do it. I already feel dead."

"I think she's waking up," Kiersten whispered.

Something cold touched my forehead.

I blinked once, then twice. My eyes felt heavy. The first thing I saw was Kiersten's worried gaze and then Saylor's. They were on either side of me. I was in Tristan's bed. Something confined me, kept me from moving. No. Panicked, all I could think of was being tied to the bed. But no, it was just blankets. Still, I had to get out of there.

I thrashed, kicking at the covers and pushing at them. I had to get them off me. I didn't want any part of him touching me. Just the thought that he'd even touched the sheets that now touched me held me down, disgusted me. Bile rose in my throat, and my stomach twisted. I was going to puke.

"Stop." Kiersten gripped my hands. "You're going to pass out again."

"Shit." Gabe ran over to the bed and gripped my shoulders. "Breathe, Lisa. C'mon, tell me you're okay. Tell me you aren't going to scare me again."

I nodded, tears sliding down my cheeks.

Gabe examined my face then tilted my head to the side. "Bastard. I should kill you!" He lunged for Tristan again, but Wes stopped him, pushing him away so hard Gabe almost fell over.

I should have blushed. I knew I had a few hickeys; I'd seen them in the mirror when I'd used the bathroom.

More tears fell.

And silence.

I hated the silence because it was always impossible to interpret. Were they pitying me? Scared? Sad? And why the heck were they even here like they knew—?

My head snapped up as I met Gabe's guilty face then Wes's.

"All of you," I croaked. "All of you *knew?*"

"It's not what you think." Tristan took a step forward, only to be stopped by Wes's hand.

"Explain." A slow chill rolled through me as I rubbed my arms and tried to calm my body down.

Tristan looked to Gabe and started toward me. "I came to Seattle for you…"

My breathing hitched at his bold admission then picked up again.

"The journal was sent to me a month ago, but the last entry was two years ago." He swallowed. "It had your picture in it, and when I saw you on the news—"

Gabe snorted.

Tristan shot him a glare and continued, "—I knew you were the same person in the journal, the girl he'd talked about."

"So you felt the need to find me and torture me?" That couldn't be my voice bordering on hysteria.

"No." Tristan shifted on his feet. He glanced up at the ceiling, then settled his eyes on me. "I found you because he's my half-brother. I went looking for you because, until six months ago, I didn't even know he existed. I searched for you because he was sick…" Tristan's voice cracked. "He was really sick, Lisa, and I needed to know…" His eyes pooled with tears. "…I needed to know if I had the—"A shudder wracked his taut body. "—the same thing."

The knot in my stomach became a huge, coiling rattlesnake, ready to strike and kill with its venom. And I was the target. I swallowed, but my throat was dry. "The same thing?" I croaked.

Tristan cursed and ran his fingers through his thick, messy

hair. "He-he had narcissistic tendencies, schizophrenia, and a—" He squeezed his eyes shut then pushed them open again. "—a god complex. He took medicine, medicine I think my father's company provided for him. I couldn't find the paper trail, even though I tried." Tristan heaved a sigh then shrugged. "Six months ago, I confronted my father about Taylor, and he mentioned that I had the same bad seed. He said I was the same, and the last thing I want to be is the same, Lisa. I just needed to know what set him off, what killed him, what drove him to insanity."

Hearts don't make sounds when they break, but there's pain — God is there pain. One minute everything's fine; you're able to breathe, able to feel blood pump through your veins. And the very next minute? You're unable to focus on anything but the tightness in your chest as the world falls from underneath your feet and takes your heart right along with it.

"Well, you should have just asked, Tristan." I looked around at all the faces in the room. "It was me."

FORTY-FOUR

I'd killed him. It finally occurred to me one night when I woke up from another nightmare. Had I not gone along with that first dare, to embarrass that kid, to post the video to Shame... to hit on him then dump drinks all over his lap... I shook my head, knowing the truth. I'd said yes to Taylor the first time, and the second, even the tenth and eleventh. So by default, I'd killed him. Because I'd helped feed the monster that he was, and in the end, I'd simply run out of food. —Mel

Tristan

"**N**o." I shook my head, refusing to believe her words. My heart was breaking at her expression — she actually believed that to be true. "Lisa, it wasn't you. He was sick."

"*I* was sick," Lisa said in a hollow voice. "A while ago, you said that you can feed fear. He was my fear." She swallowed. "I fed him on a daily basis, and when I finally stopped... he lost his mind. When he died, I walked away. And I wish I could say I regret it." Her eyes flashed. "His death was the best thing that ever happened to me. And I'm not sorry."

"Lisa." Gabe moved in front of me. "Nobody says you have to be sorry that he's dead. He was a horrible person."

"You knew." Lisa sniffed. "You all knew about Tristan?"

Gabe stared right through me, his eyes blurry, his face tight. He remained completely still.

Wes looked away and then down.

"Right." Lisa moved out of the bed.

Nobody stopped her, but God, I wanted to reach for her, to apologize, on my hands and knees if necessary.

When she walked by me, I grabbed her hand. "Lisa, please don't go. I'm sorry. I didn't want to tell you. I couldn't. What he did to you, I didn't want to be a reminder. That was selfish. I know that now, but in my mind, I thought I was protecting you."

Lisa hung her head. "Protecting someone by lying about who you really are isn't protecting. It's the most selfish thing you can do because, in the end, you're still not giving a hundred percent to the person who deserves it the most. Please let me go."

Hands shaking, I let her go. I let her walk out the door.

The girls hurried after her. Kiersten grabbed the keys out of Wes's hands, and they were gone.

I slumped to the floor and banged my head against the wall.

"So…" Gabe groaned. "She's going to hate us forever."

"Or longer," I added. Fiery agony pulsed through me with every heartbeat. My heart wouldn't stop hurting; my entire body hurt. How was it possible for someone so sick and twisted like Taylor to keep impacting people's lives even now? Two years after his death. I hated that guy, freaking *hated* him, but maybe not as much as I hated myself for not rising above it, for not telling her the truth she had deserved to hear.

"If it makes you feel better," said Gabe, lifting the journal in the air, "you look nothing like him."

"No," I snapped. "What would make me feel better is the girl I could possibly love for the rest of my life, not hating me until I'm eighty."

Wes whistled and shoved his hands into his pockets. "So, what now?"

"I won't stop trying." I squared my shoulders. "I can't."

"Good." Wes nodded. "That's what I wanted to hear. Because a girl like Lisa doesn't deserve a guy who's willing to give up just because he screwed up so bad it might take a lifetime of apologies to get it right."

"Are you guys trying to make me feel better? Because you really suck at it."

Gabe and Wes shared a knowing smile with one another, though by their body language, I couldn't tell if they were going to attack me or were just exhausted with the day's events.

"What?" I glared at both of them.

"Ah, it always comes full circle." Gabe shook his head. "Wes has issues, then I have issues, and then look, Dr. Blake's sitting on the floor looking like a kicked puppy."

"I will kick you," I said, then swore and pounded the floor.

"Keep fighting for her." Wes held out his hand to me. "It's in the fight that you prove your worth."

"And if I lose?"

"If you're really worthy, you won't lose, and you won't quit, even when it looks like you're about to."

I peered around Wes to look at Gabe. "He do this often?"

Gabe shrugged. "What?"

"Make you feel stupid and insensitive all at once but wrap it up in a really nice quote, so you feel warm and fuzzy while he's saying it?"

"No," said Gabe with a snort. Then he shook his head. "I

get no warm fuzzies when he Hallmarks me… just supreme irritation because most of the time he's right."

"Bastard," I mumbled.

Wes grinned. His hand was still held out to me. I took it and pushed to my feet as he slapped me on the back. "Just give her time."

"Right now, we should probably talk about her security since I highly doubt she's going to want to come back here."

"I'll make her." A muscle worked in Gabe's jaw. "I'll freaking tie her to my car and make her, damn it!"

Wes sighed. "Gabe's more of a tough-love sort of guy."

"Yup." Gabe nodded. "We're like good cop, bad cop."

"Which makes me?" I asked.

"The villain." Gabe grinned.

I, however, did not.

"He's kidding." Wes shot Gabe a glare and led me out of the room. "But really, every good story needs a villain. May as well be both the hero and the bad guy. That way you're kickass."

"Some heroes be weak," Gabe said from behind us. "All the princes in the fairytales? They don't even have pecs."

"It disturbs me that you look at their naked chests." I sighed. "On so many levels."

Gabe just barked out a laugh while I numbly walked through my own house. It felt empty and cold without her, and I knew I didn't want to keep living that type of existence. I wanted her to fill it, and I wanted to share it with her. So I would fight. I'd fight until she got so sick of me she had to get a freaking restraining order.

Okay, so maybe I wouldn't fight in that way.

But I'd be there for her... for as long as it took her to trust me again. I'd be there.

FORTY-FIVE

I thought everything was over with… until the threats started again. They reminded me of who I'd been, and the crappy thing about that reminder? Suddenly you realize that somewhere along the way, you never really changed, just exchanged one life for another without ever really dealing with the past. I'd pushed it so far back into my consciousness that I'd slipped into denial. And if there's anything scarier than fear, it's denial… because when you can't face the truth, you're left with nothing. —Lisa

Lisa

I didn't talk to the girls the whole way home. Kiersten kept trying to cheer me up while Saylor rubbed my arm. But I didn't want them talking to me. I didn't want them touching me. I didn't want someone saying it was going to be okay. See, that's the worst thing you can do to a girl. Say it's going to be okay when she knows it's not, when she knows that the only real ending to the story is heartache.

"Do you want us to stay with you?" Kiersten asked after pulling up to the dorms.

It was on the tip of my tongue to say yes out of habit, but I just wanted to be alone, and, in that moment, being alone totally trumped the fear that someone was able to sneak into my room. Besides, Jack hadn't seen a thing, and had Gabe seen anything on the cameras, he sure wouldn't have let me go back. I made a mental note to send him a text in the morning. Right now, I was too pissed to even think about talking to him or Wes. And Tristan? Well, I was heartbroken.

Simply put, he'd encouraged me to trust again, and he'd made me fall for him knowing full-well that I was going to get burned. But he'd let me anyway. That wasn't love. Love isn't the expectation that eventually you'll end up in heartache; it's the expectation that you can fully trust another human being with everything and still hope for a happy ending.

He'd destroyed that by not telling me who he was.

I was never one of those girls who allowed emotions to control my actions. I think that was why Taylor had chosen me in the first place, so I wasn't stupid. Part of me understood why Tristan had done it, but that didn't make me feel any less hurt or devastated.

What kind of relationship could we have if he was constantly trying to protect me from things? That wasn't love. That was control. And I was tired of control.

So tired.

"I'm good." I waved at the girls. "Thanks, though. I'll see you later."

"Lisa…" Kiersten gripped my wrist. "You don't have to be alone… not tonight. You can come stay with us."

"Or us," Saylor agreed.

Kiersten tugged her lower lip with her teeth. "I just — I don't feel good about leaving you in that room alone."

"It's fine." I gently removed her hand. "Besides, what else can happen to me?"

Saylor and Kiersten shared a look.

"It's fine," I repeated, meeting their uneasy gazes with what

I hoped was more assurance than I actually felt. "I shouldn't live in fear. Right, Kiersten?"

"No," she said slowly. "But I do think there's wisdom in being cautious."

I pulled out my pepper spray and Taser. "I'm cautious. Promise."

"Call us…" Kiersten's eyes reflected worry. "At least call us in the morning, so we know you're okay."

"Right." I forced a smile that felt totally foreign, given the circumstances and got out of the car.

My legs may as well have been full of sand as I shuffled to the dorm. The wind picked up, fluffing my hair and sending it flying around my face. I could have sworn I heard someone say my name again… just like the day before. I quickly turned around, but nothing unusual was there. Just people walking and talking, and, of course, the trees next to my building.

Don't be ridiculous, Lisa, I scolded, and let myself in. The stairs nearly overwhelmed me as I slowly trudged up them, carrying the proverbial weight of the world on my shoulders. My heart, my chest was heavy. I felt like crying, but I wasn't sure if it was because I was ashamed or because Tristan had hurt me so deeply.

When I finally reached my door, Jack was leaning against it.

"Jack?" I squinted. "What are you doing here?"

"Leaving you a note." He pulled a slip of paper from his pocket. "But now that I can hand deliver it… here."

I accepted it then read the inscription to myself: *Do you like me? Circle yes or no.*

I burst out laughing. "If you're trying to cheer me up, it's working."

He joined in the laughter and then tilted his head. "Something bothering you?"

"No, it's…" I sighed heavily and looked away. "…it's not a big deal."

"Want me to come in?" he offered. "I can make a mean cup of hot chocolate, and if it's guy problems, I'm pretty sure I can give you some awesome advice."

Something about his expression was too eager.

"No." I pressed my fingers against my temples. "I have a killer headache, and I'm really tired. But thanks."

"Oh." He snorted. "I see how it is. You let Dr. Blake in, but not me? What? I'm not old enough for you?"

The abrupt mood change took me back. "No, that's not it at all. I would say no to anyone right now."

He took a step forward, a mocking sneer in place; his eyes were wild. I'd never seen him like that. His eyes darted back and forth, unable to focus.

"Rumor has it you don't say no — ever."

My heart started racing. "Jack…" I tried to smile. "…let's not fight, alright? You're a friend, a really good friend."

"Friend?" he spat. "Friend?"

"Look, if I gave you the wrong impression, I'm sorry. I just—"

Jack gripped my wrists and slowly backed me up against the hallway wall. A few girls giggled and walked past as he winked at them. But I was terrified, terrified that he could switch from happy to pissed so fast.

"And if I want more? Hmm?"

The way he tilted his head reminded me so much of Taylor that I almost threw up on his shoes.

"What would you say then?"

"No." I swallowed. "Because I value your friendship too much."

"Bullshit!" He slammed the wall above my head. "It's Dr. Blake, isn't it?"

"Don't be silly. He's our professor."

"Exactly," Jack hissed. "Our professor." He shook his head in disgust, then jabbed a finger into my chest. "Just remember, you did this to yourself. You know I could have protected you. You know I had the power to protect you. That it was me all along that wanted to save you, despite what you did?"

"What I did?"

"Professor Blake," Jack sneered. "Right. Well, have a good night, Lisa. I'll be sure that he knows I'd like to switch partners. Yeah, I'll make sure he gets that memo."

Jack charged down the hall, leaving me gasping for air. A few girls poked their heads out of their rooms but said nothing. That was the thing about college. There was so much drama, and the school was so big... well, it was my fault I'd never really made friends with the people on my floor. That, and the fact that I'd opted out of having a roommate once Kiersten had moved in with Wes.

I gave the girls a watery smile and let myself into my room. With a cry, I slammed the door. Hands shaking, I twisted the lock and leaned my back against the wall.

All the lights in my dorm were off. I quickly flipped them on and was horrified to find that I hadn't been robbed.

No, that would be too easy.

Instead, there were pictures — hundreds of pictures — scattered around the floor and attached to the walls. I knew who they were of before I even looked closely... me with Taylor.

With shaking hands, I dialed Gabe's number.

"Lisa?" he barked. "Thank God, are you okay?"

"No." My voice wouldn't stop shaking. "No, I'm not, I just… I need you. There's pictures, and my study partner just freaked out on me and…"

"Shh, I'll be there. Lock the door and windows and keep your cell phone on you, alright?"

"Okay."

Fifteen minutes later, Wes, Gabe, and Tristan were in my room picking up all the pictures while I sat quietly on the couch.

I didn't even feel the warm mug as Tristan forced it into my hands and told me to drink. Shaking, I lifted it to my lips and would have spilled it all over me had he not gripped my hands and helped me.

Feeling like a child, I wanted to lash out and throw the cup at his face, but he was helping — he was trying to help, at least. But his touch just reminded me of what I would never have with him again.

"We called the police, Lisa." Gabe sat next to me and put his arm on mine. "They'll be here in a few minutes. We wore gloves to pick up all the pictures, so there should still be prints on them, hopefully. Until then…"

"I'm staying." I nodded my head, convincing myself and hopefully them as I glanced at each one in turn. "I need to stay. I'm not running away because some bastard is trying to scare me. I'm staying."

"I'll stay with her," Tristan whispered. "I'll sleep on the couch."

I didn't argue. I was too tired to argue.

By the time the cops showed up and then left, it was late

afternoon. I was starving and exhausted.

I lay down on the couch and listened while everyone talked in hushed tones. Finally, the door closed, and it was just me and Tristan. It felt like the air had been sucked out of the room in a *whoosh* the minute we were alone. I wanted him to kiss me as much as I wanted to push him away for hurting me. It was a toss-up.

Tristan made his way over to the couch and pulled me into his lap. I didn't say anything; I just let him. The silence was comforting. My eyes fluttered closed, and I didn't object when his hand caressed my face. Instead, I shifted into it and drifted off.

FORTY-SIX

I never imagined I'd fall for someone so soon after Taylor had ripped me to shreds, but the feelings I had for Tristan were beyond normal. They were... terrifying, and for once, I didn't turn away. I walked toward the very sun that had the potential to burn me. —Lisa

Tristan

She was exhausted.

And I was pissed. The police had nothing, but that was nothing new. They'd been on the case for weeks now and still had no leads. Wes's team was doing better than the police department, and it pissed me off that Lisa was in constant danger until we figured more out.

The police had tried to calm me down, saying ridiculous shit about how stalkers rarely make physical contact.

Right. Tell that to the girl shaking in my arms.

I knew better. I knew the mind of sociopaths. I knew what they were capable of, and, unfortunately, Lisa was doing nothing more than pissing whoever it was off. The minute the victim found a sense of confidence and stopped reacting to the fear, the stalker got braver and braver until contact was made. Half the time, the object of their obsession was only slightly harmed. The other half? My stomach filled with dread.

I refused to let that happen to her.

It was nearing eight at night. I'd let her sleep for a few hours while I mulled over all the possibilities. I needed to somehow convince her to live with me, even if it meant I was going to be near her but never with her. Hell, I'd even give her the entire first floor of the house if she needed space, but I could never live with myself if anything happened to her. I wouldn't survive it.

She moaned in my lap. Her eyelashes fluttered before opening. "Wh-what time is it?"

"Late," I said hoarsely. "Want me to order some food?"

She nodded and pushed herself away from my lap. After stretching a bit and driving me crazy, considering I couldn't stop staring at her, she went into the bathroom. I heard the shower turn on and decided to stop staring at the door like she was going to open it up and invite me in.

Cursing, I paced the room and quickly put in our order for pizza, extra cheese for her.

When the shower turned off, my ears perked up. Damn, I was pathetic, but I couldn't help it. She was a part of me now, whether she liked it or not, and I wasn't going to leave. I was going to grovel if that's what it took.

Wrapped in nothing but a towel, she exited the bathroom.

I sucked in a deep breath, my eyes roaming over her body, remembering what she looked like beneath the towel.

A blush rose to her cheeks before she quickly padded into her room and slammed the door.

Groaning, I covered my face with my hands. It was going to be a hell of a long night.

Another fifteen minutes later, she emerged, wearing a pair

of black yoga pants and a pink tank top.

I answered the door, nearly yanking it off its hinges, and was shocked to see Jack again.

"Hey," I said awkwardly. "Um, how much do I owe you?"

Jack tilted his head. "How much you got?"

"Very funny."

"Twenty-five even." His eyes narrowed as he peered around me. "Another late-night study session, hmm? Her headache must have gone away."

"Ibuprofen and a three-hour nap."

"Ah." Jack nodded his head and handed over the pizzas. "Heard some loser broke in again."

"Yeah."

Jack didn't move.

"Is there anything else you need?"

"I think—" Jack grinned. "—I've got all I need, but thanks for asking. See you in class."

I could have sworn he'd said *or not* under his breath. The kid was getting creepier and creepier every time I saw him.

When I slammed the door and locked it, Lisa was shaking on the couch. I quickly dropped the pizza onto the table and pulled her into my arms. "What's wrong?"

"Jack…" Her teeth chattered. "…when I came home late this morning, he was at my door. He said he was leaving me a note, but…"

"Shit." I pulled out my phone to dial Gabe. "Has he ever been inside your apartment?"

"Yeah, once."

"Yeah, Gabe," I barked into the phone. "Do a background check on Jack McHale."

"Spell it."

I spelled out the name, ready to chase after the kid and wring his scrawny little neck if he'd had any involvement. "That all you need?"

"Yup. I should have some info to you by morning."

"Cool, thanks."

I hung up and faced Lisa. "Gabe's on it."

She groaned. "He really freaked me out earlier, but maybe he's just… temperamental."

"Tell me exactly what he did."

The more she shared, the harder I clenched my fists. My teeth ground together. I don't even remember how many curse words escaped my mouth, but I had to have set a record.

"But I'm fine," Lisa urged, putting her hand on my arm. Then, as if remembering we weren't exactly on speaking terms, she pulled back. "Really. I'm good."

"I'll kill him."

"Don't." She gave me a weak smile. "After all, who'd deliver us pizza?"

"I'm not laughing. It's not funny." I crossed my arms. "He's a jackass, and if he touches you again, you use your Taser, got it?"

"I'll Taser his ass." Lisa nodded. "But he did say something about switching partners, so… yeah."

"Thinking about him even spending time with you makes me want to rip his head off. Let's eat… or something."

"Before you go hunt him down?"

I shuddered. "Yeah, eat."

Lisa pulled out a piece and started taking tiny nibbles.

I rolled my eyes and pinned her in my stare. "Take bigger bites. You need food. You haven't eaten all day."

"If I take big bites, I may choke."

"Then I'll cut them for you."

"You're really abrasive tonight."

I looked down. "Sorry."

"It's fine."

Her eyes were haunted, not clear like they'd been before the world had come crashing down on our relationship.

We both finished dinner in silence.

"I'm tired." Lisa stood. "I think I'm going to go to bed."

"Right." I stood, unsure if I could hug her or if I should just stay away. I finally settled on nothing and watched her shoulders slump as if disappointed.

Cursing myself, I cleaned up the mess and tried to get comfortable on the couch. I was exhausted, so at least I'd sleep through the night.

The last thing I remembered before dozing off was a vision of Lisa in her yoga pants.

A blood-curdling scream erupted from Lisa's room. I jolted awake and damn-near ran into her door, trying to get it open.

Lisa was tossing in bed; she was covered in sweat. "No, no! Just leave me alone!"

I rushed to her side and tried to wake her up.

With a scream, her fist went flying — directly into my jaw.

Cursing, I almost fell to the ground. Who knew she could punch like that?

"Oh my gosh!" Lisa covered her mouth. "I'm so sorry. I thought… I thought you were him."

"Taylor." Defeat surrounded me.

"Yeah."

"I'm sorry," I croaked. "I heard you screaming and thought there was someone in here and…"

Lisa burst into tears.

"Aw, sweetheart…" I didn't give a damn if she hated me. I was holding her. I was going to hold her until all the tears dried. I tugged her into my lap and rocked her back and forth.

"I'm so mad at you."

"I know."

"You ruined everything."

My chest felt like it was cracking. "I know."

"But I — I think I love you. That's why it hurts so bad. It won't go away, the pain in my chest. It won't go away, and I keep hoping that when I close my eyes and wake up again, it will go away, but—"

I kissed her into silence, putting everything I had into it, molding my lips to hers, forcing her to feel what I felt for her. When we broke apart, I was out of breath. "Lisa, look at me."

Tears pooled in her eyes.

"I love you, and I'm not going anywhere."

"Even if I punch you in the jaw?"

"Yes, even then."

"Even if right now, my anger overshadows everything else?"

"Even then," I whispered. "I'd rather you hate me forever yet let me in your life than love me for a moment and push me away."

She nodded, wiping at her tears. "I don't know if I can… if I can trust you again. You hurt me s-so bad."

"Lisa, if I could take that hurt from you and carry it for the rest of my life, I would. I know that's not how life works, but know I'd do it in an instant. If I could take all that guilt and shame? There would be no hesitation, but because I can't, at least let me hold your hand while you walk through it."

Nodding, she slowly lay back down in bed. "Will you lie down with me?"

"Yeah." Some of the anxiety of the day lifted. "I can do that."

Tucking her in against my body, I kissed her forehead as she drifted off to sleep and vowed I'd never let anyone hurt her for as long as I lived — even if that meant keeping her from me. I'd die before I hurt her again.

FORTY-SEVEN

You aren't born with fear... you're born with love. Fear develops as you realize that the world isn't as perfect as you'd once assumed. Fear is a learned habit — and I was its student. —Lisa

Lisa

I woke up alone. Immediately, I jolted upright and looked for Tristan. He wasn't in the living room. Just as I turned around to go back into my room and grab my cell, the bathroom door burst open.

Tristan stood there, dripping wet and naked.

Completely. Gloriously. Naked.

His jaw went slack.

My eyes went wide.

Neither of us said anything.

Until finally, I cleared my throat and folded my arms. "Well, I'd say good morning, but you beat me to it."

He scratched his head, the V from his abs flexing as water fell to the floor. "No towels."

"They're in my room."

"Because you like naked men running around trying to

find things to dry themselves with?"

"First naked man in my dorm." I tried to hide my smile but ended up bursting out laughing.

"Stop laughing."

It felt good to laugh, so I laughed harder. He looked so hot and pathetic standing there.

"That's it." In a blur, he charged toward me and threw me onto the couch. He hovered over my body, his eyes heated.

And this time, rather than overthink, I did what felt natural. I jerked his head down and kissed him hard on the mouth.

With a groan, he relaxed against me and then pulled my body tightly against his. I could feel every muscle, every breath he took as if I was breathing with him. I didn't want the moment to end; I wanted it to last forever.

Moaning, I scratched down his back.

With a growl, he reached for my tank top, just as the phone buzzed on the table.

"Phone." I breathed.

"I don't care."

"It could be important."

"This is important."

"Tristan…"

Cursing, he pulled back and snatched his phone from the table. "This better be good," he barked.

His entire face paled within a few seconds, and then he was off me, diving for my computer.

"Are you sure?" he asked.

I watched in horror as he pulled up the same webpage I'd helped create, the same web page that had ended up being my downfall.

The homepage had changed.

Instead of having videos of other people...

It had nothing but videos of me and Tristan.

Everywhere.

Holding hands. Kissing. Making out in my dorm room.

And that wasn't the worse part.

Because there was a live feed, and he'd just been naked, with me, on school property.

I gasped, covering my face with my hands, while Tristan slammed the computer shut, then ran over to all the cameras and pulled the wires from them.

His chest was heaving.

I was too shocked to cry. "How?"

Tristan cursed and looked away. "I don't know, but... I think it's safe to say our relationship is no longer illegal."

"Because you're fired?"

"I'm guessing the dean would frown upon the idea of me screwing my student."

I hissed out a breath.

"That came out wrong."

"You think?" I fought the urge to throw something at his face. "And this isn't just about you! That's me! That's my reputation!" With shaky legs, I collapsed onto the couch. "What are we going to do?"

Tristan joined me on the couch and pulled a blanket over his lap. "We're going to find the bastard and destroy him, and then... you're going to move in with me. Even if you fight me every step of the way, I'm going to keep asking until you give in. Whoever did this..." He swore. "...knew your every move. Who knows where else the cameras—"

Tristan jolted up from his seat, ran into the bathroom, and

started pulling things from the cupboards. I slowly walked after him and froze when he pulled a camera from a spot behind one of the fake plants I'd put on the shelf for decoration. "That's not from Gabe."

"No." Tristan sighed. "It's not. We need to check your room."

All in all, we found six more cameras. I had no idea how much they'd caught, but it was enough to make me feel more than terrified. I was dirty, shameful like I'd been performing for someone without even knowing it.

"I'm going to kill that guy..." Tristan pulled on his jeans and threw a T-shirt over his head. "...with my bare hands."

"Don't." I shook my head. "We have no proof it's him... none. If you go after him, it could make things worse, just... we need to just lay low. I can drop out of school and—"

"Hell, no!" Tristan roared. "You aren't dropping out of school just because some psychopath has a sick obsession with you."

His phone went off again. "Shit."

"What?"

"The dean."

I cringed.

"Hello?" He blinked, his shoulders tense. "I'll be there in fifteen minutes...yes...yes." His eyes found mine. "A few weeks. Alright."

When he hung up, the room was tense.

"Are you fired?"

"I have a meeting..." Tristan sighed. "...where I'll most likely sign papers of resignation if the dean's pissed-off tone was any indication. It seems all the money in the world can't protect you from giving the university a bad rep."

"It's my fault." Tears started pooling in my line of vision. "If you wouldn't have seen my picture... if I wouldn't have fallen for Taylor."

"No!" Tristan rushed to my side and gripped my face with both hands. "Look at me, Lisa! None of this is your fault! None of it! You're perfect. He was sick, a sick kid, alright? It's not your fault. Don't let him win. We're going to be okay... I swear. Just... damn it, I don't want to leave you alone."

"Starbucks." I nodded. "It's not like the whole world has seen the website yet, unless it's gone viral, which that's always possible, too. I'll hang out at Starbucks. I'll put on a hat, and I'll read or something. Nobody would attack me in public."

"Okay." Tristan sighed, running his hands through his reddish-brown hair. "I'll drop you off and pick you up when I'm done. I don't want you going to class today, not with a lunatic running around. I'll send an email to your professors, explaining the situation."

I nodded.

"It's going to be fine." He kissed my mouth hard. "I won't let anything happen to you. Do you understand?"

"Yeah." My lower lip quivered. "And this isn't your fault, Lisa. Please, it destroys me when I see that look on your face. Now, put on something hideous, so people don't notice you, and grab a hat."

Minutes later, I had a quad-shot latte and a romance novel in my lap. Starbucks wasn't that busy, and, for the most part, nobody seemed to even notice me. I kept my phone in my lap with my book, just in case I needed to call Tristan. I knew it was bad… he was going to be fired. But what was worse, I knew that if it leaked out into the media who he really was, who I was? It would destroy his father's career, and to me, it just seemed like a matter of time before that happened.

The freaking Secretary of State was going to know my name.

Because it looked like I was in a sex tape with his son.

I groaned and leaned my head back against the couch.

"Rough night?" a smooth voice said next to me. I didn't turn around, but all the hairs on the back of my arm stood on edge.

"Yeah."

In my peripheral vision, all I saw was a guy in glasses wearing a Yankee hat. I couldn't make out his profile because part of the hood of his sweatshirt was pulled up to cover the side of his face. "That sucks. Hope it gets… better."

"Thanks," I muttered as he stood and left the coffee shop, shoving his hands into his pockets.

Chills ran down my arms. I rubbed them and then reached for my coffee, just as Jack sat down across from me.

"So." He put his legs up on the table. "Tell me, how does an orgasm from a teacher feel? I've always wanted to know. Is he better in bed because he's forbidden…?" His eyes gleamed. "Off-limits?"

"Jack." I looked around to see if there were enough people in the coffee shop to notice if he made a move. Three. Three people. "Look, I don't want to fight."

"Found you a new partner." He ignored me. "You know since you find me so disgusting."

"You're not," I said quickly. "But you did scare me last night."

"Good." He nodded. "Fear is good."

"Pardon?"

"Fear is learned… and you… you've been such a great student. You know, I wanted to save you, but I can't anymore, Lisa. I can't save you." His eyes pooled with tears. "Just remember, you did this to yourself."

"Jack, you're scaring me." I fumbled with my phone, trying to unlock it so I could call 911. "Are you okay?" Keep him talking; keep him from doing something crazy.

"I'm scaring you?" He laughed. "Oh, that's right, coming from the girl who ruined my life… coming from the girl who took a video of a fifteen-year-old boy getting rejected in front of a hot model… pants wrapped around his ankles… looking all kinds of aroused for all the world to see. Do you remember? Well, do you? Or how about the second video? You know, the one that was posted of me in the bathroom? I'm sure that should jolt something."

The phone dropped out of my hands.

"Oh, so she remembers. He asked you to do it… to put me up on the website, but what's so funny is I know something you don't know. I know so much, and your time… is up."

"You?" I sputtered. "You've been sending the notes? Breaking into my apartment?"

"Let's go for a ride." He stood and held out his hand.

"No." I shook my head.

He showed me the blade of a knife. "Well, hell, this wasn't in the plan, but I don't give a rat's ass anymore. You scream, and I move so fast that you don't even feel the pain as I slice your throat open. Get up."

I stood, gripping my phone in my hand as I frantically looked for help. I made eye contact with several people, but they looked away.

"Let's go." Jack hit my butt. I scurried away, but he gripped my arm and led me out the door. "I've studied you... like a book. I know everything about you, and the thing is... I was totally sane until you ruined me... and slowly it turned into an obsession finding you, destroying you."

He led me to a brand new blue Mustang. "Get in."

"Jack," I tried, using a calming voice. "Whatever I did, I'm sorry. It was so long ago and—"

He slapped me hard across the face. How did nobody notice? Why didn't anyone come to my rescue? I vaguely recalled a social experiment where a woman was screaming *rape* in the street, and no one had helped; it wasn't until she said *fire* that they'd come running.

I opened my mouth to do just that when he covered it with his hand. "I don't think so." The knife touched my throat. "Now, we do this the easy way or the hard way..."

FORTY-EIGHT

Terror is something a person experiences when fear is long gone, and in its place is nothing but the evidence that you aren't going to make it out alive. —Lisa

Tristan

The meeting was going too long. I was fidgety, and my phone kept buzzing. Finally, I held up my hand. "One minute."

The dean looked ready to swallow his tongue.

"Gabe, sorry I'm in—"

"It's Jack, one of your students!" Gabe's yell split my eardrum, and I winced away from the phone. "He owns the damn website!"

"Shit!"

"Where's Lisa?"

"Starbucks. I left her there since there's a crowd."

Gabe swore. "Wes was closer to campus. He's about a minute away. I'm on my way too."

I hung up and started walking out of the room.

"We aren't finished," the Dean barked after me.

"I quit. My family still donates money. We're finished." Leaving him with his jaw dragging on the floor, I sprinted from the room and raced down the hallway. In the parking lot, I jumped into my car and prayed that Jack hadn't figured out where Lisa was hiding in plain sight. Hopefully, he'd go back to the apartment.

Hopefully, I wasn't too late.

FORTY-NINE

Sometimes you spend your whole life being a victim — until you decide you want to be a survivor. — Lisa

Lisa

"**J**ack!" I pushed against him. He was too strong to move very far, but I knew if I got in that car, I was dead. He'd kill me. He was crazy, not thinking straight. And something else was very, very wrong.

I squinted. His eyes were wild, like pinpoints like he was high on something.

"Jack…" Tears clogged in my throat. "…did you take something?"

"To make me feel better after you chose *him* over me? Hell, yeah, I did!"

The knife dug deeper, raising a stinging sensation. I wasn't sure, but that wet sensation trickling down my neck might have been blood.

"And I feel great. Now I know what I have to do. I'm sorry. If you had just listened to me, let me save you… I could have saved you!"

"So save me now," I said, trying to fight crazy with crazy. "Don't hurt me. Save me now."

"I can't have you," he whimpered. "He promised I could. He promised me!"

"Who? Who promised!"

"*He* did!" Jack yelled. "You promised! You promised!" The knife moved away from my neck as Jack stepped back, tears streaming down his face. "All I ever wanted was you." He looked at me, his face twisted in rage. "And now you're going to—"

In a blur, Jack was on the ground. Wes was on top of him, beating the crap out of his face. I didn't pull Wes away, just watched as blood splattered everywhere. Another car pulled up. Gabe jumped out and pulled Wes off Jack, just in time for arms to brace me came from behind.

I screamed and jerked against the arms.

They tightened. "Shh… sweetheart, it's me, it's me. You're going to be okay. It's just me."

I turned into Tristan's embrace and sobbed.

The next hour moved by in a blur as we all gave our accounts of what had happened to both the campus security and the police department. Jack had had no record, no history of violence, or psychological issues. It was just like… he'd snapped.

The year before, he'd been on the dean's list.

The guy wasn't the typical guy to go on a killing rampage. Nothing made sense, but Tristan said that those cases rarely did — that it's people you least suspect.

We learned that Jack didn't even work at the pizza place. All in all, two of the workers had been beaten senseless each time we'd ordered. Each delivery he'd used as a time to try to gain access into my room, but because Tristan had been there, he hadn't been able to get past the door.

"You okay?" Tristan whispered into my hair once we were back in my room.

I was packing up another bag to take to his house. Shrugging, I shook my head. "It just doesn't make sense."

A soft knock on the door made me jump.

Tristan left me with a steadying pat and walked across the room, and opened it. Gabe came through, followed closely by Wes, both of their expressions grim.

Wes spoke first. "They searched Jack's room and found this."

He threw a worn leather journal onto the table.

I gasped. "That's... how did he get the journal?"

"He didn't." Tristan looked at the journal, his face pale. "There's no way he got into my house. The security is too good. Besides, Taylor... he wrote about making more than one copy. I just didn't know it was Jack who had it all along."

A tingling chill worked its way into my knees, weakening them. I slumped onto the couch. "He knew everything about me... why? Why would he do that? He kept saying he wanted to save me. From what?"

Tristan put his arm around me. "Maybe himself? Who knows, Lisa? He was bat-shit crazy."

"Yeah." The knot in my stomach tightened. We were missing something. We had to be missing something. It just... it didn't make sense. I mean, who spent half their life going after someone only to change their plans? I shivered.

"You guys ready?" Wes asked. "The car's downstairs."

"Yeah," I whispered and took Tristan's hand. "We're ready."

The week flew by. The story, unfortunately, had leaked to the media, but by the time it had, the videos weren't of me and Tristan naked, just kissing. The damning one of me and Taylor had been taken off the website. I didn't ask him if his father was pissed because I knew that was probably a very firm yes. But Tristan didn't seem to care.

If anything, he seemed happier that his dad knew what was going on… like he was finally able to be himself. I spent every night at his house — I'd never felt safer.

But something was still bothering me about the whole situation. I couldn't explain it or put my finger on it. I stopped bringing it up whenever Tristan gave me the impression he was worried about me. He'd give me that look like he knew I was thinking too hard, and I'd flash a smile and pat his hand like nothing was wrong. But something was very wrong. I'd thought Jack was a friend, but clearly, he'd been watching me the whole time; yet he kept hinting that he was protecting me from something. I mean, why tell me to move and then attack me that very next day? Things didn't make sense, and when I broached the subject with Tristan one night, he said that crazy didn't ever make sense and left it at that. I could tell that talking about it bothered him just as much as it bothered me, and maybe I would never have the answers or closure I needed.

I still hadn't kissed Tristan since the incident. I couldn't. I felt dirty… but more than that, I felt like if I did, I wouldn't be able to stop, and I didn't want my first time with him to be something I did to take away the fear or the pain. I wanted it to be something we shared because we loved each other. I had too many demons and ghosts haunting me. I knew it would turn into something different, and my heart couldn't handle that possibility.

Tristan was a perfect gentleman. He cooked for me, made me laugh. We watched movies… I mean, it was like living with the perfect man. Except at night, I still had bad dreams. Tristan said I should talk to someone, but I wasn't sure I was ready for that.

On Friday, I finally returned to class.

When I walked into Tristan's old classroom, another teacher stood behind the desk. It felt… wrong to have someone take his place. I kept my eyes averted the whole class period.

"Lisa?" the professor asked at the end of class. "I have a new partner for your end-of-the-semester project. He wasn't able to make it to class today, but he did send me an email and say he's available to meet you at Starbucks before your next class. He wanted to at least introduce himself."

"Right." Starbucks. The bane of my existence.

"Remember, Lisa, your grade depends on this."

"Starbucks, it is," I said, mumbling *"bastard"* under my breath. Since it was Friday, I had around an hour before my next class. I hightailed it to Starbucks and shivered as memories of the incident washed over me.

"Cold?" a voice said from behind me.

I jumped about a foot.

"Didn't mean to scare you." The voice was so smooth… so familiar.

I turned around, ready to offer an apology and a polite smile. I lifted my head, and the smile froze on my face.

"Or maybe..." He leaned in. "...that's exactly what I meant to do."

"Taylor." I couldn't breathe.

"Miss me?"

FIFTY

It always comes full circle — life. The choices you make, even the ones you don't make on purpose. They always come back to haunt you. They always come back. —Lisa

Tristan

"She's not answering her phone," I barked into the receiver while Gabe swore on the other end.

"She could be in class," he said in a hopeful voice.

Urgent rapping on the door sent a blast of relief through me. It must be Lisa; she could have forgotten her key. I quickly ran to the door and jerked it open.

"Dad?"

"Son…" He shook his head. "I'm so sorry… I'm so sorry."

He collapsed into a fit of tears, holding on to me like I was his lifeline.

"Dad, what—?"

Then I looked behind him.

Lisa was crying softly.

I reached out to her just as my dad stepped to the side,

revealing a very pissed-off looking Taylor. He held a gun to her head, his eyes blazing with fury. I recognized that face; it was the same face in the picture, the same one that looked like it was hanging on by a thread.

In a cold, detached voice, he said, "Brother, we finally meet. Tell me, did you like the nighttime reading? I always thought it was kind of heavy stuff, but you never know, to each his own, I suppose. Oh, by the way, I hope it's alright for us to come in."

He stepped past me and my sobbing father and jerked Lisa toward the living room. She met my gaze briefly and then averted her eyes as she stumbled with Taylor.

I followed them but not before dialing Gabe's number and leaving the phone on; my only prayer was that he'd still be available, that it wouldn't go to voicemail — that he'd hear everything.

"Get ahold of yourself," I snapped to my father, grabbing his arm. "What's going on?"

"Well, damn!" Taylor shouted from the living room as I dragged my father with me. "This place sure is nice. Did Daddy buy it for you?"

"No!" I barked. "I bought it myself. How kind of you to ask."

"So…" He released Lisa, throwing her onto the couch, then sat down across from us, scratching his head with the gun. "…tell me everything."

"Everything?" I repeated, making my way toward Lisa. Her arms were wrapped around her middle as she rocked back and forth.

"No, no." Taylor laughed. "I don't think you get to touch her… that might make me angry, and you do *not* want to see me angry."

I held my hands up and stepped back while my dad sat on the couch near Lisa. His face was tortured, pulled tight. Swear, it looked like he was about ready to have a heart attack. Where the hell was his security detail?

"Was she good?" Taylor asked.

"What?" I snapped.

"In bed." Taylor nodded encouragingly. "I remember some good moments, some not so good. Then again, when someone's unconscious…" His voice trailed off as he winked at Lisa. "She liked it, though."

Her entire body started convulsing as her face paled.

"So?" Taylor folded his arms, the gun resting against his shoulder.

"We didn't sleep together," I said honestly. "Not once."

"Aw, big brother, don't lie to me."

"He's not." Lisa's voice sounded strong to my ears. I almost sighed in relief. "We didn't have sex."

"Because you still love me," Taylor said in a serious voice, leaning forward. "I waited for you. I planned all of this…" He brandished his gun through the air. "…for you."

"It's… nice." Her smile was forced as her eyes met mine briefly before looking back to him. "Thank you."

"I knew it!" Taylor jumped into the air. "Wasn't it beautiful? The perfect plan. There were so many players, so many conditions I couldn't control, so many factors." Taylor sighed as if he'd just accomplished world peace. "But, all good things come to an end… and Jack," he added with a sigh. "… he needed to come to an end."

"Jack's in prison," Lisa said tightly.

"Easily manipulated." Taylor waved us all off. I didn't

recognize the man in front of me; he looked like the guy in the picture, but his mannerisms were so… off, so sporadic, not human, just plain crazy. He looked normal but spoke with such weird tones like he believed himself to be a god among men.

"I should have died, you know." Taylor shrugged. "I knew if I lived, it meant what I'd suspected all along… that I'm unstoppable, unbeatable." He spared a glance at the sniveling man I knew as Dad. "Even my own father couldn't keep me down."

"Taylor…" Our father spoke for the first time. "…you know I never meant to hurt you. I was helping you."

Taylor pointed the gun at my father and smirked. "Drugs? Is that the answer? *"Here, Taylor, take this it will make you feel better. Oh, and if you could just write down your damn symptoms and the side effects, that would be great!"* I was your own personal lab rat! You put me through hell!"

"Taylor!" Tears streaming down his face, my dad held up his hands. "I tried to help you. Please, you have to believe me. We tried everything."

"You tried to keep me quiet!" Taylor shouted, spit falling from his lips. "You tried to weaken me! But you can't do it! I should have died! And I'm alive! I'm alive because I'm indestructible!" He pounded his chest. "And now I have the perfect revenge…" He smiled. "…on the brother who was always better than me, no matter what I did… and the father who drugged his dirty little secret then didn't even have the balls to claim him once he was in ICU for six months. And finally…" His demented eyes turned to Lisa. "…the broken girl who I fixed, the girl who I'll spend eternity with, even if it *is* in hell."

Lisa stood, holding her hands out in front of her. "Taylor, is this really how you want the story to end?"

His head twisted to the side. He shook it twice as if he wasn't seeing us clearly. "What — what do you mean?"

"You worked so hard, baby," she soothed. "You worked so hard... for years, the perfect revenge. And look, we don't even have any proof. No video... nothing but your own admission. This is big — huge. It deserves a massive stage."

"Yes." Taylor nodded, his gaze becoming even more feverish. "Yes. You're right. I should be on TV."

"The world should see it," Lisa agreed. "They should see how powerful you are."

Taylor's eyes narrowed. "You're not afraid?"

Lisa uncrossed her arms and answered softly. "I feel nothing."

"Me too." Taylor nodded a few times. "Me too. But you make me feel. It's why I wanted to hurt you. You make me feel now... I don't like feeling. The pills didn't make me feel."

"Taylor," Lisa held out her hand. "Give me the gun... you don't want the story to end, do you? After all your hard work?"

He hesitated, the gun held high above his head as if he was either going to throw it or shoot the ceiling. "I don't know... you're confusing me. You're supposed to be... I don't know... this isn't right, something isn't right."

"Taylor," I tried, knowing exactly what Lisa was doing, playing into his fantasy, making him feel like a god. "You win. Take her."

"She isn't yours to give!" he yelled, pointing the gun wildly in my direction.

"I know..." I shrugged. "It was always you."

"How's it feel!" He laughed. "How's it feel being the other

loser of the two brothers! How's it feel?"

"Horrible," I choked. "I may not survive it."

"Ha! And I did! So what does that say about me?"

"You're amazing, baby…" Lisa took another step forward. "Now, give me the gun."

Taylor swallowed and looked down at my dad. "But we can't have witnesses. They need to be punished, punished for hurting me, for doubting me."

"Not having Lisa is punishment enough," I said quickly.

My father moved to stand. "And knowing my son has bested me in intelligence is… more than a father can bear."

"Ha!" Taylor did a circle in place. "I win. Don't you see? Regardless, I win, I win, I win! I'm better than all of you. I'm not sick, Dad." He spat out the name like it was a curse. "I'm healthy. I've died and been reborn!" He turned his gaze to Lisa. "You know I still have to punish you."

Lisa gave him a pout. "But I always enjoyed your punishments."

"Which is why I have to make it hurt, love. I'm so sorry. But I need to make you understand that I'm the only one for you. Not my brother, not Jack, just me."

"Jack helped you?" I asked.

"Jack was a fool. I promised him Lisa… I promised him revenge, and then I drugged him. Guy was tripping."

"That's okay," Lisa said quickly. "He was horrible to me. He tried to take me from you."

"I know." Taylor nodded. "I know."

He brought the gun slowly down over his head and grimaced, shaking his head back and forth. "Now, you know… the voices are quiet. It's because I finally finished my task, but one more thing… one more thing. Lisa, I'm sorry, but you need to hurt like I hurt."

My breath hitched as Taylor pointed the gun at Lisa and pulled the trigger. She fell back against the couch just as the door burst open and police in SWAT gear exploded through the opening.

Shouts of "Drop the gun!" reverberated off the walls.

Taylor didn't move.

He didn't run. Simply watched in fascination as Lisa's chest rose and fell slowly. Crimson blossomed on the right side of her chest, spreading in a downward pattern as it soaked into her gray T-shirt.

"Drop your gun!" shouted the cop closest to Taylor.

A tear ran down the side of Taylor's face, and he shook his head. Before I realized what he was going to do, he pointed the gun at his temple and pulled the trigger.

Through a slow-motion filter, I watched blood and brain tissue blast through the air and settle around me like ruby rain. The splatters and splotches landed everywhere, but I stopped seeing the gory horror show as I rushed to Lisa's side and covered her wound with my hand. "Stay with me! Stay with me, Lisa! Stay with me!"

Around me, the SWAT team buzzed like bees in a hive, securing the scene, I supposed. "Clear!" one of them called out.

EMTs arrived four minutes later and shoved me out of their way. I knew I should step back, but I was terrified that if I left her side, I'd lose her, and I couldn't lose her.

Finally, it was my father who pulled me back and then stumbled to the floor, weeping.

"She has to make it." Tears streamed down his face. "I'll never forgive myself... she has to!"

The last sound I heard was one of the EMTs yelling, "She's suffocating!"

FIFTY-ONE

I'd always thought death would be peaceful — it's not. Especially when the last thing you see before you close your eyes is that of a person ending their own life. You have to wonder. Is anything ever so bad that death seems the only option? —Lisa

Lisa

My chest hurt.
My legs hurt.
Everything hurt.

And it was almost impossible to open my eyes. I tried, but they seemed too heavy like something was pinning them shut. Flickers of the dream I'd just had resurfaced.

"Tristan?" I sniffled. "Say something!"

"You want me to say something?" he sneered. His blue eyes might as well have been steel as they pierced through every inch of my body. "Fine."

I braced for impact.

"I hate you." He said it slowly as if he wanted me to hear each word and commit it to my memory. "I love you."

"What?" Tears fell across my lips. "What did you say?"

"Both." He put his hands on his hips. "I feel both."

I took a tentative step toward him. "Which wins?"

"The one you give power to," he said seriously. "The one I choose to give power to."

"Love?" I begged, pleaded, my voice hoarse.

Tristan's smile was sad as he took a step back and gave his head a solid shake. "No, sweetheart. I'm sorry, but no."

He left.

Hope died in my chest.

I stared down at the ground, closing my eyes, wishing for snow, wishing for a do-over. Wishing I could go back and make the footprints straight in the snow, wishing I wouldn't have chosen death.

Because that's what I was experiencing. Death. Taylor had killed me, and in killing me, he had taken away Tristan.

My eyes stung with unshed tears. Why couldn't I move?

"I hate hospitals, freaking hate them." Gabe's voice trickled into my consciousness.

Wait a second, I wasn't dead? My fuzzy mind started gaining more consciousness.

"Right." Wes laughed. "Because out of the two of us, you have a better reason than me?"

"Touché."

"Shh," Tristan grumbled. "She's still sleeping."

More voices, this time from Kiersten and Saylor, and then another voice, a deep one I didn't recognize. I tried to open my eyes again but finally gave up. Too exhausted to care. Sleep was coming for me again, but I wanted to stay awake. I strained to stay awake.

Instead, I drifted in and out of the fog of sleep, not sure

how much time had passed. When I finally got one eye open, it was to see Tristan and another man — the Secretary of State? His dad? — talking in the corner.

"You tested products on him?"

His father sighed. "Nothing was working. His diagnosis was... well, at the time, everything seemed to make him more erratic. The only reason I gave him his freedom when he turned eighteen was because he begged for it, said he'd do better. And I believed him because, until his attempted suicide, he did fine. Stayed out of trouble, spent money, even said he had a girlfriend. I thought things were fine."

"And the drugs?"

"I kept sending them." His father shuddered. "I sent the newer ones, hoping they'd be stronger, hoping they'd work better."

"But they didn't."

"A week after Taylor's attempted suicide, I went to the hospital to check on him. He was in a coma... the doctors said he'd never wake up. And when he did... a year later, I panicked. Your mom never knew he even existed. You only found out because of the journal that was mailed to you and... I didn't know what to do. His real mom had passed away from a drug overdose, so he had nobody, nobody but me."

"So you let him go?" Tristan cursed.

"After several rounds of psychological therapy and being at the institution, he was showing such great progress that he was released, got a job working on his own, and... he was... good. For a while, he was good."

Tristan exhaled. "Until he saw the news."

"I remember that night so vividly. He called me, asked if I knew about his ex-girlfriend, could I make some calls, he thinks she's in Seattle and wants to surprise her. Her picture was everywhere — Melanie Faye, found! He said he was in love with her, thought about her all the time. I believed him."

"So all his planning…" Tristan let out a heavy sigh. "He sent the journals truly thinking he was going to die… and when he didn't… when he saw her picture on the news, he snapped all over again."

"A psychotic break," his dad repeated. "I've been trying to reach him for weeks. When he finally called and said he was in Seattle, I panicked, more worried for *you* than anyone. I arrived at the house just as he pulled up with Lisa in tow. I had no idea…" Things went silent, and then he spoke softly. "I told security to stay at the hotel, that I was going to the pool for a swim. I begged for some private time when I should have had them follow me. If I would have had them with me, none of this would have happened."

"Dad…" Tristan put his hand on Mark Westinghouse's arm. "…we all made mistakes here."

"A young girl was raped, tortured, and almost died because of me." His dad shook his head. His voice sounded more tired than I felt. "Not to mention, I lost one son, only to see the look of disappointment on another's face. No… this is on me, Tristan. This is all on me."

He slowly got up from his seat and walked out of the room.

"You can stop pretending you're asleep now," Tristan whispered as I opened my eyes.

"Sorry." My throat ached. "I didn't mean to."

"It's probably good for you to hear. At least you know that Taylor wasn't stewing for the past two years, thinking about ruining your life."

I snorted. "No, my picture just caused him to have a

mental breakdown."

Tristan smiled sadly and sat on the bed. "How are you feeling?"

"I hurt."

"I almost had to give you a lung."

"You can't give people lungs."

"I know," he whispered. "But for you, I'd have died to give you a lung." Tears pooled in his eyes. "You can't do that to me again. You can't be brave. I'm begging you, just be weak for the rest of your life. If I ever have to see you stand up to a psychopath again, I'm going to be the one that needs to be institutionalized."

"Tristan," I croaked. "I had to... he had a fantasy. I was playing into it."

"Yeah, well, stop listening so well in class. Better yet, I hereby revoke all criminal minds' privileges."

I smiled, but it hurt. "Sorry."

"Don't be. You probably saved all our lives."

With a soft chuckle, I said, "I always wanted to be a hero."

Tristan leaned down and kissed my forehead. "Think you could let me step up to the plate next time?"

A big grin tugged at my mouth. "You were too slow."

He swore. "I can't believe we're joking about this."

"If we don't joke, I'll just cry," I admitted, tears already starting to form. "So let's joke until reality sets in... or until these drugs wear off."

"Anything," Tristan whispered. "Anything for you." His eyes narrowed. "Is there something else? You look... upset, not that I blame you. Are you in pain? Do you need a nurse?" He started to stand, but I pulled him down.

"No." I exhaled loudly. "I'm just curious about one thing.

Do you really still think you're capable of doing what he did?"

"No," Tristan said quickly. "Do we all have darkness within us? Absolutely, but you can't live in fear. You always have a choice, and I choose to continue to focus on taking medicine that I know will help me with my own struggles. Taylor... not only did he struggle with bi-polar from my father's side, but his biological mother had severe mental issues. She was eventually hospitalized because she was unsafe to herself and others. But Lisa..." A nervous expression crossed his face as his eyebrows pinched together. "...I do take meds for bi-polar, you should know that. I was never diagnosed with what Taylor had. When my dad mentioned a bad seed, he was just trying to warn me away, trying to make me angry enough to drop it. I'm healthy, I'm fine. My medicine helps keep the highs and lows normal. It's not like it's a death sentence or anything, but I know, after everything with Taylor, it probably scares you. I'm... sorry."

I gripped his hand and squeezed. "You're sorry for actually taking medicine to help you? If I had cancer, I wouldn't apologize for getting chemo, would I? If I had the flu and needed to take ibuprofen to help my fever, would you judge me?"

He swallowed. "No."

"Then why is this any different?"

"Because it's close to home," he whispered. "And I couldn't live with myself if you were afraid of me... because of him."

"I'm not afraid," I said boldly. "Not anymore. And not of you. Not now, not ever."

His head slowly rose as his eyes searched mine. "Promise me... promise me we'll discuss things if I do something that reminds you of him. I can't..." His voice cracked. "...I can't lose you, Lisa."

"Sorry." I smiled. "But you're kind of stuck with me, especially after offering to die and give me your lung and all that."

He cupped my face and kissed my mouth softly. "You're so brave."

"I don't want to be brave." Our foreheads touched. "I just want to be in your arms."

"Done."

Tristan slept in the chair that night. Gabe had threatened to do the same, or worse yet, sleep on the floor, but I kicked him out. I needed time alone, time to breathe, time to be with Tristan.

I wasn't sure why I was so calm. Maybe it was because everything was out in the open. When I closed my eyes, I still saw Taylor's face. I still saw the blood. But instead of fear, it was just pity I felt. I felt sorry for him, sorry that he couldn't live a normal life, sorry that he was sick because everyone deserves a chance to live.

I truly believed, in that moment, that having a psychological illness was just as bad as being physically ill, maybe worse. When you're physically ill, people can see what's wrong; they can help you fix it. When something's wrong inside the mind, all doctors can do is guess, and people can't tell if you're sick. They don't believe you a lot of times until they see the outward signs of your sickness. Maybe you're walking aimlessly on the street talking to yourself, or you hurt someone you love. That type of sickness is harder to define, harder to fix, and scary because, in the end, the sickness is you.

That's a tough pill to swallow. Knowing that what's in your head might not be right — but not having any idea how to fix it.

My mind was going into overdrive, thinking about Taylor, what had led to his madness, what had led to his end.

Tristan stirred in the chair, and his head tilted back. I smiled at the sight. He was so beautiful. Moonlight lit up the side of his face, showing off his strong jaw, his perfect profile.

I was done.

Tired of waiting for life.

And I refused to be the type of person that held a grudge like Taylor had, the type of person that let madness consume me, or maybe even bitterness, revenge — they were all a type of poison, a type of sickness that if allowed in your body, would destroy you from the inside out.

"Tristan," I whispered.

He jolted awake. "Are you in pain? Are you okay? What's wrong?" He moved to my bed, his hands caressing my face.

"I love you."

He closed his eyes, and his shoulders relaxed as he bowed his head and kissed me on the forehead. "I love you too."

"Dr. Blake."

"Really?" His voice was hoarse from sleep. "You wake me up just to turn me on? Thanks, Lisa, really, I appreciate that. Not like I've had enough shock to my body these last few days."

"Sleep with me."

"Okay." He moved next to me, his muscled body moving to lie down on the bed.

"Not like that." I was thankful it was night.

His eyes squinted together, and then all of a sudden

widened. In an instant, his mouth was on mine, and his shirt was on the floor.

"That was fast." I laughed against his lips.

"I've wanted you since the first day I saw you, and damn if I'm ever going to let someone come between us again."

I let out a hoarse cry as his tongue plunged into my mouth, his hands sliding up my body, lifting my hospital gown. Pausing, he whispered, "Sorry, I'm being rough, and you did just get shot."

"Stop talking!" I tugged at his jeans.

With a curse, he jumped off the bed and threw them to the floor, then joined me again, totally naked.

"Later…" I arched beneath his touch. "…I'll stare at your sexy body later, Dr. Blake, but right now, I need you. I need you so bad."

"I'm right here." He kissed me hard against the mouth, again and again, slanting at a different angle as if he couldn't get enough of me.

Finally, I couldn't take it anymore.

"Tristan!"

"I thought I was Dr. Blake," he teased, his hands sliding across my hips, and then, I felt him.

My body shuddered with pleasure.

"Ah, so she likes calling me Dr. Blake." He inched into me.

I clutched his shoulders, digging in with my fingers as his mouth moved to my neck.

"Why are you going so slow?" I whimpered, my body tightening, threatening to explode, wanting to move against him but afraid to do anything.

"Say it again."

"What?"

"Say my name."

"Tristan."

"Wrong name." He started pulling away.

I gripped his shoulders and moaned, "Dr. Blake," just as he plunged all the way into me. My head fell back against the pillows as a lone tear ran down my face.

FIFTY-TWO

Finally… I found peace. In the arms of someone who looked at me like I was his air. —Lisa

Tristan

"You're beautiful." I could barely speak, but she needed to hear it. "And I love you more…" I moved within her. "…and more…" She gasped. "…with every passing day." Her body tightened around me. "And I'm never letting you go. For as long as I live, I'm never letting you go."

"Are you promising me forever?"

I stopped moving, nearly killing myself in the process, and reached up to touch her face. I tasted her with my lips, trailing them down her cheeks, kissing away the tears.

"The broken pieces are the prettiest ones, Lisa. The demons, the proudest scars."

"Touch me," she breathed. "Please, I need you, I need you."

"I love you… I love you." I stroked slowly, taking my time to feel every part of her, not wanting to rush a perfect moment. "You're going to marry me, by the way."

"Tristan," she hissed.

"Dr. Blake."

"Dr. Blake…" she moaned, her fingers digging into my shoulders as her body spasmed around me. "I may have to say yes… but you'll need to ask when I'm not ready to scream your name."

"In pleasure, I hope." I grinned, then she jerked me against her, and my own release overtook me.

Gasping, body sated, I waited for her to tense, to possibly regret her actions. Instead, she pulled me closer, kissing my lips softly.

"In pleasure, always in pleasure, Dr. Blake."

"Say it again, and I may just have a repeat performance."

At a soft knock on the door, I paused and glanced over my shoulder. A gray-haired nurse waltzed in with a smile pasted on her face. The minute she saw us, she stopped dead in her tracks, gasped, then nearly ran into the door trying to leave.

"I think we just gave her the shock of her life," I mused.

Lisa tugged me closer. "Well, at least now I can scream since she's probably telling everyone on this floor. Dr. Blake…"

I kissed her hard across the mouth. "Louder."

I was ready for her again. Hell, I wasn't sure I'd ever not be ready for her.

"You're sexy…" She ran her fingers through my hair.

I had to keep myself from purring.

"…when you're out of control."

"You're sexy," I nipped her lower lip. "…when you think you have it."

And then I gently moved within her again and winked.

EPILOGUE

Sometimes the most beautiful things are the ones that pose the most danger, just like the ugliest of the world turn into objects of absolute beauty. The cancer was ugly, but Kiersten turned it to beauty. The death of Gabe's fiancée was horrendous, but Saylor made the death redeeming, precious. And Lisa... her past was ugly, but look at the beauty of the disaster that struck: Tristan, redemption within their family, and finally, love. I think the world has it wrong when it strives after the beautiful. It should fight for the ugly; it should hope for the damned; it should seek the lost — because in the end, if there weren't tears, if there wasn't fighting, then do you really deserve to feel satisfied and happy? —Wes Michels

Wes

"**G**abe!" Saylor yelled. "I mean it! Drop the water gun."

Gabe ran around the pool, aiming for her face like a toddler.

Naturally, it was in my best interest to stop him, considering all the girls were warring against him, but I was too relaxed to care.

I lay back... watched Kiersten, my wife, join forces with the other females, and laughed at all their expressions. I laughed out loud.

It felt good to laugh; it felt good that it was real. My friends made fun of me for always spouting out nonsense and wisdom, but how could I be any different after going through what I had?

Funny, because out of all the people in my life, the one person who understood the most was Lisa. The most unlikely of partners. She sat quietly next to me and whispered, "I like laughing again."

"It gets easier," I whispered. "The laughter."

She smiled and turned to face me. "I know."

She'd been through hell. The media hadn't been kind once the story had broken about Taylor and her involvement. We'd tried to protect her as much as we could, but in the end, she'd been made out to be a bully, just like he had been.

Tristan had done his best to defend her; even his father had defended her. But once the storm died down, she'd approached the media with her story. She'd bravely broken her silence. She'd spoken so eloquently that day, explaining the dangers of emotional bullying, how it turned into physical abuse, how she'd been raped. She'd left no stone unturned, and with all our help, had started her own non-profit in honor of online bullying.

"Tristan," Lisa warned as he made his way around the pool with a squirt gun. "Don't! Don't you dare!"

"Do it, do it!" Gabe chanted while Kiersten and Saylor squirted him in the face with the water guns.

It probably didn't help that it was a chilling fifty-five degrees outside, hardly pool weather. Then again, the water was heated, so it wasn't a huge chore to swim.

"I love you." Tristan nodded. "But it's time... for revenge." He squirted her leg. "That was for hiding the label maker."

Lisa burst out laughing.

He squirted her stomach. "And that was for making labels that had words like breasts on them when labeling chicken."

"In my defense, it was still accurate." Lisa laughed harder.

"She's right."

"Stay out of this, Michels!" Tristan roared, then lunged for Lisa and pulled her into the pool. Her laughter was more than I could have hoped for.

Laughter meant healing.

Healing was more than just being cured of cancer or finding the one who actually saw you for you. It was more than getting over your past, embracing your future. Healing's waking up every day when you'd rather stay in bed; healing's when you smile instead of cry; healing's when you can hold your head high, despite what demons try to pull it down. And life was full of it, full of opportunities to cut and run, rather than stay put and face the storm.

They never teach you that in school. They never teach you that the fish that survive are the ones that swim against the current.

My name is Wes Michels, and I'm a survivor.

Now it's your turn to live, laugh, and love.

Live… like Kiersten, and I chose to do.

Laugh… at all the little things along with way, like Gabe and Saylor did.

Love… like Lisa and Tristan were finally able to do.

Yeah, I chuckled as I watched my friends continue to tease and yell at one another.

Just thank God.

And live.

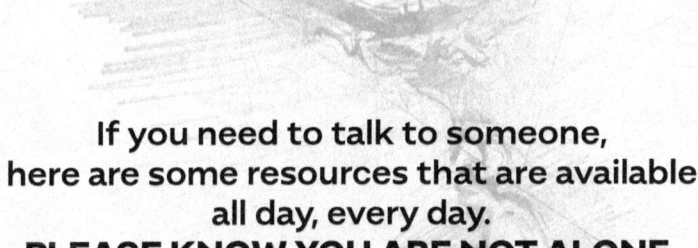

If you need to talk to someone,
here are some resources that are available
all day, every day.
PLEASE KNOW YOU ARE NOT ALONE.

The National Sexual Assault Hotline

*RAINN (Rape, Abuse & Incest National Network) is the nation's
largest anti-sexual violence organization.*
Telephone: 800.656.HOPE (4673)
Online chat: online.rainn.org

The National Suicide Prevention Lifeline

*The National Suicide Prevention Lifeline provides free and
confidential emotional support to people in suicidal crisis or
emotional distress*
Telephone: 1-800-273-8255
For Deaf & Hard of Hearing: 1-800-799-4889
Online chat: suicidepreventionlifeline.org

The National Domestic Violence Hotline
*We answer the call to support and shift power back to people
affected by relationship abuse.*
Telephone: 1-800-799-SAFE (7233)
Online chat: thehotline.org

loveisrespect
*loveisrespect's purpose is to engage, educate and empower young
people to prevent and end abusive relationships.*
Telephone: 1-866-331-9474
Online chat: loveisrespect.org
Text: LOVEIS to 22522

WANT MORE RUIN?

I hope you enjoyed Shame!
Haven't read enough Wes and Kiersten?
Want to know Gabe and Saylor's story?
Here is the reading order!

Ruin (Wes Michels & Kiersten's story)
Toxic (Gabe Hyde & Saylor's story)
Fearless (Wes Michels & Kiersten's story)
Shame (Tristan & Lisa's story)

WANT MORE YA ROMANCE?

If you enjoyed this book, then you will also love these Young Adult Romances:

Ruin Series
Ruin (Wes Michels & Kiersten's story)
Toxic (Gabe Hyde & Saylor's story)
Fearless (Wes Michels & Kiersten's story)
Shame (Tristan & Lisa's story)

Seaside Series
Tear (Alec, Demetri & Natalee's story)
Pull (Demetri & Alyssa's story)
Shatter (Alec & Natalee's story)
Forever (Alec & Natalee's story)
Fall (Jamie Jaymeson & Pricilla's story)
Strung (Tear + from the boys POV)
Eternal (Demetri & Alyssa's story)

Other Titles
Every Girl Does It (Preston & Amanda's story)
Compromising Kessen (Christian & Kessen's story)

AUTHOR NOTE

I started this series as a way to honor my Uncle Jobob. Those of you who have read *Ruin* know that it was a tribute to him while he fought cancer. I never imagined it would turn into what it's turned into, and I'm so overwhelmed and blessed that readers have attached to the characters as much as I have.

Writing *Shame* was different for me. I had a lot of anxiety going into it because I wanted Lisa's story to stand apart from Wes and Gabe, but HOW do you do that? It's almost impossible. Needless to say, I went through a lot of stress before I started the first chapter, but after typing that first section, I knew her story needed to be told. I think this one hits home to so many women who have been in abusive relationships. I know this is an extreme, but when I look back on my relationships in high school/college and even relationships of my friends, it amazes me how many went through similar controlling situations where they were almost shut out from their friends and family because of the control the boyfriend had on their lives. Know that, if this is you if this story speaks to you in that way, there is hope. Emotional bullying is just as wrong as physical abuse.

Bullying is bullying, plain and simple. To those women, I hope this story gives you courage, to ones who have already walked that road, bless you for enduring and coming out on top; I hope this story helped you heal.

Readers/bloggers, you guys amaze me. Thank you so much for all your support and encouragement. Inkslinger PR, yeah you guys rock my world, Danielle you have to be the best PR lady around; thank you so much for your countless hours!

To my agent, Erica, for being a bulldog on my behalf and always supporting my crazy ideas—you rock.

If you want to catch up with me, just add Rachel's New Rockin Readers on Facebook. I'm always in there talking and sharing excerpts of stuff.

ABOUT THE AUTHOR

Rachel Van Dyken is the #1 *New York Times, Wall Street Journal,* and *USA Today* bestselling author of over 90 books ranging from contemporary romance to paranormal. With over four million copies sold, she's been featured in *Forbes, US Weekly,* and *USA Today*. Her books have been translated in more than 15 countries. She was one of the first romance authors to have a Kindle in Motion book through Amazon publishing and continues to strive to be on the cutting edge of the reader experience. She keeps her home in the Pacific Northwest with her husband, adorable sons, naked cat, and two dogs. For more information about her books and upcoming events, visit www.RachelVanDykenauthor.com.

ALSO BY RACHEL VAN DYKEN

Mafia Royals Romances
Royal Bully (Asher & Claire's story)
Ruthless Princess (Serena & Junior's story
Scandalous Prince (Breaker & Violet)
Destructive King (Asher & Annie)
Mafia King (TBA)
Fallen Rotal (TBA)
Brroken Crown (TBA)

Rachel Van Dyken & M. Robinson
Mafia Casanova (Romeo & Eden's story)
Falling for the Villain (Juliet Sinacore's story)

Wingmen Inc.
The Matchmaker's Playbook (Ian & Blake's story)
The Matchmaker's Replacement (Lex & Gabi's story)

Bro Code
Co-Ed (Knox & Shawn's story)
Seducing Mrs. Robinson (Leo & Kora's story)
Avoiding Temptation (Slater & Tatum's story)
The Setup (Finn & Jillian's story)

Liars, Inc
Dirty Exes (Colin, Jessie & Blaire's story)
Dangerous Exes (Jessie & Isla's story)'

Cruel Summer Trilogy
Summer Heat (Marlon & Ray's story)
Summer Seduction (Marlon & Ray's story)
Summer Nights (Marlon & Ray's story)

Covet
Stealing Her (Bridge & Isobel's story)
Finding Him (Julian & Keaton's story)

The Dark Ones Series
The Dark Ones (Ethan & Genesis's story)
Untouchable Darkness (Cassius & Stephanie's story)
Dark Surrender (Alex & Hope's story)
Darkest Temptation (Mason & Serenity's story)
Darkest Sinner (Timber & Kyra's story)

Curious Liaisons
Cheater (Lucas & Avery's story)
Cheater's Regret (Thatch & Austin's story)

Red Card
Risky Play (Slade & Mackenzie's story)
Kickin' It (Matt & Parker's story)

Players Game
Fraternize (Miller, Grant and Emerson's story)
Infraction (Miller & Kinsey's story)
M.V.P. (Jax & Harley's story)

The Consequence Series
The Consequence of Loving Colton (Colton & Milo's story)
The Consequence of Revenge (Max & Becca's story)
The Consequence of Seduction (Reid & Jordan's story)
The Consequence of Rejection (Jason & Maddy's story)

The Bet Series
The Bet (Travis & Kacey's story)
The Wager (Jake & Char Lynn's story)
The Dare (Jace & Beth Lynn's story)

The Bachelors of Arizona
The Bachelor Auction (Brock & Jane's story)
The Playboy Bachelor (Bentley & Margot's story)
The Bachelor Contract (Brant & Nikki's story)

Waltzing With The Wallflower — written with Leah Sanders

Waltzing with the Wallflower (Ambrose & Cordelia)
Beguiling Bridget (Anthony & Bridget's story)
Taming Wilde (Colin & Gemma's story)

London Fairy Tales

Upon a Midnight Dream (Stefan & Rosalind's story)
Whispered Music (Dominique & Isabelle's story)
The Wolf's Pursuit (Hunter & Gwendolyn's story)
When Ash Falls (Ashton & Sofia's story)

Renwick House

The Ugly Duckling Debutante (Nicholas & Sara's story)
The Seduction of Sebastian St. James (Sebastian & Emma's story)
The Redemption of Lord Rawlings (Phillip & Abigail's story)
An Unlikely Alliance (Royce & Evelyn's story)
The Devil Duke Takes a Bride (Benedict & Katherine's story)

www.rachelvandykenauthor.com